THE
WEREWOLF
WEARS PRADA

A SAN FRANCISCO WOLF PACK NOVEL

THE WEREWOLF WEARS PRADA

A SAN FRANCISCO WOLF PACK NOVEL

KRISTIN MILLER

Entangled Publishing, LLC
2614 South Timberline Road
Suite 109
Fort Collins, CO 80525
Visit our website at www.entangledpublishing.com.

Covet is an imprint of Entangled Publishing, LLC.

Edited by Candace Havens
Cover design by Erin Dameron-Hill
Cover photos from 123rf and Shutterstock

Manufactured in the United States of America

First Edition April 2015

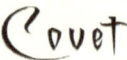

To Justin,
for braving this faja girl's fire.

Chapter One

Life is *not* a fairy tale.

Melina Rae Rosenthal had lived her entire life repeating that mantra to herself. She'd kissed a long list of frogs, and put up with a lot of B.S. Today, however, made her question whether she'd been wrong, and incredibly bitter, all those years. She'd been asked out by one of the most eligible bachelors on the planet.

Prince Charming had finally arrived.

There was only one thing missing: a fairy godmother who'd wave a glittery wand in front of her face and turn her yoga pants into a puffy blue dress.

"I've got nothing to wear." Melina dove into her walk-in closet, tossing leather pants and a fur poncho onto the bed behind her. "What am I going to do?"

Her best friend Colleen squealed from the bedroom, probably ducking for cover. Not very fairy-godmother-like. "Just calm down. You've been skipping around all day like Little Red Riding Hood on Redbull."

"Not Redbull. *Espresso.*" Throwing hangers behind her,

Melina huffed and shoved two coats apart. "I've had six today."

"Six?" Colleen laughed—one of those witchy cackles Melina both loved and hated her for. She really was more like the Wicked Witch of the West than any fairy godmother Melina had ever seen. "You and Hayden must've really hit it off."

Merely hearing his name made the hair on Melina's arms stand on end.

Hayden Dean.

He was a San Francisco business mogul, millionaire, and model magnet. He was also scorching hot. Dark brown hair parted perfectly down the center with silky strands that nearly brushed his ears. Creamy chocolate eyes set against golden tan skin. Thick, swooping jaw, and a set of plush lips.

Totally Prince Charming material.

Before today, she might've settled for far less. She hadn't had a date with a real man in months. The ones she'd gone out with had turned out to be mama's boys, cat-callers, loud eaters, snorters, and scratchers. And if she went out with another guy who called her "Doll" she was going to scratch out his eyeballs.

She'd started to think the good ones were either already taken or dead.

"I'm telling you, it was magic. He's not anything like you see on *E! News*." They'd painted the famous Hayden Dean to be a stupid playboy. A chauvinist who cared for nothing and no one but himself. To her surprise, he'd shown her none of those things. "He's unexpectedly…charismatic. And caring."

Two hours interviewing the drop-dead gorgeous hunk, and Melina knew he was the one she'd been waiting for. The guy plucked straight from her dreams. He was tall, dark, and unquestionably handsome—more so in person, if that was possible—so staring at him while she fired questions about his personal life wasn't the worst assignment she'd ever had.

And she could go off for hours about the trashy assignments she'd had from *Celebrity Crush* magazine. She'd worked as the *Celeb Life & Style* columnist for eighteen months, and longed to move up the ranks to *Eclipse*, the city's leading fashion magazine.

Every article was one step closer to reaching that goal and leaving the unrealistic demands of her editor behind her.

"I'm stoked you two hit it off," Colleen said, her voice laced with concern, "but they don't call him Hook-Up Hayden for nothing."

A subtle twinge in Melina's gut warned Colleen might've had a point. All those stories about Hayden's womanizing ways couldn't have been terribly off-mark. But how could she turn down the chance to see for herself? Guys like Hayden didn't come around that often, if ever.

"I think I can take care of myself." Melina squeezed between two Gucci dresses. Exactly how deep was her closet? "If you got to know him, you'd see he's different. Deep down, I don't think he wants to be that way…the way everyone paints him to be."

Colleen huffed. "You really think you know him? Deep down? After two hours in Starbucks?"

"Maybe, maybe not." Melina's fingers gripped silky-soft pleats. "Gotcha."

She yanked a Prada gown off its hanger and burst into the bedroom holding it high. The dress was a gorgeous shade of eggplant. Grecian. Long and draping, with pleats on the gown and a dangerously low V-neck.

"Ooh!" Colleen crooned, jumping off the bed, her platinum blonde locks bouncing over her shoulder. "It looks like the one whats-her-face wore to that huge awards show last season."

"Yes, but this one's better. The V-neck is deeper, the skirt is tamer. The differences are subtle, but it's striking, don't you think?" She stroked the pleats, seeing the image take form. "I'm going to pair it with glittering gold Manolo Blahniks, nude lips, and the most fabulous earrings I can find."

What better way to make a splash at the Silverlight Awards?

She still couldn't believe he'd asked her.

Infamous womanizer Hayden Dean had leaned across their tiny table in the back corner of Starbucks, gazed deep into her eyes, stirring something in her chest…and whispered the words she never thought she'd hear: *Be my date tonight?*

Not only any date. His date to the *Silverlight Awards*. She'd walk the red carpet. Mingle with celebrities. Wave to the cameras. If she was lucky, she'd show up on *E! News*. The minute she'd returned from the interview, Melina had set her TiVo to record the event. Just in case.

"What do you think?" Melina bounced on her toes and met her friend's bright blue eyes, practicing the show-stopping smile she'd give to the paparazzi that followed Hayden around. "Am I going to rock his socks, or what?"

"Wow, Mel, I don't—I'm speechless."

"Let's hope he is, too."

"I don't understand why Hayden is going to the Silverlights in the first place," Coleen said, her gaze raking up and down the dress. "He's not in the film industry."

"No, but I guess his father is on the Board of Governors and is getting some kind of honorary award for his work." She shrugged, excitement pulsing through her. "Hayden gets two complimentary tickets."

Colleen shook her head slowly. "And he asked you to be his date…"

Melina flinched at her friend's disbelieving tone. "Why wouldn't he?"

"I don't mean it like that." Colleen grabbed Melina by

the arm and dragged her to the edge of the bed. They shoved clothes aside and plopped down, dangling their legs over the edge. "It's just that…isn't he still dating that *Sports Illustrated* model? You know, the one with the rack?"

"I've got a nice rack." Frowning, Melina grabbed handfuls of her B cups and held tight. "Okay, okay, so they're not as big as the other girls he's dated, but at least they're real! Doesn't that count for something?"

"I don't know." Colleen shrugged. "I'm more of a leg girl."

Melina snorted into a belly laugh. "I don't think the size of my boobs matters anyway. He totally thinks I'm hot as-is."

"Really?" Colleen beamed, snatching Melina's hands off her boobs. "He told you that?"

"He didn't say the words, but one glance and I could feel the chemistry. It was like—" How could she possibly explain their connection? It was crackly. Sparkly. Fizzling the air between them. "—Snap, Crackle, Pop."

Colleen's smile fell, and she cocked a thinly-plucked eyebrow. "You're talking about the cereal? Sweetheart, I think we need to get you out more often. You shouldn't feel anything close to cereal when you're with a guy like Hayden Dean. You should melt. Like butter."

"Oh, there was definite melting going on."

If Hayden had been any hotter, he would've melted the panties right off her body.

"All right." Colleen nodded. "You better get your petite ass moving. He'll be here in twenty, right?"

Melina gasped, shooting a glance at the clock on her bedside table.

Six o'clock.

"It can't be that late already!"

She swept off the bed in a whirlwind, dug around in her drawer for a pair of Spanx, and dashed into the bathroom. Squeezing into the bodysuit, she leaned and tugged as the stretchy material inched up her body. With a groan, she wiggled into the stunning Prada dress. Colleen zipped up the back, *oohing* and *aahing* as Melina spun, excitement spearing through her. For the next fifteen minutes, she applied her makeup. Dried her hair. Straightened and smoothed down the fly-aways. If she hadn't drained her bank account to buy this dress last week, she might've had the money to pay for a stylist. But things were tight.

As soon as she landed a job at *Eclipse*, she'd be fine.

Six-thirty came and went.

Glad to have a few extra minutes, Melina wiggled her size eights into her sky-high shoes and had Colleen strap them. She tweaked her hair. Reapplied her lipstick. Chose a pair of long silver earrings with chunky beads hanging off them. They were high fashion, bordering on gaudy, and they were perfect.

She checked the time on her cell, and just in case, scanned the log for missed calls. There weren't any.

Nerves settled in, though there was really no room for them in her dress.

"I'm sure he's having trouble parking," Colleen said. But her voice didn't sound so confident.

"Yeah." Her lips twitched. "Parking's hellacious around here."

Melina shrugged off the doubt. As her toes protested the squeeze she'd put them under, she lowered herself onto the bed—keeping her posture straight so the dress didn't crinkle—and then flicked on the flat-screen mounted to the wall.

"Look." Using the remote as a pointer, Melina poked it in the direction of the television. *E! News* flashed over the screen. "People are already showing up."

"I think they show up early and circle the block over and over again, waiting for the perfect moment to stop." Colleen sat beside her, crossing her leather-clad legs at the ankle. She was long and lanky—probably six inches taller than Melina, who stood at five-foot-two on tiptoe—and hung her feet over the end of the bed. "I'm sure some like to be there first thing, and others like to make an entrance. From what I've heard, Hayden likes to have all eyes on him. I'm sure he won't mind being late."

It must've been Colleen's mention of Hayden that made Melina see him emerge from a limo parked at the curb. The camera angle was distant and from the side, so she couldn't be sure, but this man was the same height and general size, with the same complexion. He turned before she could get a good look at his face. He extended his hand for two blonde bombshells to exit the limousine behind him.

That couldn't be right.

Blinking quickly to clear her head, Melina leaned forward as worry hardened into a ball in the pit of her stomach.

"Mel," Colleen whispered, "is that…"

"I don't think so."

Colleen had either read her mind, or Hayden Dean was there with someone else. Two, to be exact. As the camera angle zoomed on Hayden's look-a-like, Melina's heart dropped to her Blahniks.

Hayden grinned and held up the hands of his escorts as they spun for the cameras, their green silky gowns hiding little of their curvy figures.

It was Hayden Dean. Playboy. Casanova. *Pompous ass.*

"Oh my God, Mel." Colleen grasped her shoulders. "What a jerkhole!"

Melina nodded as tears pinched her eyes. She wasn't crying for him. She wasn't. She couldn't be. She'd just been so freaking excited to be going to the Silverlight Awards. That had to be it. She'd spent all day building up tonight's experience. She'd planned it all out in her head. Of course she'd feel deflated when the fantasy didn't match the reality.

Cinderella wasn't going to the ball after all.

Desperate to get a closer glimpse of the television and Hayden's smug face, Melina crawled over the bed on her hands and knees. When she reached the end, the breath *whooshed* out of her lungs.

"Are you okay?" She heard Colleen say. "Mel?"

"I'm fine."

Oh, she was far from the bland emotion. She wanted to rip out Hayden's tongue and shove it where the sun didn't shine. The man was a snake in—oh God, was that *Prada*? They would've matched. They could've been the perfect pair.

"I should've known better," Melina mumbled. "I should've listened to my gut. Somewhere deep inside I think I knew all those magazines couldn't be wrong." She shook her head. "I gave Hayden Dean the benefit of the doubt, and two hours of my day. Those are two things he didn't deserve. I won't spend another second thinking about him."

"Good for you."

Melina sighed. "I guess I just hoped—I just thought maybe for once, the fairy tale could actually come true for me, you know?"

As her legs cramped, she sat back. The ear-piercing sound of fabric ripping hit her ears. She stilled, slowly glancing down. She brushed her fingers over a rip in the Prada dress she'd spent her entire month's earnings on.

Tears burning her throat, Melina glared at Hayden's face on the television screen and realized two things.

By ripping her Prada dress, she'd just committed a fashion sin.

And fairy tales were most definitely real. They *were*. Maybe not for her, but for the girls on Hayden's arms. They radiated happiness, their wide, innocent eyes taking in the fanciful scene around them. They smiled as she would've been smiling. If those blondes could live in a dream, she could too. She had control over her life, including who came in and out of it.

She should be blissfully happy too.

Why'd she have to wait for some dashing knight in shining armor to come riding in on a white horse and sweep her off her feet?

She vowed, then and there, in her torn Prada dress, that she'd make her fairy tale come true…without an arrogant Prince Charming like Hayden Dean on her arm, acting as if he was the one responsible for it all.

Chapter Two

ALMOST ONE YEAR LATER…

Two thunderous *bangs* on the bedroom door jerked Hayden upright. Blankets and pillows slid off the edge of the bed in a waterfall of down.

He peeked through impossibly heavy lids, using his heightened werewolf senses to scan the dark. The curtains were still drawn tight.

It didn't matter who was at the door.

He'd had a rough night filled with too many Crown and Cokes. He pinched his eyes tight, the strobes from the nightclub a familiar blinding pulse against the back of his eyelids.

"Go away!" Hayden fell back onto the mound of pillows, twisted onto his stomach, and buried his head under the thickest one. "Come back in two hours."

Bang! Bang! Bang!

"I said go away."

A key shifted in the lock.

"Get the"—He scrambled to pull the sheet over his naked body—"hell out of here!"

Two-hundred-and-sixty pounds of pissed-off werewolf barged into the room, swinging the door open wide. Once his lap was covered, Hayden exhaled heavily and leaned back against the headboard.

It was only Gabriel Park. Packmate, Hayden's assigned secondary, and most trusted friend. He'd bailed Hayden out of so many sticky situations, the guy deserved a medal.

"I appreciate the personal wake-up call." Hayden stretched. "But you could've used the phone and avoided the peep show."

"Your phone's off and downstairs security had a do-not-disturb order until noon." Gabriel marched for the windows on the far side of the room. Seemed his jaw was set on a permanent clench setting. "She's fired up and out for blood."

She could only be the infamous Lydia Hyde, packmate and co-founder of Dean, Hyde, & Hammer, and managing editor of *Eclipse* magazine. She was six-hundred years old—four-hundred years older "and wiser" than Hayden—and she never let him forget it. Alongside Angus Dean, Hayden's father and the San Francisco Wolf Pack's Alpha, she'd built Dean, Hyde, & Hammer into one of the country's most prominent law firms. She ruled the branches of the wolf pack's companies with an iron fist, and since Hayden's father passed last year, she'd taken it upon herself to make him feel like shit for what he *didn't* do.

It was the same script, set on repeat: he wasn't good enough to run the firm or rule the pack. According to Lydia, he never would be.

He was the son of the Alpha, true. But he was adopted. A turned wolf accepted into a born wolf's home.

It was blasphemy to some. To him, the pack was the only home he'd ever known.

"She's always out for blood. What's new?" Hayden tunneled his fingers through his hair, the long waves tangling in his grasp. "Is that seriously the reason you busted in here?"

Gabriel jerked open the curtains, blinding Hayden with harsh rays of daylight. He picked up a pair of jeans Hayden had strewn on the floor and chucked them at him. "What happened to you this morning?" Gabriel fired.

Hayden tossed the jeans aside and scrubbed his hand over his face. "You banged on my door. I rolled out of bed."

"It's ten o'clock, Sleeping Beauty. You missed the banquet this morning."

A mix of doubt and panic streaked through him.

"Hell, you say." Leaning over the bed, Hayden snatched his cell off the bedside table. He waited for it to turn on and then flicked his thumb over the screen. "Fuck me."

Ten-oh-three.

He was supposed to be the keynote speaker for a wolf pack breakfast honoring the guards of the pack. For the last year, they'd been on high alert, working double-time to rein in the rogue wolves who'd split from the pack the few months before the Alpha died. They'd made their stance known right away; they believed turned wolves were inferior to born wolves and shouldn't be under the protection of the pack. Hayden's father had vehemently believed otherwise. Four turned wolves had already been kidnapped from the city's streets. Two of the victims were still missing. They'd amped up the search efforts, but a safe return wasn't looking good.

The rogues' agenda hit too close to home.

This morning, Hayden was supposed to put on a happy face. Boost morale. Give 'em a pep talk that'd breathe new life into the search for the rogue wolves and the turned wolves they'd abducted.

Even though he hadn't been declared Alpha yet, he should've been there.

"Lydia covered for you," Gabriel offered.

Of course she did. She always had the pack's best interest at heart, and had always been there to pick up the pieces when he dropped them.

"I'm sure it was fine." Regret soured Hayden's stomach.

He'd have to make it up to them. During his induction ceremony at the end of the month, he'd have to honor the guards. Discuss their courage and tell tales of their heroism on the streets.

He'd have to do better—*be* better—from here on out to earn their respect.

He'd have to be a better man like his father.

"You're in it deep this time, and not only with Lydia." Gabriel sat on the edge of the bed and stared at the blank television on the wall above the stone hearth. "The council is questioning your ability to take the role of Alpha seriously. They're not sure you're the best for the job."

As Hayden shot upright, tiny stars danced in front of his eyes.

"What are they going to do? Ask someone else to be Alpha?"

Gabriel leveled him with a humorless stare. "Exactly."

"They wouldn't do that." Even as he said the words, doubt trickled in. "They couldn't. I'm Angus's only son. According to pack law, the position of Alpha should pass to me."

"There's a clause in his will stating the council has the right to vote on another Alpha if the heir to the throne is deemed unworthy."

"*Unworthy?*" The word escaped as a growl. "The council thinks I'm *unworthy?*"

How could they not see how much he did for them?

He'd give his life to any one of his packmates. Any. One. Of. Them.

Gabriel shrugged, his sport's jacket tightening over his

bulky shoulders. "They haven't said the words officially, but they demanded Lydia hire someone to improve your public image before the ceremony. They want no more parties, no more drinking, no more—"

"Is that all they see when they look at me? A sloppy drunk?" Hayden interjected. "I may not have the desire to run the law office like my father did, but that doesn't mean I'm unworthy. I'm a *Dean*, for Christ's sake. He taught me to rule from the moment he took me into his house." He flopped onto his back, the air in his lungs coming up short. "Once I'm Alpha, everything would change. It'd have to, and I'd gladly accept the responsibility"

Gabriel shot him a slanted glare as he strode to the door and swung it open wide. "You party hard, Hayden. You can't deny it."

"No, I can't. But that doesn't mean I won't be the best damn Alpha the pack has ever seen."

"I agree with you," Gabriel said, nodding. "But my opinion doesn't change anything. Lydia hired a columnist who specializes in improving celebrity images to do a piece on you for their December magazine."

Hayden's eyebrows pitched for his hairline. "I'm not exactly a celebrity, Gabriel."

"You're in the public eye." His friend shrugged. "Between your father's legacy, the money, parties, and the models you date, you've trained the spotlight on yourself. Anyway, this columnist is going to follow you around for a while. It's not a choice, celebrity, public figure, or otherwise."

"This is bull."

"It's not going to be every day," Gabriel said, throwing up his hands. "Two weeks, maybe. A month tops."

"Is the council really going to get rid of me because I like to have a good time every now and then?"

Gabriel stared.

"I don't have time for this. The rogues need to be controlled now. Before they go too far. The council should be focused on them rather than my reputation."

"I'm having the columnist meet you at the game tonight." He went on as if he hadn't heard what Hayden had said. Maybe it was because it really didn't matter. The wheels were already rolling in a different direction. "I already sent her editor the ticket to get into the pack's luxury suite. You can spend the game chitchatting. From what I hear, she's into fashion."

Hayden suppressed a growl. Game nights were *his* nights. He drank cheap beer, screamed at the refs, and rooted for the red and gold.

"You're determined to ruin the game for me, aren't you?" Hayden bit out.

"What do I care if your Niners lose? I'm a Cardinal fan." Gabriel smirked. "Anyway, she's going to get the real Hayden Dean story—minus the hairy wolf details, of course—and then she's going to write an article, painting a better picture."

Hayden swallowed down the bile rising at the back of his throat. "And what does the council plan to do with this article?"

"It's going public, like every other article the press has ever done on you," he said simply. "Only this one will have a good spin. It'll be posted to the e-entertainment website, *Celeb Crush*, first, and if Lydia thinks it's good enough, it'll go to print next month in *Eclipse*. Thing is, Hayden, from the outside, it looks as if you're teetering between rock-star status and disaster zone. The council merely wants to rebuild a bit of that image before they declare you Alpha."

Hayden stared, unmoving, his mouth hardened into a straight line. "Do you think there's anything wrong with my public image, or how that affects my ability to rule the pack?"

"As your friend, I say no. This is your life. Live how you want, doing what makes you happy. As your secondary, I say you need to get your shit together before they steal the Alpha seat from you and hand it over to someone God-awful."

He'd sacrifice himself to the pack before that happened.

Looking on the bright side though, if he had to be shadowed by someone from the magazine, maybe he could have some fun with the hot little writer. He could give her a *real* sneak peek into his life…and maybe, if he was lucky, his bed.

He struggled to suppress a grin. "So what's her name?"

"Melina Rae," Gabriel said, as he strode into the hall.

Hayden's bed disappeared beneath him as the sound of the familiar name hit his ears. He'd tried to bury the tantalizing memory of that temptress beneath a year's worth of partying and dating other women. Judging from the scorching pinpricks of unease spreading through Hayden's gut, it hadn't worked.

There was no way he could allow Melina Rae to hang around for a month. Her mouth-watering scent had followed him into his dreams, and had messed up his sniffer for days.

Not happening.

Nuh-uh.

No way in hell.

• • •

Melina held up a ticket to a private luxury suite at Levi's Stadium, and fought to hide her grimace.

49er versus Cardinal game.

Something wasn't right, Melina thought. She hated the *Whiners*. Anyone who spent more than a few minutes with her during football season knew she'd grown up in a Raider Nation family. A tiny Raider flag was propped in the desk-supply caddy on her desk, for crying out loud. Beyond all that, Sylvia Reinhart, editor-in-chief of *Celeb Crush*, never gave gifts. Ever.

Melina waved the ticket in front of her face. "Thanks…I haven't been to a Niner game in ages."

Because they sucked.

"They're not a gift, Ms. Rae." Leaning over her cluttered desk, Sylvia Reinhart pushed her thick-rimmed glasses up her nose and glared. "It's your next assignment."

"I'm sor—sorry?" Melina felt her face scrunch. "Is someone huge going to the game tonight?"

If she landed an interview with someone like Ashton Kutcher or supermodel Marisa Miller, it could make her career.

"Listen, whatever you do, you can't screw this up," Sylvia said, as if to herself. She ripped her glasses of her nose and tossed them onto a pile of papers to her left. "You got it?"

"You say that as if I've screwed up before."

Melina's new column in the monthly e-magazine, "A Month in a Celeb's Shoes," required her to get the nitty-gritty details of whichever celebrity she featured, and then spin those details to make him or her sound like one of Hollywood's angels. She'd make cheaters appear loyal, and scoundrels become wholesome.

Apparently, it was her secret talent.

There was no celebrity image she couldn't twist or re-tool.

"You've had the golden touch this past year," Sylvia said, "but this assignment comes from corporate."

Oh, shit.

Sylvia rested her elbows on the desk. "You nail this article and it'll be featured in *Celeb Crush* and *Eclipse*."

"*Eclipse*?" Melina's hands went numb. "It'll actually go to print?"

"Do I have your attention now?"

Melina plopped into the chair across from Sylvia's desk. "Who am I meeting?"

"The assignment is to make this guy look good. No matter

what." Sylvia paused, and bit into her lower lip. "If you can pull this off, the people at *Eclipse* want you to work for them. They said to consider this your interview."

The air sucked out of Melina's lungs on a *meep!* She placed her hand over her heavily thumping heart and fought to catch her breath. "This is my dream. It's all I've ever wanted. I'll do it. I'll put everything aside. I'll work overtime. I'll make this guy shine like a freaking diamond if that's what the editors at *Eclipse* want."

If it meant landing her dream job, she'd make a steaming pile of dog crap look good.

"Fine. It's settled then. You'll have to write the article quickly. I want to see the first draft in two weeks to make sure you're on track. Final copy goes out at the end of the month." Sylvia sighed and leaned back in her chair, nailing Melina with piercing emerald eyes. "As long as you understand the stakes, I'll tell them you're on board."

"Thank you so much," Melina gushed, slapping the ticket against her legs. "I won't disappoint you, or *Celeb Crush*." She was chomping at the bit to find out whom she'd cover. There were so many celebrities who could use the magazine to improve their image. Britney Spears…Miley Cyrus… Dare she hope for someone hunky like Colin Farrell? "So?"

Sylvia's lips twitched. "Next month's column will be titled, 'A Month in Hayden Dean's Shoes.'"

Melina's stomach fell. "Hayden Dean."

"The one and only."

She'd been right earlier. To get her dream job, she'd have to make a steaming pile of dog crap look good. Only Hayden Dean didn't look like dog crap. As a matter of fact, he had the classic good looks of a Greek god.

Dog crap, she reminded herself, as she marched out of Sylvia's office, football game ticket in hand. *Hot*—really freaking hot—*steaming, dog crap.*

Chapter Three

Standing square on the fifty-yard line, Hayden introduced players from the last thirty years into the 49ers Hall of Fame. He waved and smiled for the cameras, and shook hands with the 49er Foundation Board of Directors and honorable officers.

His father had donated his time and charity to his favorite team, using Angus Dean Investment Services, and passed along his love of football to Hayden. Now, one year after Angus's death, Hayden was honored to accept an award in his father's name.

After his duties were finished, he swept into the wolf pack's luxury suite. He expected Melina to be waiting for him. Silky dark hair falling over her shoulders. Sexy brown eyes. The petite little thing was a vixen, haunting his dreams.

The suite was empty. Not even the sight of his favorite food and drinks arranged on a long table against the wall to his right could soothe the disappointment souring his stomach. The wolf pack had followed his orders to the letter. Nachos with chili and jalapenos. Mini hot dogs. BBQ Sausage links. They even got the beer fountain right.

His stomach growled fiercely, but he couldn't eat.

Not until she showed up and he could put his anxiety to rest.

The first quarter went by in a blur. The 49ers were at the top of their game. The crowd roared, rising to their feet, swinging red-and-gold T-shirts over their heads. But Hayden couldn't celebrate the two early touchdowns with them. He stood near the back of the suite, rods of tension hardening his body to the point of pain. He was going to need a massage after this; he'd have knots for days.

All this from merely thinking about Melina coming back into his life, even if it was only for a month.

Why couldn't he have met her at a different time, under different circumstances? During their interview at Starbucks last year, he'd tried to play it cool, the way he did with every other woman. But she didn't fall for any of his lines or believe any of his bullshit. She seemed to look right through him. For the first time in as long as he could remember, he felt as if he could be himself. As if he could tell her anything. He'd felt a spark of...*something*...between them, and he couldn't exactly pinpoint what it was. It was damn strange. Acting on the primal impulse howling in his gut, he'd invited her to the Silverlight awards.

Terrible timing.

Hours before the awards show, a rogue wolf had kidnapped their first victim: a turned wolf from the Alpha's private council. Hayden's father recovered a note left behind in his office. It was a declaration of war on turned wolves and non-shifters associated with the wolf pack.

Inviting Melina, a non-shifter, to a very public event like the Silverlight Awards would've been interpreted as Hayden's official stance on the issue. It would've put a target on his back, and the Alpha's. More importantly though, Melina would've been an irresistibly sexy bleep on the rogues' radar. They would've gone after her—he knew it with every fiber of his being. And although he'd only known her a few short hours, he felt something for her. He was too involved to risk her safety.

To keep things neutral, Angus had demanded that Hayden choose a born shifter from the pack as his date instead.

He'd chosen another date to keep her safe, to keep that precious heart beating in her chest.

He hadn't called to cancel his date with her. How would he have explained it? "Hey, I can't take you to the Silverlight Awards or my Alpha werewolf father could be targeted by a group of rogue wolves. Oh yeah, one more thing. If you're associated with me, they'll probably hunt you down and rip your heart out. Sorry."

Who would believe such a thing?

He could nearly feel the burn of the slap across his cheek now.

He'd tried to brush off her memory as best he could, though it'd been damn hard.

Now, with his Alpha *worthiness* in question and the rogue wolves gaining strength, he couldn't, under any circumstances, let Melina get too close to him.

No matter how much he ached for it.

A year apart might've dulled the instant attraction, Hayden told himself as he poured himself a beer and flopped into a seat against the glass. As long as they didn't get personally involved, it'd be fine. She wouldn't have a target on her back if she were merely a columnist doing a piece on him.

Where the devil was she, anyway?

As halftime kicked off and the teams filed into the locker rooms, Hayden propped his feet on the seat in front of him. Kiss Cams cued up on the massive screens situated around the stadium, and the crowd erupted into *oohs* and *aahs*. He was half-interested, leaning back to drink his beer, when a familiar brunette appeared on the screen.

Melina.

She'd pulled her dark hair into a ponytail that emphasized the sharpness of her cheeks, the sweet pout of her lips, and the almond shape of her eyes.

The blood lurched through his veins, and then went cold.

She wore tight black jeans, and a Diehard Raider Fan T-shirt…to the Niner game. The crowd booed at the sight of the rival's apparel. She waved an arm over her head, laughed, and kissed the old man beside her on the cheek.

Hayden growled from deep within his chest.

She'd left him in the suite waiting for her to arrive while she partied in the crowd?

Painted on the wall over her shoulder, he spotted C136.

• • •

Melina hollered as the 49ers returned to the field for the third quarter. She didn't think twice about booing, and had already moved seats twice to avoid ruining the game for the fans surrounding her.

It was a good thing the stadium was nearly empty. There were a ton of seats available to steal for a few minutes each. Another few downs and she'd head up to the suite to face Hayden.

She wasn't ready. Not yet. Nerves still rattled in her belly and her hands clammed from the thought of meeting him face-to-face.

As the Cardinals kicked off and the Niners received, the returner took off down the field with the ball. Melina held her breath as the runner ate up ground, cutting this way and that, until he reached the twenty-yard line. A few more strides and he'd earn them another touchdown.

"Get 'em!" Melina screamed, cupping her hands over her mouth. "Come on!"

Out of nowhere, a Cardinal defensive player darted in from the left side of the field and dove into the red-and-gold runner, knocking him to the ground. The ball came loose. The Cardinal player landed on it and curled into a ball.

The crowd went silent in disapproval. Or shame, she guessed.

Whooping, Melina threw her arms into the air, knocking into someone next to her.

"Oh my gosh, I'm so—" She spun, and her words died off.

Hayden stood in the aisle beside her chair, his arms in the air, an empty pint glass tilting in his hand. And a giant wet spot soaked his 49er T-shirt. The liquid smelled like beer from where she stood, though that could've been the old guy next to her.

He removed his gaze from his beer-drenched shirt, sucked in a short breath, and leveled her with a heated gaze. "What are you doing?" His words were clipped. Harsh and cold. She'd be cold too, if she'd just had an entire pint of beer poured down her chest.

What *was* she doing? How to answer… "Umm…I'm root-root-rooting for the home team?"

He made a growling sound—*who does that?*—and wrung out the bottom of his T-shirt. "You were supposed to meet me in the suite." Two long pauses, and then, "Did you lose your ticket?"

She shook her head as the crowd went wild behind her. "No, I have it."

"I was waiting," he said. "I didn't think you were going to show."

"Sucks, doesn't it?" She smirked, and watched as his gaze landed on her mouth. Her insides trembled. "I'm here now. Want to get started?"

His jaw clenched, and a wall went up behind his eyes. "I have to change. You should too, before you get jumped. The fans here don't take well to black and silver. Did you bring anything to cover up with? A coat or a blanket?"

"Cover up?" A laugh bubbled out of her as she turned her attention to her rocking ensemble. "There's no way I'd cover this up. Besides, even if I did bring something, it wouldn't be the color you're obviously looking for. I don't own anything red."

"Nothing?"

Something about the way he spoke the word made her think of naughty red silky things he'd peel from her quivering body.

"Nope." She squeezed into the aisle, careful not to brush him. One touch and he'd feel the gooseflesh covering her arms. He couldn't know the effect he was having on her body. He was heartless. Cold. *That's the way she had to be*, she remembered. "What about you? Do you own anything as black as your heart?"

"Ouch." He pierced his lips together, and then nodded. "I guess I deserve those jabs after leaving you behind at the Silverlights."

At least he remembered the extent of his douchebaggery. "You think?"

The crowd erupted. Another 49er touchdown.

He leaned in close, catching her off-guard. She held her breath as he whispered, "I'm sorry for the way that went down, and I don't have an explanation other than I was an inconsiderate ass. I know you probably won't believe it, but I did you a huge favor that night." He pulled back, leaving her shaking on unsteady legs. "You deserve way better than a guy like me."

He stared, waiting for her to answer.

She shook her head, speechless at the sympathetic tone

in his apology. And it sounded sincere, damn it. She softened, despite the anger she tried to summon.

"I'm going back to the suite," he said, turning to head up the stairs. "I'm going to change, get another beer, and then we can talk about the boundaries of our agreement."

Hayden was notorious for ditching out on his responsibilities. Yet here he stood, eager to talk about their agreement?

She hadn't prepared her defenses for that.

She should still be angry with him, shouldn't she? In spite of everything, she didn't feel that way. She felt surprisingly, *stupidly*…intrigued.

"Okay," she said, a bit rattled. "I'll be right behind you."

As she watched him march up the stairs, Melina got the feeling Hayden expected this article to be written on his terms. Saying exactly what *he* wanted to say, showing only the parts of him that *he* wanted to show.

Well, he had another thing coming.

She'd write the article *Eclipse* wanted. She'd make Hayden look like a golden warrior of virtue if that's what earned her a job there. But along the way, she'd try to dig up every single dirty deed he'd ever done. And then, when the time was right, she'd expose Hayden Dean's dirtiest secrets to the world.

She hid the smile curling the corners of her lips, steeled herself against his natural charm, and trudged up the stairs behind him.

Chapter Four

Hayden struggled to control his breathing as he marched up the last stair and turned toward the direction of the luxury suite. From the moment Melina bumped into him, her drugging aroma had assaulted him. He felt winded, as if the air refused to fill his lungs. Even in human form, he could sense hints of the lavender in her shampoo and the honey fragrance in her lotion. He wanted to drag her against him, bury his face in her hair, and take a deep, heavenly breath until she consumed him.

Note to self: have Gabriel stock up on nose plugs. Melina's scent was bound to drive him mad.

He could sense other things about her, too. She was stalking behind him, her stride slow and sure, her gaze measuring everything around them. He could almost feel her eyes on his back. If he listened closely, the strong, strumming sound of her heartbeat whispered to him, calling him closer.

He'd never been so in tune with a woman before.

Why couldn't things have been different? If she'd been born a werewolf, they could've been together. The pack would've accepted her with open arms. But as a non-shifter, she didn't belong in his world. And the timing was horrible considering there were rogue wolves roaming the city streets, determined to do anything to keep people like her out.

If they got together—*damn,* what he wouldn't give to toss her over his shoulder and carry her to bed, even once—she'd be in danger.

He couldn't do that to her.

She didn't ask to be a part of his world.

He'd have to keep his distance. Leave her be. Keep her safe.

"We're almost there. It's the second door on the left." He craned his neck around to meet her gaze, and then pointed to a cart selling 49er gear. "You want to pick something up? I can spot you twenty."

She puckered her lips in defiance and kinked her head to the side. "Not hardly."

"There he is!" Screeching voices brought Hayden's gaze back to center. A group of twenty-something women huddled near the door to the suite, hands covering their mouths. "Oh my god!"

"It's him!"

"Hayden Dean!"

High-pitched screams bounced off the walls and lanced through his eardrums. He froze as the group rushed him, circling like hungry predators, anxious to overwhelm their prey. Melina fell back, out of sight. Hayden's nose tingled, as if instinctively searching her scent out among the others.

"How are you ladies doing tonight?" he said to one. She giggled and squealed to the friend beside her instead of answering—the usual response he received from a female. "I'm doing great too, thanks. Enjoying the game."

"Are you still with Heidi?" the redhead at his left asked. "You two were the hottest couple in Hollywood."

Except he didn't live in Hollywood. Dean, Hyde, & Hammer didn't have offices there, either. And he'd never dated Heidi. She was simply a woman he'd driven home after she'd had one-too-many drinks at a club in the Lower Haight. A handful of e-magazines had snapped a photo of the woman in his arms, her head resting on his shoulder, as they headed out of the club. The magazines crafted the headlines to make it appear as if Hayden was escorting the woman back to his place to take advantage of her inebriated state.

It seemed no one cared about the truth.

And that might've been all right. Because if people focused on the lies, they wouldn't dig deeper to know the *real* truth. It was better to be seen as a playboy than a werewolf.

"Are you enjoying yourself?" he asked a blonde. He grinned. She winked and reached for his crotch. "Easy, now. There's enough of me to go around." Redirecting the bold move, he grabbed her hand, kissed the back, and replaced it at her side. "Ladies, it's been a pleasure meeting you all." As he skirted toward the suite, they followed, their words jumbling into giddy shrieks. They smelled like a cocktail of sin, hairspray, and vanilla lotion. It burned his nose, the way a non-shifters scent usually did. Well, with the exception of Melina's. "Unfortunately, I have to run. I've got some important business to take care of." He waved, blew a kiss — his signature move — and backed into the suite. "Ms. Rae, are you lost?"

"No, I'm coming," she said, pushing her way through. "Just swamped back here."

Nothing could drown her out; she was foolish to think it. A gigantic spotlight might as well have been trained on her. Her lips were plush — though pinched in irritation — and her dark hair shone with honey highlights. God, those strands would be silky-smooth weaving through his fingers, wouldn't they?

"She's writing an article on me for *Celeb Crush*," he told

the crowd, pushing the door open to let Melina in. "Look for it next month."

And then this would be over. He'd never have to see Melina Rae again.

His stomach tightened.

• • •

Melina waited for the door of the luxury suite to *click* closed before turning around to face him. "Don't you have bodyguards to take care of your groupies?"

He seemed to pause, staring at the closed door as if he was lost in thought. Maybe he was thinking about escaping. If he knew how bitter she was about being stood up, he'd be smart to do it.

"I don't like bodyguards tailing me to games. Makes too much of a scene." He strode to a bucket of jerseys in the corner, swiping his hands on his dark-washed jeans as he went. He swung open the door and took a deep breath. "And they're fans, not groupies. Big difference between the two."

"Which is?"

"Groupies have psychotic tendencies."

"Sounds like you know something about it." Too bad security wouldn't let her bring her purse into the stadium. She would've liked to take notes on her iPad for the article.

Oh yeah, here comes the dirt.

"Believe it or not, I've never dated a groupie. Doesn't mean there haven't been a few who've *thought* they dated me from something as simple as a hello or good morning."

"If you don't want to give the wrong impression, you might want to rethink, you know—" Melina shrugged, kinking her head to the side to play the part of a ditzy blonde. "—leading them on and dating a new one every month."

It wasn't rocket science. If he wasn't interested, he

shouldn't play with a woman's emotions.

Without saying a word, Hayden stripped the beer-soaked shirt from his torso. Layer upon layer of glistening gold muscle twitched and flexed as he flung it to the floor near the jersey bucket.

"Jesus," Melina breathed, and spun around to check the scoreboard. The Cardinals were up by sex. *Six,* she corrected mentally. They were up by six. She plopped onto one of the barstools near the glass and looked out over the field. "You're certainly not shy, are you?'

"No, not anymore." He spoke slowly, the tiny hint of a drawl escaping his lips. "There's no room for shyness when you grow up in the spotlight. Since I was twelve, I've gone to nearly every charity event associated with my father's companies. Know what it's like to have a publicly documented history of your awkward years?"

She shuddered at the thought.

"Yeah," he said, appearing beside her. "That's my reaction, too. If the world wants to take pictures of me now, so be it. Nothing can be worse than the others out there."

Out of the corner of her eye, Melina watched Hayden yank a dry 49er jersey down his abs. She forced her body to chill out. One glimpse of those ridges on his stomach, and she'd started to sweat.

He took the barstool next to her and faced her, his legs spread slightly, one foot kicked up on the bottom rung. His dark hair was stylishly disheveled, his eyes narrowed. Damn, if she had a camera, she'd snap this shot of him and sell it to *GQ.* It'd make front page, and earn her a killing.

He was effortlessly sexy, a model of powerful grace.

"We should set the ground rules for this article," he said, his voice a sexy rumble.

Melina almost fell back from the heat of him. The intensity and smolder in those chocolate-brown eyes.

"You can ask anything about me, my habits and food preferences or whatever, but the focus remains on me and me alone. My family and close circle of friends are not to be discussed." He tipped back his glass. "Period."

"That's fine."

She didn't want to destroy their reputation. Just his. It was oddly chivalrous of him to want to protect them from the scrutiny of the public eye. The thought struck her as honorable, but she dismissed it. He must've had another reason for the request.

"I don't want any mention of my home," he went on, "and I don't want anything discussed further back than the last fifteen years."

Control issues, much? "I don't quite understand the part about your home, but if that's what you want, it's doable."

"Perfect. Glad we're clear on that." He stretched his leg out and tapped his foot against her stool. "Did your editor give you any direction for the article?"

"She told me to make you look good." Melina watched absentmindedly as the 49ers charged downfield and scored. "My job is usually pretty easy, but you've got a track record, so it's not like I'm working with a blank slate. People already have an opinion of you in their mind. I'll simply have to tweak it."

"What's their opinion?" He fist-pumped the bar when the 49ers kicked their extra point. It was good, slicing through the uprights. "What do people think about me?"

She took a long, hard drink, hoping she wouldn't have to be so direct, especially to his face. Although she couldn't turn down the job offer from *Eclipse* to make Hayden look good—especially if they were offering her a stab at a print run—writing an article exposing Hayden as a chauvinistic pig sounded much more appealing.

"I'm sure you know what everyone is saying. You can't go into a grocery store without seeing your face on the cover of a dozen magazines."

"Oh, I see those magazines, and I read some of the articles. They're rather comical, actually." He stared, his fingers tapping along the length of the bottle. "But I'd like to hear it from you. What do you think?"

If he cared so much about what she thought of him, maybe he should've thought twice about standing her up without so much as a phone call last year.

"I'm not going to put my opinion into the article, if that's what you're worried about," she mumbled into another drink. "I'm going to report the truth, add a lot of fluff, and a glossy veneer."

"Believe it or not, there aren't many people in my inner circle who'll even give me that much. They think I'll fire them for being honest. They say one thing to my face and another behind my back. Something tells me you'll be honest with me, and I'm not talking about the 'truth' that you're going to write later this month. I believe you'll give it to me straight."

Fine. He wanted it. He was going to get it.

Sighing, Melina closed the distance between them, and held her breath so she wouldn't lose the nerve to say what had to be said. "I think you're a playboy, the heir to a huge fortune who squanders it away on hot parties and plastic women, and buys the fastest, most expensive cars he can, because he can."

He shook his head. "Nah, beyond all that. Give it to me, Melina."

Oh, God. Her panties melted at the words.

Idiot. That's not what he meant. Didn't matter. Her mind instantly went *there.*

"Okaaay." She breathed deep, willed the tingling in her middle to subside, and braced herself for the bitter truth pushing at her lips. "I think you put yourself in the public eye so people will be so blinded by the pretty face in front of them that they won't bother digging deeper. Because somewhere inside you"—she pointed a finger toward his stone cold heart—"there's a secret you've locked away like a caged animal so no one will see it."

If people were too busy gawking and criticizing his lifestyle choices, they wouldn't see what a failure he'd become in his father's eyes. At least that's the kind of gems she'd picked up from reading *Eclipse*'s "Taking Control Over Your Past" column.

Hayden paled, his pupils widening as he looked down at the finger pointing into his chest. An electric current zinged through her finger pad into her hand. She took it back, rubbing where it had warmed. Tingles covered her body, from the back of her neck to the tips of her toes.

Tension-filled silence ballooned into the space between them.

"I want more," he whispered so softly, she thought she'd misheard.

"Excuse me?" Her heart faltered. Apparently it heard his words loud and clear. "More of what?"

"Honesty." After rubbing his eyes with the back of his hand, he cleared his throat and readjusted the jersey over his shoulders. For the first time, he looked rather uncomfortable in his skin. "I asked for the truth. I didn't expect you to save me a month's worth of therapy. What's my secret?"

"I don't know," she stated simply. "You tell me."

He rapped his hands over his knees as if he was gearing himself up for something, and then swiped his glass off the table to take a hearty drink. "I'd rather not. I would like to know what you think about my image, though. From the outside looking in."

"It's tarnished."

Outside, the crowd went wild, so she checked the field. Cardinals were down with five minutes to go, but victory was theirs with a touchdown and two-point conversion.

"Redeemable?" Hayden swallowed hard.

She hesitated, puckering her lips. On the outside, Hayden had a lot going for him—financial stability, strong genes, a sexy voice, an honest career—if only people could get past the party boy, playboy image. And that would only happen if he were through partying and manipulating women.

"Jury's still out," she said.

"Fair enough." He rolled his fingers over his pint glass, and Melina realized he was tapping in some sort of a rhythm. Did he play piano? He took a deep breath and said, "If you were in a position to give me a leadership role, a big one, let's say, would you trust it to me?"

"That depends." A nervous giggle skipped out of her. "When you say leadership role, do you mean Head of the Jelly-of-the-Month Club or President of the United States?"

His stoic demeanor cracked as he smiled into a laugh. "Somewhere in the middle. How about…mayor of San Francisco? Would you trust me to run the city?"

Her first instinct was to laugh off his question—where was he going with it, anyway?—but the serious set of his mouth and the hard clench of his jaw made her think the answer somehow meant something to him.

"No, I don't think I would," she answered honestly. "I've seen the stories about you in the papers. Responsibility doesn't suit you well. But that's why I'm here, right? I'm assuming people on your staff hired me to clean up your image so you can take over one of your father's businesses?"

"Something like that." He nodded. "If you had to get me to the point where I'd be unequivocally trusted with a leadership role, what would you suggest to get me there?"

Picturing Hayden in politics was all kinds of backwards. He needed to star in movies and be the romantic lead. He'd win hearts of women across the country, hers included.

"If political prowess is your goal, there's an image

reconstruction plan I can share with you that'll help you focus on what's important," she offered. "It's something I put together on the side for the celebrities I've covered so far. If you want to see it, if you think you're ready to take it seriously, I can email it to you when I get back to my computer."

As the Cardinals scored — a deep pass to the corner of the end zone — and the crowd screamed in one uniform roar, Hayden stood and dug through his pocket.

"How long does this usually take?" He pulled out his wallet, removed a business card and slid it across the table in front of her. "The image consulting and improving thing couldn't take that long, right?"

She chuckled. "Are you in a hurry?"

"I have an important ceremony coming up at the end of the month. It'd be ideal if things improved by then." He shrugged, though his eyes shone with determination. "So? How long?"

"I can pack everything into a week or two," she said, sliding off the barstool and pocketing his card. "The first draft has to be finished early next week, so that gives you plenty of time to improve your image for the ceremony. But it all hinges on one very important thing."

"What's that?"

"Your willingness to change."

On a burdened exhale, Hayden turned his attention to the field, where a flurry of red and white scurried to the sidelines.

"A field goal will tie, but a two-point conversion will win it." His words were deep and raspy. Nearly a growl. "It's risky, but some say 'no guts, no glory.' Do you think they're going for it?"

"I would." She finished her drink. "If you want something bad enough, you should go after it." She paused and studied the man beside her. Hayden looked tight. On edge. As if he was holding his breath. He didn't look at her. "And if your competition tries to take it from you, you should fight to the bitter end," she said. "This is the Cardinals' game if they really want it. And your father's companies could be in good hands, if you had the desire to work as hard as he did."

At the mention of his father, Hayden averted his attention from the field and eyed her with dark intensity. If she wasn't mistaken, desire sparked behind his eyes. It was the same look he'd given her in Starbucks last year, when she'd mistakenly believed they had a connection. Her insides tumbled and squirmed, and her core warmed under the heat of his glare.

"You are one special woman, Melina. I can see why they chose you for this assignment." He licked his lips and caught the bottom one with his teeth. He eyed her mouth, and the temperature in the suite hit an unnatural high. "There's fire in you. It's a rare quality."

Wow. The world fell away beneath her feet and her heartbeat kicked into overdrive. Nothing existed beyond the walls of the suite. The football game could've been replaced with World War III and she wouldn't have been able to tear her gaze away from his.

"I need your help."

Her heart stuttered at the sound of her name on his lips.

"I need someone beside me, guiding me through this, and it has to be someone who'll be honest with me, no matter the cost. Someone who doesn't work for my father's lackeys so their opinion isn't tainted by the business. I need someone who can see what needs to be done to get me that position—job." He stuttered, and then seemed to catch himself. "But more than that, if we're going to work together, we have to set up strict guidelines. What's going to happen between us is business and nothing personal."

"Fine with me," she snapped, folding her arms over her chest. "I wouldn't have any reason to suspect it'd be otherwise."

Oh, she heard him, loud and clear.

"Nothing personal" translated to "not interested."

He was only going along with the article because she was good at her job, and knew how to get him out of a bind. He wasn't happy to see her, as she'd secretly—and stupidly—hoped. Nothing had changed since last year. *He* hadn't changed. He'd do anything, and use anyone, as long as it meant he could get ahead.

Playing with women's emotions had clearly become a game to him.

Swallowing down what she *really* wanted to say, Melina shifted her attention to the game. The Cardinal's center snapped the ball, except the kicker didn't drop back to kick. He palmed the ball, cocked back, and threw to a receiver in the end zone. He was wide open! They were going for the long-shot win!

Melina gasped, the breath catching in her throat.

Distracted by the defenders rushing him, the receiver took his eye off the ball. It bounced off the tips of his fingers and dropped to the ground. As one team lowered their heads in defeat, the others leapt off the ground and ran to the sidelines, relishing in the crowd's excitement.

"Raiders would've clenched the win." Melina shrugged nonchalantly, and strode toward the door. "Maybe next time."

"You're just upset the Niners won," Hayden said, swiveling to face her.

"They didn't win…not really." Melina waved, blew a kiss—Hayden's own cheesy signature—and then whispered a single line that'd haunt any hot-blooded man. "The other team just *sucks harder*." She spoke the last words slowly, drawing the primal meaning from them.

Hayden stared, his mouth falling open as she winked slowly and marched out of the room.

He wasn't the only one who could play games.

Girl power, for the win.

Chapter Five

As Hayden pulled his jet-black Bugatti into the underground parking at the Dean, Hyde, & Hammer building in the center of the bustling business district, he revved the engine and slid into the first RESERVED spot on the right.

It was noon, a full two hours before he normally arrived at the law firm. He didn't practice law, but he kept an office in the building. Any San Francisco Wolf Pack business passed over his desk—as it had his father's—and pack meetings were held in the Dean, Hyde, & Hammer boardrooms. Hayden didn't come to the law offices unless there were pack matters to handle, but he'd be spending nine-to-five there once he was officially inducted as Alpha.

Today, he wanted to make sure Gabriel had followed his instructions: swipe everything from the top of Hayden's desk into the top drawer so Miss Nosey wouldn't be inclined to snoop.

She'd texted late last night, saying she wanted to tag along on his typical workday.

Little did she know, a part of her had tagged along with

him long after the football game ended. He'd tossed and turned all night long, with two little words spiraling through his head.

Sucks harder.

Freaking woman.

He could still hear the way she'd said it. She wasn't as innocent and fragile as she pretended to be. *Oh, no.* She was a pistol, that one. A firecracker that'd explode in his hand. Still, he'd risk losing his hand to feel her, to traipse his fingers over her smooth, fragrant skin.

Would touching her again elicit the same spark, or had it been a one-time thing?

When she'd pointed her finger against his chest at the game, he felt as if he'd been shocked with high-voltage power cables. Only the current that passed from her body to his had been fiercely sexual, and had sent sizzling rods of lust straight to his groin. Desire bloomed hard and fast, and if Melina hadn't removed her finger as quickly as she did, he might've pinned her against the glass in the luxury suite and pleasured her until she broke apart.

Bet that would've been great feed for the Jumbotron.

Would've given "Kiss Cam" new meaning.

What made Hayden push her away wasn't the thought of embarrassing her in front of the entire stadium. It was the fact that he'd heard Luminaries—the non-shifter equivalent of soulmates—felt the same zinging connection upon first touch.

Fated mates came around once in a wolf's lifetime, if he was lucky. Some found their mates young, some not at all. And up until recently, Hayden had never heard of an Alpha finding his fated mate with a non-shifter. Not until Drake and Emelia Wilder from the Seattle Wolf Pack. They'd settled their differences and were blissfully happy and in love, from what he'd heard. But Seattle didn't have the same stigma associated with being a turned-wolf. After Emelia Wilder's transition, his pack accepted her with open arms.

The San Francisco Wolf Pack wouldn't be so forgiving. With escalating tensions between born and turned wolves in the city, there was no way in hell the council would vote him in as Alpha.

Not with a non-shifter at his side.

The pack would be too divided.

If Melina was his Luminary—another touch and he'd know for certain—their lives were about to be forever intertwined. He'd force himself to tune in, to use his heightened werewolf senses to search out his mate within her.

As he killed the engine and exited the sports car, Melina's scent assaulted him.

She was already here.

He spun, scanning the dark garage. With his keen eyesight, he spotted her immediately, striding away from a midnight-blue Jetta. Just when he thought she couldn't be more beautiful, she showed him he was wrong.

She wore black leather pants, short black boots, and a gray fur coat with a collar that brushed her chin. She'd let her hair down, layered around her heart-shaped face, and had painted the brightest shade of red on her lips. Most surprising—and disturbing—of all was the closer she got, the more Hayden realized the color of her coat was exactly the shade of his fur in wolf form.

"Thought you said you had to work today," she said as she approached, her hips swaying seductively.

He struggled to find his voice. "I do."

"It's noon, in case you haven't noticed. Most people start work first thing in the morning. That'll have to change for the next couple weeks, but we'll go over my list later."

"Your *list*?"

Nodding, she handed him a Starbucks cup. He hadn't even noticed she held two in her hands. He grabbed the cup, and tried to brush his fingers over hers.

One touch.

That'd be it.

She slid her hand off the cup before he could touch her.

"I read that you like Starbucks' Macchiatos," she said. "It's cold, since I bought it at eight this morning. You can trash it, if you want. I just didn't want to leave it in my car all day."

"No, thank you, this is great." He took a sip and refrained from spitting the drink onto the concrete. "I like my coffee cold."

She eyed him disbelievingly. He may have been lying about his coffee preference, but she'd been thoughtful to get him his favorite drink. People usually bought him drinks because they were told to. Not many did so because they *wanted* to.

She chucked her empty cup into the trash and said, "Do you usually start your day at this hour?"

No, usually it was later. "Depends if I've got work to do or not."

"With an empire as vast as Dean, Hyde, & Hammer, it's hard to believe a day would go by where there *wouldn't* be work to do." They moved toward the elevators, their strides in-step. "I mean, you're set to inherit the company that includes two hundred attorneys in the city alone, and another eight hundred worldwide. Aside from the law firm, Dean Enterprises owns an architectural company, a construction company, a financial corporation, and a magazine. It's almost as if your father had a hand in everything in the city, from the buildings to the media outlets. It took hours of work for me to research his legacy last night, and I barely brushed the surface. I can't imagine what you go through on a daily basis."

He pushed the button to whisk them to the fifteenth floor. "You've really done your homework."

"What can I say? I'm thorough."

Keeping the truth about the wolf pack away from her was going to be more difficult than he thought.

"Here's a question for you," she said, leaning against the elevator handrail. "Why do you show up here at all? You're not a lawyer, so what do you do all day?"

From the outside looking in, that was a good question.

As Alpha, wolf pack business was his father's main concern. For that reason, the Dean, Hyde, & Hammer building provided a believable front. Inside the building's doors, Angus had made sure turned wolves handled transitions appropriately, the wolves in the pack kept their world secret, and any rogue wolves were brought in and tried for their crimes against the pack. They'd spread roots in the city as deep as they could, and established their empire one corporation at a time.

A non-shifter wouldn't know any of that.

"Even though I haven't had any say in my father's businesses to this point, he wanted me to be included from a young age so I'd instinctively know how to run everything when he died." Hayden paused, listening to the hum of the elevator and the pounding of his heart. Tears stung his throat as memories of his father flooded him. "Now that he's gone, I'm supposed to slip into my role, but it's easier said than done." He hadn't expected to say the last part. "None of this should be included in—"

"I'm not writing any of this for the article," she interrupted. "I'm just curious. It's not every day I get a personal escort into one of the most diversified companies in the world."

As the doors opened on his floor, Melina held her breath. He shouldn't have been so in tune with her, but he couldn't help it.

"Wow," she breathed as the lights kicked on, illuminating the entire floor: the pool table and bar on one side, the free-weight gym that wrapped around the corner, and the piano lounge in front of them. "Bachelor pad office?" She nodded, smirking. "I should've expected this from you."

He brushed past her, holding his breath so her scent didn't follow him, and used the monitor near the elevator to turn off the security alarm.

"Is there some kind of bachelor magazine you used to order this stuff?" he heard her say while he punched in his code. "Leather couches, candles everywhere, grand piano… I bet you've got a bed in here, probably on the opposite side. It's round and zebra striped, isn't it?"

She was right. He did keep a bed here, though it wasn't covered in zebra patterns. It was black satin, and where he brought his overnight guests, so he didn't have to take them to his home. Better to keep everyone at arm's length.

With a start, Beethoven's Final Symphony echoed all around them from the surround sound system.

Melina spun slowly, glancing up at the speakers in the ceiling. "Classical?"

Frantic, Hayden jabbed at the buttons on the monitor to change the music to something more fitting…and less personal. He chose Stone Temple Pilots and prayed to God she didn't probe about his music choice. He should've remembered to tell Gabriel to turn it off before they arrived.

"This way," he said, turning along the wall housing the elevator shafts. It was the only wall in the office. Not a single wall blocked one room from another, and the glass on the outside wasn't glass at all. It was a huge one-way mirror. The entire face of the building was reflective, which meant Hayden could shift in his private office anytime he wanted without feeling as if someone was going to peek inside.

"These are great," she said from behind him. "I bet they're originals."

She must've been talking about the artwork on the central wall. She was right on that mark, too.

"I'm starting to think you're in the wrong business," he said over his shoulder as he opened the glass door to his office. "You should've been a detective."

"Nah, too much pressure. My deadlines are about all I can take." A smile spread over her face as she strode through the door, keeping her distance, and plopped into the leather chair across from his desk. She dropped the bag from her shoulder, set it at her feet, and then pulled out an iPad. "I sent over the image improvement plan while I was waiting for you to show up. Do you mind if we go over it before you get started for today? After that, I swear I'll disappear. You won't even know I'm here."

"Sounds great." He sat in his chair, rolled back, and rested his feet on the empty top. "Hit me with it."

"I wish I had a hard-bound copy to take you up on that, but I emailed it to you."

Hayden rolled close to the desk, and then cued up his email. "Hayden Dean's Image Improvement Plan" in the subject line stared back at him.

He opened the mail and scooted closer for a better look. "Phase One deals with the traits on the outside that scream laid-back and non-committal," he read aloud, "Clothes and hair should reflect business attitude. Schedule appointment with a stylist. Suit and tie, and briefcase suggested." He met her expectant gaze. "What's wrong with my hair?"

"It's got that tousled look, like you just rolled out of bed," she said. "It's sexy and wild. Not the vibe you want right now."

"You think my hair's sexy?"

She rolled her eyes, though a rosy pink blush bloomed over her cheeks. "Keep reading, would you?"

"Car of choice should be responsible instead of fast and fun." His world spun. "After work, time should be spent out of the public eye, in reflection or some private activity that does not involve bars, women, parties, or anything destructive."

He stared. She stared back, batting impossibly long lashes.

"You want me to be a monk?" He forced out a laugh. "Not happening."

"It's only for a month, right?" Her lips twitched as if holding back a smile. "Keep reading. You haven't reached Phase Two."

He'd agreed to let Melina follow him around and improve his image, but damn. Wasn't there anything he'd done right on his own?

He scrolled past a long list of To-Do's, Shouldn't-Do's, and Never-Do's. "Phase Two deals with change on the inside, that reflects on the outside. Learn to unwind using acceptable forms of relaxation such as mediation, yoga, and acupuncture. Work hard, after hours, taking on extra projects. Learn to compromise. Make time for friends and family. Trust your instincts, as long as they reflect the new and improved image." *Holy shit.* "You want me to trust my instincts? They say delete this email and never think about it again."

"I was thinking about you last night, and…"

Hold the phone. She thought about him last night? *Was she in bed when the thoughts struck her?* He wondered. Did she toss and turn and dream of him, too? He went hard at the thought of her in his bed, tangled in his sheets.

Shit, she'd been talking as his thoughts veered into the gutter. He shook his head. "I'm sorry, what?"

She groaned. "I'm supposed to improve your image with my article, but if nothing has changed in your life, from the outside or the inside, the business associates you want to impress will see through it. You've got to make changes to how you live your life if you want to earn their respect."

Gabriel had been telling him the same thing for years, long before his father had passed on. Sad truth was, Melina's words sank deeper than Gabriel's ever had. Maybe it was the fact that the council had threatened to take the Alpha seat from him. Even though Hayden knew he could handle pack business, if he didn't prove it to the council within the month, his opinion wouldn't matter.

"There are so many things wrong with this email, I don't even know where to start." His head ached. "Firstly, we've got to address—"

The elevators *dinged*, silencing him.

He wasn't expecting anyone, and although Gabriel came in and out, he always left a message stating when he was coming up, and for what purpose.

"Be right back," Hayden bit out. "Stay here."

Without waiting for an answer, Hayden swept out the doors and charged around the corner. Anita Cross, fellow packmate and Lydia's secretary, emerged from the elevator, and then backpedaled at the sight of him. "I'm sorry, Mr. Dean, I wasn't expecting you here."

"Which means you've invaded my privacy before," he said, standing in front of her, arms folded over his chest. "How many times?"

Her gray eyes went wide. "Never, s—sir," she stuttered. "I mean, never before now, sir."

He could smell her fear. It was bitter, tingling his nose. "What are you doing here?"

"I'm so sorry, sir, but the council is in the middle of a meeting and Lydia needed the newest report on the rogue attack. Gabriel had it sent to you, since you're, well, you know who you are, or who you'll be next month." Damn, she was stumbling all over herself. "He didn't want an electronic trail, so it was sent paper only, and Lydia couldn't find her copy. She sent me to retrieve it for the council. I was going to replace it on your desk as soon as the meeting was over."

Hayden couldn't stop the growl rumbling through his chest. "The council is meeting now? With Lydia?" It was all he could force out through the haze of anger rolling over him.

"Where? The boardroom?"

Anita shook her head. "Her office."

The fury rose in him, hot and vicious, nearly triggering the urge to shift into wolf form. He swallowed down the heady impulse. Barely. "I'll take the report to the meeting myself. Do yourself a favor. Disappear from the building for the next twenty minutes, and never step foot on my floor again."

Anita nodded into a bow, and then ran to the elevators. If he even sensed her in the building before his anger died off, he was liable to combust and take his aggression out on her. Although he was pissed off as hell that she'd even *think* about sneaking into the future Alpha's office and stealing something off his desk, she didn't deserve the brunt of his hatred.

She was simply following Lydia's orders.

How dare Lydia schedule a meeting with the council without him present! Hayden wasn't a genius, but he knew the reason she scheduled it now. He never came in this early. She'd planned to get close to the council, prove she could handle the Alpha's business, and squeeze him out completely.

To hell with that.

Focused on nothing but Lydia and the rogue report, Hayden burst into his office, jerked open his top drawer, and sifted through the papers until he found the one she'd wanted. He slammed the door closed and mumbled something to Melina about keeping herself busy—out of his office—until he came back.

Chapter Six

"What the hell, Lydia?" Hayden burst through the doors of Lydia's office and threw the report across the table. "How dare you call this meeting without me!"

"Hayden, great to see you," Lydia said, her face an apathetic mask. "Take a seat."

She was a beacon of poise and elegance—always had been. Raven-black hair cut to fall around her chin, beady black eyes with glasses perched on the edge of her nose. She sat at the head of an oblong table, *damn her,* with the three council members seated around the curves.

The council members had been some of the Alpha's most trusted friends. Before his passing, he'd appointed them himself. Reagan, the shortest and squattiest, had also been a loyal friend to Lydia's mother. White, the oldest on the council, had worked for Hayden's grandfather and was extremely faithful to the Dean family. The final member, "Mad Dog" Maddox, had joined the San Francisco Wolf Pack late in life, and had befriended Angus Dean almost immediately. Since the pack saved him from a life on the streets, he was loyal to them as a whole, rather than any one leader—that reason alone was probably why Angus had chosen him for the third council seat.

Hayden's fate, and that of the ruler of the pack, rested in their hands.

"I'm the pack's future Alpha. Any meeting having to do with pack business should include me." Hayden paused, trying to strangle Lydia with his stare. Why couldn't looks kill? Just this once. "Wouldn't you agree?"

She stared back, returning fire with a challenging gleam in her eye.

"Hayden, join us." White spread his arms to the opposite end of the table, where Hayden would be seated across from Lydia. "We were going to call the meeting later, when you'd be available to attend, but Lydia informed us of another attack this morning. We thought it best to discuss it now, while the coals burned hot."

They burned hotter in hell, where he wouldn't mind sending the snake on the opposite end of the table.

He leaned back in the chair and crossed his legs, propping his ankle up on the opposite knee. "Who reported the attack?"

"A non-shifter discovered the turned wolf bleeding behind a Dumpster in Haight-Ashbury," Reagan answered, templing his fingers as he leaned over the table. "The woman called the police first, but we intercepted the call and sent in the guards to clean up the mess before officers arrived."

"The wolf is in critical condition at Howlands," Lydia continued, "though he's not expected to make it. A silver rod is lodged in his chest, inches from his heart"

Shifting was the easiest way for a werewolf to heal—transitioning from wolf back to human form usually cured all wounds. But with a silver rod lodged in the wolf's chest, changing back to human form was risky. The rod could remain stuck, and could damage major organs during the process.

And while Howlands was a private facility built to house and care for critically injured werewolves with abnormal wounds, there wasn't much they'd be able to do for that wolf.

"Were there any witnesses?" Hayden asked, looking to minimize damages.

"Not that we know of," Mad Dog said, his voice booming through the office. "We're listening to scanners for breadcrumbs that'll lead us to witnesses or the wolf responsible."

Seemed as if they'd covered every issue. Without his involvement.

The council members should've tried harder to let him know what was going on, but he couldn't shrug off the burden weighing his shoulders. If he'd been here earlier, if he'd gotten into the habit of coming in early every day, Lydia wouldn't have been able to move the meeting without him knowing about it.

If he took it more seriously—all of it, every damn thing— maybe they'd take *him* more seriously…

"How do we know the rogue wolves are the ones responsible?" he probed. "Have they contacted us yet to—"

"We've already covered all of this." Lydia closed the laptop in front of her and sighed exasperatedly. "The leader of the rogue pack, a Were who identifies himself as Archer, called Howlands about an hour ago. They've claimed the attack as theirs and accepted responsibility."

"If you've already covered all this, why'd you need to send someone snooping through my office to nab the report?" Hayden flicked it further down the table.

"The operator at Howlands called to report that they'd received a message from Archer, but we didn't know what was said until now. They didn't want to discuss it over the phone line." Reagan scooped up the report and scanned quickly. "Well, now I know why they had a messenger deliver it by hand."

"Why's that?" Lydia pressed.

Reagan slid the paper to the snake running the show.

Lydia read, and then met Hayden's gaze. There was something hidden behind her onyx eyes...

"What's it say?" He slammed his fist over the table. "Out with it!"

"The rogues won't stand by and watch you—a turned wolf—rule over the wolf pack. They'll kill one turned werewolf or non-shifter associated with our pack every day until a new Alpha is voted in. If the newly-chosen Alpha is a born wolf, they'll disappear from the San Francisco Bay Area and never return."

Hayden's stomach ached as if he'd been sucker punched. He willed his expression to remain unreadable, and his blood pressure to drop to normal levels. But inside, a war raged, boiling his blood and stealing his breath.

Angus had been a true Alpha, born with wolf blood in his veins. Rather than go on some crazy power trip against turned wolves, he embraced them. He'd found Hayden attacked and left for dead on the street. Instead of turning away, he'd saved Hayden and adopted him as his only son.

If only others could be as kind-hearted and understanding.

Hayden stood, pushing back his chair. "If my father were here, he'd say we should never bow to threats made by rogue wolves. We must protect the ones who cannot protect themselves. My father would call out the entire army of guards and hunt down the rogues, starting with the area of Haight-Ashbury. If we send out a team now, we might still be able to pick up their scent." He went palms down on the table. "But he's not here. And we won't have a designated Alpha to make these calls until the end of the month. Don't think for one second the timing is coincidental, either. The rogue wolves know that without an Alpha, the council has to vote on pack movement. They're trying to take advantage of a split vote so they have more time to instill fear and cause chaos to rumble through the pack."

The council went quiet except for the tap-tap-tapping of Lydia's fingers as they rolled over the table.

"What is the council's stance on this issue?" Hayden forced down the fury rising in his throat. "Do we send out more guards and continue on the path we're on, or do you move to vote in a new Alpha?"

The vote was split down the middle. White and Mad Dog voted to induct a new Alpha, while Reagan and Lydia chose to wait.

As inherent heir to the wolf pack throne, Hayden didn't get a vote.

One thing became crystal clear as he took the elevator back to the fifteenth floor: the council didn't need him to hold meetings, and they didn't care to hear his voice in the boardroom. To top it off, thanks to the rogues' threats, Hayden's presence as a leader meant more deaths for their packmates.

He'd become more of a liability than an asset.

And it didn't take a business degree to understand what happened to liabilities.

Chapter Seven

Melina was absolutely, positively blown away by Hayden's private workspace.

Not that she'd ever tell him that.

After eyeballing a few things on Hayden's desk, she left his office. She strolled around the floor, checking things out, and didn't feel bad about it. Not one bit.

Hayden had pretty much ordered her to stay put. He'd have to learn she didn't take commands well. And she never would, least of all from him.

Besides, now was the perfect opportunity to dig up some dirt on her hunky subject. She already knew the basics about him. He was breathtakingly good looking, and frequently used it to his advantage. He was also filthy rich, drove a hot car, and had a reputation for being extremely...*generous*...in the sack.

Gooseflesh blanketed her arms, chilling her to the core, even though the air was warm and comfortable. She *hated* the fact that her body had such a traitorous reaction to the mere *thought* of Hayden Dean. She really couldn't stand him and his cocky attitude, and the way he acted like he was God's gift to…well, *everything*.

"Focus," she said aloud to herself as she wandered over the fifteenth floor, "and keep your eye on the prize." Thoughts of Hayden invaded her brain. "He is *not* the prize."

The prize was her dream job, and she couldn't forget it.

She took mental notes of everything as she ambled through his personal space.

Although the room had the definite feel of a bachelor pad, with shining hardwood floors, plush rugs, leather couches, fully-stocked bar, and floor-to-ceiling windows—man, the view of the sunset must've been stunning—there were parts of the office that were uncharacteristically elegant. Classic and regal, even.

Guess that's what "old money" did for people.

Before writing her column, "A Month in a Celeb's Shoes," Melina penned the tiny, nearly unnoticed column titled, "Moguls Among Us." It was the reason she'd interviewed Hayden last year in Starbucks. Although the article was surface level, detailing how millionaires spent their day-to-day lives, Melina had researched Hayden's father and the businesses in his portfolio. She'd discovered Angus Dean owned some of the most influential businesses in the city. If he didn't own it, his construction company had built or remodeled the building. Either way, Hayden's father had his hand in every part of San Francisco's business structure.

Hayden had monstrous shoes to fill.

He put on a front, as if nothing bothered him, but every now and again he'd say something that made Melina think otherwise. In the elevator, he'd started to open up. He'd started to talk about stepping into his father's role and how it was easier said than done.

There was depth to him, she realized. And his bachelor pad spoke volumes to that.

After brushing her hands over the piano—it was glossy and clean, as if he rarely played it—and sifting through his stash of alcohol—scotch and vodka, mostly—Melina studied the paintings on the walls. A few frames down, she lost herself in the unexpected blend of colors and brush strokes. She didn't know art very well, but she knew the collection was contemporary and very expensive.

One piece of art in particular caught her eye, stirring something in her chest.

She stopped, and felt compelled to step closer.

The painting depicted a gigantic gray wolf, standing in the middle of a dark forest. Its coat was full and fluffy with tinges of black streaking through it. Its snout was thick and formidable, and its lips were curled in anger. The ridge on its back was arched, as though ready to attack, but the gleam in its eye was soft. *Pleading*, even.

Everything about the wolf was menacing—one she wouldn't want to come across in the forest—though Melina got the bizarre feeling that the wolf was only dangerous if it was protecting its own.

How she knew that, she couldn't explain. She just *did*.

Her stomach tumbled as she reached out and brushed her hand over the wolf's coat. Ridges of the dried oil on the canvas scraped against her fingers. Disappointment, followed quickly by embarrassment, speared through her when she realized it was a painting and nothing more.

Ridiculous.

She felt dizzy. Had she been holding her breath? Instead of moving on to another picture, she sat on the ground and got comfortable, crossing her legs. If she fainted, she'd be closer to the floor, too.

She stared at the painting, at the wolf. Her heartbeat hammered against her ribs. He seemed to be looking back at her, though that was a stupid thought, wasn't it? He gave off an air of dominance, firm and unyielding, but still, she ached to feel the softness of his fur.

It was magnificent.

"What are you doing on the floor?" a deep voice said from beside her.

Hayden.

"Admiring the painting." Jumping to her feet, Melina dusted off her backside and then pointed at the picture. "Who's the artist?"

His dark eyes narrowed. "Why?"

"I don't know." Because she wanted to do a Google search for him and ask if he had any other paintings of the animal for purchase. She probably wouldn't be able to afford it, though. Unless she gave up her monthly shoe allowance. Shrugging, Melina tried to play it cool. "I like this one. It's not like the others you have up. He's…cute and cuddly."

"Cute and…*cuddly?*"

She nodded and clamped her mouth shut, though she wanted to say so much more.

"I think cold and reckless might be more fitting," he bit out.

"What are you talking about?" She glanced back at the wolf. He wasn't cold at all. She could almost feel the warmth radiating from him. And when had the wolf become a "he" rather than an "it?" "That wolf is *not* cold. He's majestic and regal. You can tell he's the leader of the pack."

Hayden grumbled beside her, though she couldn't take her gaze off the painting.

"I bet he'd lead effortlessly," she added. "The other wolves would fall in line and bow down."

"Yeah, you'd think so, wouldn't you?"

Hayden left her side, and stormed into his office. The sound of drawers slamming closed caught her attention. She followed him, and stopped in the doorway when he jerked open a drawer so hard, it fell to the floor.

"The council is so full of shit," he mumbled.

What council was he talking about? And what did they

have to do with the painting?

"My father painted the wolf, a really long time ago." He dumped the contents of the drawer into a backpack leaning against the side of his desk. Then with a heavy sigh, he planted his hands on the desk and lifted his eyes to hers. "Things have changed—everything has changed since then."

"Your father painted that? Really? He was very talented. I had no idea." She longed to touch it again. "Was it painted from life, do you think?"

"Could you not show so much interest in the damned wolf? It's not a good idea to ask so many questions, and it's not making this"—he gestured between them—"any easier."

Was he talking about the article?

He slung the backpack over his shoulder and charged past her toward the elevators. He moved like a force to be reckoned with, his hands clenched into fists, his boots thundering against the hardwood.

He was strung tight, his jaw clenched, his eyes blazing with fury. Why had he gestured between them? Was it really the article that had him so upset? Was it the meeting he'd just had? A knot in Melina's stomach warned it might've been about something more.

"Hayden?" Nervous energy shot through her veins. "Make *what* any easier?"

He dropped his bag, and turned back. And then he came at her with the same strength in his stride. She didn't feel fear—far from it. She felt stalked, in the sexiest way. He exuded sexuality and control, a dizzying combination. She shuffled back, resting against the doorframe. He stood in the doorway across from her, his dark eyes burning like coals.

Something about the way he glared reminded her of the wolf in the painting. His eyes were almost the same shape, color, and depth.

She was silly to think it, but the thought wouldn't leave her.

He sighed, and then clenched his jaw tight. "Would it kill you to not be so—damn it, so…"

"So…what?"

"*Intense*." His nose twitched. He rubbed it, grimacing. "Can't you go anywhere without wearing that perfume? You make every single room smell like you after you leave."

"I don't wear perfume." She pulled a strand of hair to her nose and sniffed. "It must be my shampoo. Is it bad?"

"Far from it." He groaned as if a giant burden rested on his shoulders, and his eyes churned with need. "It makes me want to eat you up."

A wave of desire rolled over her. She shuddered beneath the weight of his stare, hyperaware that his chest heaved as if he'd lost his breath. She was having trouble finding air, too. He stepped closer, eliminating the space between them. They couldn't be any closer without meeting hip-to-hip. Wobbly on her legs, Melina leaned against the doorframe, looked up at him, and held her breath.

Time froze.

"Don't move, Melina," he said, and wrapped his strong hands around her neck.

She jumped from his touch, and the fire it ignited in her middle.

"Did you feel that?" he asked, his lips nearly brushing hers.

She nodded, trembling, reaching up on tiptoe to capture his mouth.

He sucked in a short breath as if he felt the spark too. He dragged her mouth to his in a seductive rush, ripping the air from her lungs and the floor from beneath her feet. It was a kiss of pleasure and shock, and as his lips parted, her stomach fell. She whimpered as she melted into him. He consumed the little mewing sounds, feasted on her mouth, and hauled her against him.

She couldn't detach from him, couldn't catch her breath,

and didn't want to. Not ever again.

With a moan, Hayden removed his mouth from hers. His eyes were unreadable, his jaw tight. "You look like innocence," he said, breathing hard, "but you taste like the sweetest sin."

She stared, swaying against the wall and then into him.

He searched her face, his head tilting, his mouth hovering over hers. "Your heart is racing a mile a minute."

"You can hear it?"

"Every beat. Every promise." He shook his head as if trying to wake himself from some kind of spell. "If you know what's good for you, you'll write the article as fast as you can and forget you ever met me."

Melina's ego wilted.

Forget him? Like that could happen. Now that she'd kissed him, her mouth had been spoiled for any other. "Why would you wish something like that?"

She didn't know what else to say.

"I don't know. It doesn't even matter."

Doesn't even matter?

He scrubbed his hands through his hair. "I should make an appointment with a stylist. You said that was first, right?"

"Right." Reality thundered down around her. "Stylist. Of course."

How could one little—*smoking hot*—kiss make her forget the reason she was *hired* to be here in the first place? Her assignment had been clear-cut. Clean up his image. Write a killer article. Simple.

She would've slept with him if he'd asked her, she thought with chagrin. But if news got out that she had while on the job, that'd only cement his playboy status rather than improve it. And what kind of journalist would she be then? A slutty one, that's for sure. A sketchy employee no one would trust. Goodbye *Eclipse*.

Regardless, she couldn't help but want him.

More than she'd ever wanted anyone.

Ever.

"I've got a magic worker who'll do wonders for you," she said as her heart cracked in her chest. "Clear your schedule tomorrow afternoon."

He nodded, his gaze honing on her lips. "Make the call."

She couldn't have misread their connection. Couldn't have. But if he felt the same thing she did, how could he push her away so easily?

Holding her head high and feigning confidence she didn't feel, Melina turned away from him and marched to the elevators. She tightened her bag over her shoulder as the heat of his gaze warmed her back.

Was he watching her walk away? If he were, wouldn't that mean he didn't really want her to leave?

Don't look. Don't look back.

Curiosity niggled at the back of her mind.

Slowly, she glanced over one shoulder.

Hayden stood in the center of the doorway where she'd left him, but now, a stunned expression marred his features. His mouth dropped open. His hands clenched to fists at his sides. *Hunger* burned in his gorgeous eyes. He looked as if he wanted to eat her up.

Melina smiled coyly, as if it hadn't been a big deal to walk away. But the moment she disappeared into the elevator and the doors hissed shut, she blew out a shaky breath.

"You may say one thing, Mr. Dean," she said, resting against the elevator rails, "but your eyes say something completely different."

Why did he date women left and right, as if he didn't care for any one in particular, but stand her up the night of the Silverlights? Why did he taste like an intoxicating mix of heat and promise, yet his words were clipped and cold?

She was determined to figure out *why*.

Chapter Eight

Tuesday afternoon, on the drive from his office to Vision Amore, the stylist's boutique in Pacific Heights, Hayden mumbled two phrases over and over again.

Melina Rae is your Luminary.

Being with her isn't an option.

He repeated them to absorb them. So he wouldn't forget them when he was with her, surrounded by her drugging natural fragrance. Something deep inside him warned it wouldn't matter how many times he repeated the lines.

He wanted her.

The wolf part of him—the crazed, howling part that instinctively wanted to possess her body and bond with her soul—would simply have to cool it.

The rogues and their threat to her safety were one thing, but beyond that, Hayden had never wanted to find his Luminary. He'd realized early on that it wasn't in the cards for him.

His parents, Cara and Angus, had been completely, hopelessly in love with one another. They were one—mind, body, and soul—and had completed the Luminary bond young. But after Cara died, Angus had become a recluse. He wouldn't eat. He'd hide in his office and stare into the space for hours. Leave in the middle of the night. Find an empty park, and shift into wolf form. He'd howl at the moon until daybreak.

He was a ghost of a man without his mate.

Why would anyone jump into that kind of bond, where you'd experience that kind of loss, that kind of soul-tearing pain?

He didn't want to find out.

All the more reason he needed to keep Melina at a distance and forget all about that kiss they'd shared yesterday.

That kiss…

As the limo pulled up to the curb, Hayden's mouth still tingled with the delicious taste of her. Distracted beyond belief, he checked the sidewalk. Quaint neighborhood. Locals crossing the street with reusable shopping bags in hand. Women tightening scarves around their necks. A homeless man begging for money in front of the store next door.

"Go ahead and return the limo, Eugene," Hayden said to the driver. "I'll get back on my own."

Glancing through the rearview mirror, Eugene nodded and stepped out.

"No, I got it." Hayden shoved the rear door open himself. "Thanks, though."

As he charged onto the sidewalk, he dug through his pocket and pulled out a few dollar bills folded over a stack of business cards. Unfolding the cash, he handed it to the homeless man who smiled in thanks.

"If you're in the same place later tonight, I'll send someone back with food," he said, and then shook the man's hand.

As he stood, the bitingly-sweet aroma of vanilla and sandalwood wafted from somewhere behind him, overtaking the smell of the dirt on the man in front of him.

Melina.

"What are you doing?" she asked, approaching his side.

"Helping someone who's down and out." It was the least he could do after his father had helped him, pulling him off the streets. He opened the door to Vision Amore. "After you."

With a puzzled frown, Melina swept inside, and then waited for Hayden to enter behind her. The narrow shop had a distinct floral scent that tickled Hayden's nose. Black-and-white pictures of celebrities lined the walls, along with what appeared to be thank-you letters. A long counter had been placed in the center of the shop, separating it into two parts. Behind that, a curtain blocked their view of the back half of the space. And over the speakers, Jeff Buckley played guitar and moaned lyrics in a slow, painful rhythm.

"Giving money to that man was a front, right?" Melina said as they approached the counter. "Something to help me improve your image for the article?"

"Is that what you think I was doing? Putting on a show?"

"Giving to charity *was* part of the improvement plan we went over," she said simply. "Maybe you're a better study than I gave you credit for."

The way she said *study* made Hayden think of tutors and homework and studying late night over coffee. He would've done a hell of a lot better in law school had Melina been his tutor. Great. Now he was picturing Melina dressed as a schoolgirl. White shirt knotted below her breasts. Short plaid skirt. Thigh highs.

"What happened out there had nothing to do with your improvement plan." He swallowed hard to return the moisture to his mouth. "Dean, Hyde, & Hammer donates millions each year."

"I'm not talking about your company. I'm talking about you." She shook her head. "If what I saw just now wasn't an act, if you are truly that generous, I wouldn't have been hired to improve your image in the first place. You wouldn't need it. It had to be a show."

He rang the bell beside the register. The high-pitched sound echoed through the store and pierced his sensitive ears. Someone shuffled around behind the curtain. Must've been Oz.

He snickered inwardly at the thought.

"You can't believe everything you read about me in the magazines," he said. "But you work for one of them, so I'm preaching to the choir."

"Tell me one thing we've gotten wrong."

"Only one?" He tapped his fingers on the counter, suddenly anxious to get today over with. Their banter only amplified their connection. "According to *Celeb Crush*, how many celebrities have I dated?"

"This month?" Melina's lips twisted into a smile.

He stared, fighting the urge to kiss that smile.

"Okay, okay," she said. "Celebrities you've dated this year? Probably…twenty?"

He rested his elbow on the counter. "Twenty? Really?"

"What's the real number?" she pressed. "Is it higher?" She shifted her weight from foot to foot. "Lower?"

Before he could answer, a woman pushed through the curtain, living up to the name of the shop. She was a vision in white. Bleached white hair. Pale skin. White pantsuit. The only color on the six-foot-tall woman was her bright red lips.

"Good to see you, Melina," the woman said, shaking Melina's hand. "Hayden Dean. I'm Ruby." Her red lips spread wide as she set her sights on him. "Pleasure to meet you. I have to say, right up front, if you're working with Melina, you're in great hands."

Her hands really were great. Delicate and soft.

Melina Rae is your Luminary.

Being with her isn't an option.

Keep distance. Keep it business.

"What's the plan for today?" he asked.

Ruby shifted her weight side to side, crossed one leg over the other, and then measured him up and down. "I'm thinking Armani. Black on black. A few inches cut off the top. Maybe a facial."

"Whoa." He threw up his hands. "Nobody said anything about a facial."

Melina belted out a laugh, and then covered her laugh with a cough. "It's up to you, but Ruby is the best."

"Yeah, I bet."

"It all boils down to how badly you want the position you're after," Melina said. "I bet the mayor of the city gets facials.".

Son of a...

He was ready to rule, completely prepared to step into the position of Alpha and bring down the rogues threatening to terrorize his city. Angus wouldn't have bent to pressure from rogues, and he wouldn't either. Although they'd threatened to kill turned wolves if he ruled, he refused to live on their terms, fearful of their demands. If the council succumbed now, there'd be no limit to their influence over the pack. What demand would be next? Eliminate all turned wolves from the pack, or else?

It wasn't too far-fetched to image the slide in logic.

He'd prove he could bring down the rogues before they harmed a single hair on an innocent's head. If he had to overhaul his wardrobe, cut inches off his hair, and dance like a puppet to somehow demonstrate he was worthy to rule, so be it.

"Fine." Hayden rubbed his hands together briskly. "Let's just get this over with."

• • •

Two hours later, Hayden was seated in a chair in the corner of Elegance Salon. He went back and forth on the facial and manicure but finally refused. No matter how many times Ruby pressed after he'd made up his mind, he'd declined with a stoic expression on his face. He'd grumbled and cursed under his breath while Melina failed to control her laughter.

Torturing Hayden was turning out to be her favorite form of entertainment.

He squinted and rubbed his nose, as if the chemicals in the salon really bothered him. He looked downright miserable, staring into the mirror as Ricardo—hair stylist extraordinaire—snipped his hair. Ruby stood beside Ricardo, guiding him in his masterpiece. Hayden closed his eyes, scrubbed his hand beneath his nose, and winced.

"How long has it been since you've been in a salon like that?" Melina asked, sitting on one end of the bench next to his chair.

"Never." He sneezed. "The barber comes to me."

"Seriously? Must be nice when the world revolves around you."

"It's not a Prima Donna thing." He rubbed his nose harder. "The chemicals in here are too strong. They burn my nose."

Her attention shifted to the pile of magazines on the bench. She tossed a few onto his lap. "Want some reading material to take your mind off it?"

He looked down. Ricardo jerked his head back to level and continued cutting.

Hayden held the magazines in front of his face. As he flipped through, he read aloud, "*Hayden Dean: Womanizer Strikes Again, Hayden Dean's Night Club Brawl; Two in Hospital, The New Dean Girl Exposes Hayden's Nitty-Gritty*

Secrets." He tossed the last magazine onto her lap. "Women, fights, secrets. Are you sure your article is going to be able to turn this all around?"

"It has to." She met his eyes in the mirror. "There's a lot riding on this."

Her dream job at *Eclipse.* Hayden's new position in his father's company...or whatever he was after.

"I think the only way we can change the public image of you," she explained, "is if we give readers a completely different version of you to believe in. For that to happen, though, I have to see you in your element so there's a ring of truth to it. I have to know what makes you tick. I have to know the reasons behind certain things."

Yeah, like why he kissed her, and then sent her away.

He nodded, and got smacked in the back of the head by the ridge of Ricardo's comb. Melina bit back a smirk as Hayden growled, and then held his head straightforward and still.

"Six," he said, giving his nose a rub. "That's the answer to your question."

She knew exactly which question he meant.

But that didn't mean she wanted to miss the opportunity to screw with him.

"Six sexually transmitted diseases you have?" She laughed as Hayden's eyes went wide, Ricardo dropped his comb, and Ruby backed away from the chair with her arms in the air. "Joking. Joking. Six...inches long is the size of your—"

"Six celebrities I've dated this year," Hayden blurted, laughing. "Jesus, Melina."

Ricardo waggled his eyebrows. Hayden paled. Ruby shrugged, and glanced at Melina as if waiting for an answer on the true length of his manhood.

Total embarrassment.

"How would I know?" Melina mouthed, cheeks burning.

Although she couldn't attest to exactly how big Hayden's *ego* really was, when he'd pressed against her in the doorway and ground his hips into hers, she'd felt something... *impressive.* Her knees weakened and her tummy went fluttery at the memory.

"You probably wouldn't believe most of those women broke up with me," he said, "but that'd be the truth. Not that the magazines would report that."

She'd have to remember to research his past girlfriends for the article. Maybe she could do a small section on his past and the real reasons some of those relationships failed. If he were telling the truth, it'd take some of the womanizing heat off him.

As she puzzled over Hayden's words, and tried to shift them into place in her mind, Ricardo slicked Hayden's hair back. He parted it down the side. And before Melina realized it, Hayden had transformed into a total Hemsworth.

"What about you?" he asked.

She met his eyes in the mirror once more. "I'm sorry, what?"

"How many men have you dated in the last year?"

A sudden rush of blood burned her cheeks. "We're not improving my image with this article."

"I know that."

Ricardo and Ruby discussed colors Hayden should wear to accent the dark highlights in his hair as Melina fought to find a way out of the conversation.

Why did it matter how many men she'd dated in the last year? Why did he care?

In truth, there'd only been one date. Well, it hadn't even really been a date, but the same first-meeting feelings had been there. When she looked into Hayden's eyes, they were *still* there.

"A few," she lied. "They were mostly casual dates."

Casually running into friends here and there, and talking to the guys at the *Celeb Crush* offices.

God, the truth was pathetic.

A soft humming sound—almost like a growl—came from Hayden's chest. His shoulders rose toward his ears. His hands clenched around the arm of the chair. He coughed loudly, and then glanced up into the mirror.

What had him so on edge? Must've been a buildup of the chemicals in the salon.

"What's next, Ruby?" he asked, his voice strangely tight.

"Next is the fun part, darling," she said, running her fingers through Hayden's shorter hair. "Thursday after you get off work, we go shopping."

"Thursday?" He exhaled heavily. "Can't we get this all over with today?"

"Rome wasn't built in a day, sweetheart." Ruby put a hand on each shoulder and stared down his reflection in the mirror. "And you're not my only client. I have a four o'clock on your heels."

"That actually works better for us," Melina said, hyperaware of how much she liked the sound of "us." "We already have an appointment that'll take up most of tomorrow afternoon."

Hayden's lips pressed together in a hard line. "What appointment?"

"Since you're soaring through Phase One of the improvement plan, I thought we'd move on to Phase Two. We'll work on improving the inside so it reflects on the outside."

"Oh shit, here it comes."

"We're volunteering at an animal shelter. We'll be helping with the dogs."

"If working with dogs for one afternoon will rebuild my image," he mumbled as he stood and moved toward the exit,

"I'd be golden by now. I'm already surrounded by dogs all damn day."

Funny, but besides the wolf picture hanging in his office, Melina hadn't noticed signs of a dog being in the Dean, Hyde, & Hammer building.

Chapter Nine

Late Wednesday afternoon, Melina strode toward Forever Pets, an animal shelter near the Presidio. She loved the city when it smelled this way—like rain-washed asphalt. The mist hanging around for the last few days had finally turned into a dusting rainstorm that washed away the dirt and grime in the streets.

Sometime during the night—when she'd tossed and turned thinking of Hayden—Melina came to a few conclusions regarding her article. She wouldn't mention his stunning good looks since most of the articles floating around focused on it; she'd give readers something different. She'd leave out how many girlfriends Hayden had, and instead focus on one or two serious ones.

But when she woke up this morning, cued up her computer, and searched Google for Hayden's longer conquests, not a single serious relationship came up. It seemed as if Hayden had never dated anyone longer than a few weeks.

It almost seemed as if he kept everyone at arm's length on purpose.

His earlier words rang through her head.

I don't want any mention of my home.

Family and close friends are not to be discussed.

What did he have to hide?

Her thoughts were still whirling when she passed a magazine stand positioned on the edge of the sidewalk. The entertainment magazine on the top right caught her eye.

Millionaire Snubs Homeless.

A picture of Hayden striding down the street in front of Vision Amore was plastered to the front page. The homeless man in front of the shop was in the bottom corner, holding out his hand for spare change. The magazine had clearly Photoshopped Hayden's face from a photograph in his past. He appeared to be screaming at the homeless man.

Melina's stomach wrenched.

That wasn't how it'd happened at all.

She'd witnessed the scene firsthand.

He'd given the homeless man money. He'd shaken his hand and promised to send him food. She'd heard him right, hadn't she?

Disgusted with the lies plastered in front of her, Melina snatched a copy, paid, and then marched away from the stand. When she pushed through the doors leading to Forever Pets and approached the front counter, her blood was still boiling hot.

"Good afternoon," she said to the brunette at the front. "I made an appointment to volunteer today at four. I'm still waiting for someone else to arrive, but if you'd like me to get started with the dogs, I can—"

"You're with Hayden Dean, right?" The woman blushed. "He's already here."

"He is?"

She nodded. "Around back."

After showing her ID and signing in, Melina weaved

around the front counter, clutching the magazine in her fist. She passed through a set of doors leading to the veterinary section of the shelter, and continued down along a long hallway that smelled of wet fur. As she turned right and passed through another set of doors, a jerky symphony of barks and howls hit her ears.

She reached the canine section of the shelter and her heart tingled with warmth.

She loved working with the dogs.

She volunteered on a weekly basis, taking each one out to play, and cleaning out their kennels. There was something soothing, almost rejuvenating about spending time with the animals. Some were broken, scared, and skittish. Others were loud and excitable, needing more time to run.

All it took was quality time with each of them, and they loosened up, opened up, and trusted her to care for them.

She wouldn't hurt them. They simply had to come to that conclusion on their own.

A few of the dogs wouldn't trust Hayden at first—having never met him before—but he could wash out the kennels while she took those timid few out to play.

As she pushed through the final door leading to the unit, she stopped and held it open with her palm.

Hayden stood against the back wall, his arms folded over his chest. He wore dark-washed jeans and a black T-shirt pulled tight over his chest. His jaw was clenched tight, and his eyes were focused far off. He almost looked…scared. Or maybe lost in thought. He couldn't be afraid; what reason would he have to fear the dogs? They were in kennels, for crying out loud. It wasn't like the shelter housed Cujo.

"Hayden," she said, letting the door close behind her. "What are you doing?'

Louder and sharper barks echoed off the cement walls as the dogs went wild.

Hayden's eyes shifted, and zoned out. As if he was listening to something in the distance rather than her words. He didn't answer, though he stared at her mouth.

"Hayden?"

Still, he stared, his expression a blank slate.

She approached him, and then smacked him in the shoulder with the end of the rolled up magazine. "Hello?"

With a hard shake of his head, Hayden snapped out of his daze. "There are too many of them," he hollered. "They're too loud!"

And then the strangest thing happened.

The dogs quieted. One by one. As if he'd ordered them to.

She spun, watching each of the dogs in the kennels simmer down. And then nothing. Golden silence.

"God," he said, rubbing his hands over his ears, "that's better."

She squinted, staring at each of the dogs. "What the hell happened? I've never seen them do that before."

"Must've gotten all the barks out of their system." He shrugged. "What'd you hit me with?"

"Oh." She held up the magazine, though she kept her eye on the dogs and their stranger-than-stranger behavior. "I bought this on the street."

He took the magazine from her and read.

"That's par." He plopped down on the bench seat along the wall. "I'm surprised they didn't say I stole his blanket while I was at it."

"How can you be so calm?"

"This is normal, Melina. Same thing every day. It's fine."

"It's not fine." One of the dogs in the back yelped. Hayden leaned around Melina, and seemed to zone far off again. "Can't you look at me when I'm talking to you? Can't you stay focused for one second? This is serious."

He sat straight again, and the dog quieted.

"This is the last thing we need right now. Can't your law firm sue the magazine for misrepresentation or something?"

"And dump a ton of money into the suit? Settle out of court?" He rested his head back onto the cement wall and sighed. "How long would it take for another magazine to print another, equally-hideous story about me? It'd be like Whack-a-Mole. Smack one, only to have another two rear their ugly heads."

"So you're just going to let it go?"

He exhaled heavily. "As long as my closest friends and family know me—the real me—I don't care what they assume from the outside looking in."

Could he really be that level-headed?

He was a businessman, and maybe he had to be composed about rumors like these. But he seemed so damn confident. As if nothing got under his skin.

If someone printed an article like that about her, she'd flip.

"So what do we do first?" he said, tossing the magazine in the trash.

"I have to love on Minnie over here. She's my new favorite." From the small kennels on the right, the tiny pup yelped. It was the squeakiest, sweetest sound, and broke Melina's heart every time. She strode over, unlocked the gate, and picked up the Golden Retriever puppy. She held Minnie against her chest and spun around. "Here she is. Isn't she the sweetest?"

Hayden eyed the pup, but didn't make a move.

"She was rescued from an apartment in Glen Park last week." She stroked the dog's fur as she burrowed her head in Melina's sweater. "The owner had more dogs than they could care for. Someone in the building finally reported the conditions to the authorities when they realized the owners had moved out, leaving the animals to fend for themselves."

"That's terrible." He stood, and moved in front of her.

"Tell me about it. Minnie refuses to eat. The shelter has run all kinds of tests on her, and has tried all kinds of different food, but nothing's working." She nuzzled the dog against her. "She's losing weight fast. If she doesn't eat soon, they don't think she'll make it. Here." She held Minnie out for Hayden to take. "If you wouldn't mind, I want to get a picture of you for the article."

He blanched. "What?"

"Hold her." She cupped Minnie in her hand and moved closer. Hayden backed away. "It'll only be for a second. I want to mention your charity and volunteer work. I think a picture with Minnie would really win people over."

Shaking his head, Hayden thrust his hands into his pockets. "I'm not sure that's a good idea."

Melina couldn't help but laugh. "She's not going to bite."

He lifted his chin. "I'm not afraid of her biting me."

"Then what?"

He exhaled heavily and then searched right and left, as if looking for an escape route.

"Nothing," he said. "Never mind. Hand her over."

He took Minnie in his hands and held her against his chest. The dog gazed up to stare at his face, her tiny black eyes blinking innocently. His touch was gentle, his fingers softly raking through Minnie's silky-soft fur.

His behavior was so starkly contrasted from the guy she'd kissed in his office—all possession and anger and intensity—that she went dizzy.

He was hot and cold. A womanizer in the magazines but someone else when he was with her. A brash businessman, yet someone who could cuddle up next to a puppy.

"Okay, that's...perfect." Melina took out her phone and snapped a few shots.

The dog quivered and shook, whimpering in his arms.

Melina took a handful of other pictures, in case the first few didn't turn out.

And then Hayden leaned down and whispered something into the dog's ear. Minnie looked up at him again. Although it was the craziest thought, she could've sworn the dog nodded, and then bowed her head into Hayden's hand. He felt along her neck, right under her jawbone, and around the back.

"Have the vet do a biopsy on her lymph nodes," he said simply, and then he handed Minnie back.

Chapter Ten

Hayden hadn't wanted to hold the Golden Retriever yesterday at the shelter. What if Melina picked up the connection he had with canines? Would she know he could hear them? Understand them?

Once the dog trusted him enough to relax in his hands, he knew he had to do something about her pain. If the vets at the shelter didn't know what was wrong, why not guide them in the right direction?

After they'd finished their volunteer duties at Forever Pets—washing out the kennels and refilling their food and water—Hayden had the company limo pick them up and drop her off at her place. He ached to go with her. Take her to dinner. Wine and dine her the way he did the other women who'd come into his life.

Business only.

The article hanging over their heads was a constant reminder that their time together was limited. And every time he thought about it, something pinched in his side.

She's better off away from you.

Even as he thought the words, they felt hollow.

When their Thursday afternoon appointment with Ruby crept upon him, Hayden directed his driver into Union Square. He'd never actually shopped there since it'd always been easier to have tailors measure him in the office, and then deliver his clothes. Saks Men was a pleasant surprise, however. Sparse shelves. Light paint. Dim lights. Wood accents. Every tie, every pair of shoes, had the smell of money.

Ruby had texted, stating she'd be a few minutes late, but to get started with Armani.

When Hayden walked in, Melina was waiting in the middle of the store with a pensive expression on her face. Her mouth was pulled down into a frown, and her eyebrows crinkled together.

"What's wrong?" He checked his watch. "I'm not late."

"How'd you know about Minnie's lymph nodes?"

Shit.

"It was a lucky guess." He approached a Saks assistant before she could probe further. "I need a tuxedo for an event this weekend. I was told to start with Armani."

Nodding in agreement, the assistant mumbled something about Hayden's stature, the estimated breadth of his shoulders, his inseam, and then disappeared around a half-wall sectioning off the store.

"Are you a dog whisperer or something?" Melina asked, suddenly at his side.

He could communicate with canines. Not every breed, and not every animal, but he'd heard Minnie loud and clear. Her throat hurt. Her neck felt puffy and swollen. She wanted to eat, but couldn't.

He laughed at Melina's comparison of him to the dog whisperer, though she wasn't far off. "I told you, it was a lucky guess."

She tapped the toe of her shoe against the dark wood

floor. "The vet ordered an emergency biopsy. Results came back earlier. It's Lymphoma, but they expect the treatment will be successful."

Relief sang through him. He hadn't been too attached to Minnie, but he'd wanted the tiny animal to be well.

"If that's a good thing," he said, studying a rack of ties, "why are you staring at me as if you want to kill me?"

"Because you act aloof, jumping from woman to woman, party to party, as if you don't care about anyone or anything. And then you give money to the homeless guy and save one of my favorite dogs at the shelter. Do you have split personalities?"

He chuckled into a belly laugh. "You think I have a disorder?"

"No, not really." She moved in front of the rack so he'd have to look at her. She'd pulled her dark hair into a ponytail today. It emphasized the plumpness of her bottom lip and the soft pink tint in her cheeks. "I just don't understand why every article that *Celeb Crush* has ever run on you has been focused on your yacht, sports cars, dating record, club appearances, yada yada. But beyond all that, there's more. There's surprising...*depth*. But it's like you only show it to who you want to, and only at certain times. The Hayden I met at Starbucks, the one at the shelter, and the one here with me now are different than the Hayden you show to the public."

"Are you just now realizing that you can't judge a book by its cover?"

"That's not it. I simply don't understand why you don't care more about the image that's out there for the world to see." She plucked a slim black tie from a hook and handed it to him. "It seems like you don't mind if your reputation is dragged through the gutter."

"Maybe the stories they create are better than the real thing."

"Better," she said, kinking her head to the side, "or safer."

He should've left it alone. He should've shut his mouth.

The Saks assistant snapped for Hayden to meet him in the back of the store. He did as he was instructed—begrudgingly thanks to the dog-like command—and disappeared behind a black dressing-room curtain. At least he didn't have to finish their conversation. As the assistant helped him into a classic one-button tuxedo, Ruby's voice rang through the store.

"I'm here!" she bellowed. "So sorry I'm late. I ran into someone outside who said he was looking for Hayden. We got to talking about—oh, I won't bother you with that. Is Hayden back there somewhere?"

She'd run into someone outside?

Someone who knew to find Hayden here?

He'd been followed.

With a growl, Hayden peeled apart the curtains and charged into the center of the store.

Melina gasped, averting her eyes. Ruby's red lips pulled into a devious smile. And Gabriel strode around the tie rack.

"Hey, boss." He nodded toward Hayden's lower half. "Nice pants."

Hayden glanced down. He'd only been partially dressed when the protective streak had pulsed through him. His pants were slung low on his hips, unzipped and unbuttoned. Black boxers peeked from beneath the hanging flaps of his slacks. And gooseflesh pebbled over his bare chest.

"Now *that's* a tuxedo," Ruby said, planting her hands on her hips.

Melina seemed to stiffen, and glanced at Hayden out of the corner of her eye.

Yeah baby, get an eyeful.

He flexed a chest muscle, and then immediately chastised himself for being such a douche. "What are you doing here, Gabriel?"

As he joined the group outside the dressing room, Hayden fastened his pants and stretched out his arms. The assistant helped him into his shirt.

"This came for you at the office," Gabriel said, holding out an envelope. "It says 'urgent.' After the meeting we had the other day, I thought it best I bring it to you personally. Just in case it has something to do with—"

"Got it, Gabriel. Thank you." Hayden took the envelope and tore through the upper seam. "It's only tickets for Saturday."

"Thank God," Gabriel breathed.

"What's Saturday?" Melina piped up.

His gaze locked with hers. "Worried I'm going to go out, get hammered, and do something stupid that'll land on the front page?"

"Someone's got to care about those things."

"That someone is usually me." Gabriel extended a hand to Melina. When she took it, he flipped her hand around and kissed the back. "I'm Gabriel Park. It's a pleasure to meet you, Miss Rae. Hayden has told me so much about you."

"He has?"

Hayden ground his back teeth together. He'd told Gabriel about Melina, but he'd left out the one thing that mattered most: she was *his* by fate's design. If his secondary had known that fact, he might've refrained from kissing her hand. Not only was it disrespectful, but—*damn it, wasn't that enough?*

Why'd Fate match him with a non-shifter anyway? On what planet would their relationship ever work? Not that they had a relationship. But if they did...

"Of course your name has come up," Hayden offered before assumptions could be made. "Gabriel is my second-in-command, I suppose you could say. He worries about the pesky details of my life so I don't have to."

She flinched when he said "pesky" as if he were talking

about her.

But the only thing pesky about Melina was the fact he couldn't get her out of his mind. If only he could tell her that…

"Anyway," he said, "when it comes to this Saturday, I won't need either of you. The craziest thing that'll happen at the aquarium is I might have too many drinks and sponsor a stingray. It might not be as cute and cuddly as a wolf, but it still has bite."

Smirking, Melina shot him a playful glare. "Everyone's a comedian."

"You two should go together," Ruby interrupted, perching on the edge of the round leather seat next to Melina. "She could make sure you don't tarnish that golden reputation by saying something stupid."

"Golden reputation?" Melina's eyes went wide. "Hayden? Um. No."

Gabriel coughed. "If that's the plan, Miss Rae better hang around 24-7."

Hayden repressed a growl.

"That's not a good idea." Melina finally detached her gaze from his and shook her head. "There's no way I could be Hayden's date. If the tabloids see him with me, someone they've never seen before, I'll be labeled as another 'Dean Girl' and that's not happening in my lifetime."

Sharp, burning sensations pinched Hayden's gut. He rubbed a hand over his stomach, but couldn't soothe away the pain. *Odd.* Felt like he'd been punched.

"I'm holding out to be a James Bond Girl," Melina went on.

Ah, there was the humor. That spark he'd come to like so much.

She was sexy as hell. Intelligent and funny.

The woman was a dream.

Not my dream, not my dream, not my dream.

"It wouldn't have worked out anyway. I already have a date." All eyes turned Hayden's way. Melina seemed to stare through him, her eyes sparking with curiosity. "She's a friend of the family and works for the aquarium. Seemed like a good fit. I'll be on my best behavior. Scout's honor."

Gabriel sat to Melina's left and leaned in close. "Don't believe a word that man says. I've known him my whole life, and he's never been a Boy Scout."

"Well I must be ahead of the curve. I've only known him a year, and I already know better than to believe anything he says." Her lips twisted in that playful, teasing way that tied him in knots.

There was nothing playful about the jealous thorn in Hayden's side. Why'd Gabriel have to sit right next to Melina when there were perfectly suitable chairs in the corners of the room? And why'd he have to lean so close to her shoulder when he talked to her, as if he was telling her a secret?

As the Saks assistant finished adjusting the coat over Hayden's shoulders, Ruby requested he bring over a white shawl collar single button dinner coat, and a bunch of other items he didn't care to think about. As long as the new threads fit him comfortably, he was good.

"Why doesn't Melina go with me?" Gabriel said. "I still need a date."

This time, all eyes turned to Melina.

And it was a good thing, too. That way, no one saw the pissed-off glare Hayden shot his "trusted" secondary.

. . .

Melina could barely breathe as Hayden stood in front of her in that Armani suit. His broad shoulders filled up that tuxedo as if it'd been sewn for him. Totally fine. GQ material. Mmm-hmm.

Distance.

God, she'd just licked drool off her lips.

But when Tall, Dark, and Handsome smiled her way, and asked her out—had she heard him right?—Hayden disappeared. Only for a second. She turned toward Gabriel and examined him for the first time. He wore a Calvin Klein suit as slick and black as his hair, and a midnight-blue tie that complemented his sapphire eyes.

He was definitely gorgeous, but didn't have the kind of sex appeal that seeped from Hayden's pores.

"I didn't know you got an invite." Hayden's voice was so deep and raspy, it vibrated the floor under Melina's feet.

Gabriel didn't seem to notice. He pulled his own envelope out of his inner coat pocket and grinned. "Two complimentary tickets from the company. I wasn't going to attend, but if you already have a date, and Melina doesn't have a ticket, why not?"

"Yeah," Hayden breathed. "Why not…"

"Perfect!" Ruby clapped, and held her hands over her heart. "Ah, to be young and in love again."

"I don't know who you're referring to," Hayden said, "but nobody here is in love."

"Not yet, maybe," she said, coming to stand beside him. "But soon."

"So?" Gabriel lightly bumped Melina in the shoulder. "What do you think?"

Although it seemed absolutely ridiculous, the idea of getting glammed up for a night out thrilled her.

"I don't see the harm in it." She raised her gaze to meet Hayden's. Damn, if there wasn't fire burning in those depths. "Our relationship is business-only, right?"

Say no. Say you want me for yourself. Don't let me go with your friend.

His eyes narrowed and his lips pressed into a hard, white

line. "Right."

She understood completely now. He was still undecided when it came to her, and he always would be. He wanted to kiss her, yet push her away. Tease her and play with her emotions. Going to the benefit with Gabriel was out of the question, but he didn't want to take her himself.

To hell with him.

She deserved someone who would want to stand at her side, and wouldn't be able to handle the thought of another man taking her out.

She deserved better.

"I'm glad we're on the same page," she said, and then turned her attention toward Gabriel. "I'd love to go with you."

Chapter Eleven

Looking out her living room window over Haight Street, Melina pounded away at her keyboard. She only had an hour before Gabriel arrived to pick her up, and wanted to jot down her notes for Hayden's article.

"Initial thoughts," she read aloud as she typed. "Loyal 49er fan...to his own detriment. Seems stressed after work meetings, which is contrary to the laid-back vibe he tries to give off." She took a long drag on the straw of her Frappuccino. It was sweet, with extra whip and absolutely perfect. She needed the caffeine to get her through the night. "Drives fast, probably recklessly. Kisses like a pro, probably does other things like one too." She deleted the last part and took a bite of the Ghirardelli square next to her coffee. She needed the chocolate so she didn't gorge on sweets at the event and look like a cow. She swiped the caramel off her lip. Better to look like a cow in private, she decided. "Long eyelashes, dreamy eyes."

Delete, delete, delete.

After making notes about the overall feel of his office,

including that amazing wolf picture, Melina crafted fanciful stores about the football game and the day at the office that made Hayden look like a knight.

He helped a woman up the stairs at the stadium and opened doors for women in the office.

What a gentleman.

On the way into the shop, he'd pulled out his wallet and handed a homeless man fifty dollars. On Thursday, he arranged for one of the top lawyers in Dean, Hyde, & Hammer to handle a large case pro bono during his morning business meeting. She hadn't been present when he made the deal, but she'd read the memo on his desk.

What a generous soul.

Someone needed to hand her a freaking crown—she was officially the Queen of Bullshit.

But then she really got down to the nitty-gritty. She researched donations and grants given by Angus Dean or any part of his company. And then she wrote about Hayden's volunteer work, about Minnie and the care he'd given her. It was only one day, one time, one dog, yet she couldn't help but feel as if he'd had a real impact that day.

She uploaded the photo of Hayden holding Minnie and saved it to her computer with the caption: Beauty and the… *Beast*?

Trying not to think about how Hayden had shifted in her mind, Melina shut down her laptop and showered for her date. After drying off, she hooked a towel around her body so she could dry and style her hair. According to Gabriel, the affair was black tie. Formal.

Eager to glam up for someone who might actually show up for their date, Melina blow-dried and teased her hair, twisting and pulling the strands until they sat on top of her head. She applied her makeup—shimmering blue on the eyes, and glossy nude on the lips—and then stepped into a designer dress she'd never worn. It was strapless, silky cerulean blue, and flared at the knee. The best part wasn't the color or the material, although both were equally gorgeous. It was the layer upon layer of faux peacock feathers at the bottom that made the dress runway glam.

A honk outside the apartment had Melina peeling apart her living room curtains. A canary-yellow Camaro waited at the curb in front of her building. Leaning against the driver's door, Gabriel was an image of composed sophistication in a black-and-white tux.

Frantically hopping into her pair of gold Jimmy Choos and snatching her matching clutch off the closet door handle, Melina exited the building and strode toward Ashbury.

As she approached her date, Melina eyed him carefully. He was handsome. There was no denying it. If she had to guess his ethnicity, she would've said he was Greek, with thick dark hair, big round eyes, and full lips.

"You look great," he said, meeting her at the back of the car. "Like a million bucks."

"Thanks." She grinned, remembering the discount she'd gotten on the eight-thousand-dollar designer dress. Maybe she should start a local off-the-runway online company—a place to borrow and exchange dresses like this for discounted prices. Only they wouldn't be ordered online and shipped. They'd be in-store. Where women could come in and try them on and return them after events such as these. "Nice ride."

"Chicks dig it."

Yeah, she bet.

Gabriel may've been suave, but he was kind of a tool. Especially if he referred to women as *chicks*.

As he led her around to the passenger side, he reached for the handle, and then stopped. He turned, staring down Ashbury one direction before the other. His nostrils flared and his shoulders pulled back. He looked as if he was taking some sort of challenging stance, but that wouldn't make sense, would it?

"What's wrong?" she asked.

"Nothing. Just thought I…saw someone I knew."

He sounded as if he was about to say something else. Melina slid into the car, and checked everything out as he walked around the hood. The interior had a deliciously new smell, and was oiled and clean, as if it'd been driven right off the lot.

"Hayden was right," he said as he slipped inside and brought the engine to life. "You do smell good."

Her mouth fell open. "He told you that?"

"He tells me everything." Gabriel shot her a mischievous grin. "You ready? He's already called twice to make sure we're on our way. He's saving us two seats at his table."

The thought of spending the evening with him had her heart beating fast. Hayden, being the alluring *him*. "At Saks, you said you've known Hayden your entire life?"

"He's like a brother to me." He downshifted around the corner of Haight and Asbury and made the car purr as he put his foot down to the floor. "We disagree on certain issues and have our moments, but that's normal when you're family."

Perfect person to probe for personal information to go into the article.

She twisted her hips so that she faced him. "What's he like?"

"What do you mean?"

"He's probably the most complex guy I've ever met. He's got secrets, but he won't share them." She gripped the oh-shit handle as he peeled around a turn. "He's like an onion with all kinds of layers built up around him. Of all people, you ought to know what's in his core."

Gabriel eyed her through the dark as they drove through the city at break-neck speed. "He's got so much responsibility on his shoulders, it's a miracle he's able to function as well as he does. Through everything, the man's got heart."

He had *heat*, raw and scorching; that much was undeniable. But his heart was something she wasn't sure she'd ever reach. He'd built up too many walls, and was too intent on keeping people out.

Gabriel turned on the windshield wipers as mist rolled through the city. There was a full moon tonight, not that she could see it through the cloud cover.

"He's probably the most generous soul I've ever come across in my two hundred and fif—" He choked, and then slammed his hands over the steering wheel, "—I'm sorry, I lost it there for a second."

"Are you okay?"

He nodded, swallowing hard. He suddenly looked clammy, his caramel skin covered in a sheen of sweat. "What I meant to say was he's the most generous soul I've met in my whole life."

"Really?" she asked. "You don't think that's a front?"

"It's not a front." His voice was stern. "He's also fiercely loyal."

Her lips quirked in disbelief. He dated women left and right. If he were loyal, wouldn't he be in a deep, committed relationship with one woman? "I don't know about the last part. His track record in the relationship department certainly doesn't show it."

"Maybe he simply hasn't found the right woman, yet."

As Melina wondered what kind of woman Hayden was looking for—if not brilliant and beautiful like the models he dated each month—Gabriel made a sharp U-turn and pulled up to the curb.

"We're here."

Chapter Twelve

A red carpet had been laid out, stretching up the steps to the aquarium, and at the sidewalk's end, two valets in tuxedos waited to park his car. They held umbrellas, protecting the event-goers from the rain. Gabriel and Melina exited in style, and strolled into the building. It wasn't the Silverlights, with paparazzi shooting pictures left and right, but it was classy nonetheless.

She admired the decorations, the flowers and candles, and tiny white lights as they entered and were immediately surrounded by groups of gossiping socialites. People milled about, drinking champagne, gabbing and laughing, and when they laid eyes on her, their gaze immediately shot to the pile of hair on the top of her head; they either didn't understand high fashion or were silently admiring her choice.

"Why don't we grab our seats," Gabriel said, brushing his hand against her elbow. "They'll be this way."

His touch was gentle and guiding, without being overbearing. What a change from the first few times she'd been in Hayden's company. Hayden gave off a possessive vibe, heady and intense, while Gabriel's mojo was calm and posed. She doubted anything could rile him up. The two men were oil and water. Open versus secretive. Suave versus cocky. Complete opposites.

She let him lead her through the foyer, to the main floor of the aquarium. Signs hung overhead, indicating the sharks, jellyfish, and rays were to the right, and coral reefs were to the left. In the center of the room though, tables and chairs covered with powder-blue linens dominated the space. Soft streams of blue and white light danced over the walls and floor, giving the feel that the entire room was underwater.

It was wicked cool.

"We're over there," he said, leading her to a table near the front. A woman's bag had already been placed on one setting, and the one next to it had a tuxedo coat draped over the chair.

Must've been reserved by Hayden and his bimbo date.

Loyal.

She scoffed silently and swallowed down her bitterness. What she really needed was a drink to wash it down. Where was the bar? *There.* In the corner.

"Can I get you something to drink?" Gabriel asked, as if he'd read her mind.

Was he always such a gentleman?

"Sure, could you get me a—"

"Lemon Drop?" a deep voice muttered behind her.

She turned around, nearly bumping into the sweet and sour drink extended in Hayden's hand. Turned out he was the gentleman, bringing over her very favorite drink before she'd even asked for it. Maybe she'd been wrong. He *was* suave... when he wanted to be. The Armani tuxedo they'd chosen Thursday afternoon fit tight over his shoulders and fell loosely to his sides. It fit him perfectly, though her first vision of Hayden in the tux—bare-chested with his fly unfastened— definitely topped this one.

"How'd you know I like Lemon Drops?" she asked, mouth drying from the sight of him.

"I'm freaking *Hayden Dean*. I just knew." He handed her the drink with a wink and a smile. "I have a sense for these things."

"Really?" Melina said, licking sugar off the rim. "Are you psychic or something?"

"No," he said, the laughter in his eyes dying down as he eyed her lips. "I saw it on your Facebook. You really should change your profile to private. Never know what kind of... *animals* could be following you on there."

Gabriel laughed tightly, and the blonde behind Hayden grinned, draping an arm over his shoulder.

"I'll try to remember that. Thanks for the drink." She reached out to shake the blonde's hand. "I'm Melina Rae."

"Laurie Harper." Hayden's date extended her manicured hand over his shoulder and shook delicately. "We're glad you could make it. Tonight's our biggest event, thanks to the generosity of people like Hayden."

There was that word again: *generous.*

If people closest to Hayden believed him to be such a generous soul, how could every single magazine get it wrong? Wouldn't there be at least *one* magazine singing his praises?

He must've only showed that side to people he was closest to...

"I love your dress," Laurie went on. "You look like you just stepped out of a magazine."

"Thank you." Melina smoothed her hands over her hips and down the puffy feathers. "I'm a sucker for high fashion, I'm afraid. Can I tell you a secret though?"

Laurie leaned in, grinning. "Please."

"I buy most of my accessories from Ebay," she whispered, touching her earrings and bracelet. "No one would ever know, though."

"That's brilliant." Laurie beamed. "I'll have to start looking there from now on."

Their conversation veered to magazines, *Eclipse*, and the article she was writing for *Celeb Crush*. Turned out Laurie was a fan of her column, which made Melina love the woman even more. She was smart too, damn it. Women as elegant as Laurie should be dumb. Wasn't fair for Mother Nature to give one woman both beauty *and* brains.

As they talked fashion and men and Lemon Drops, Gabriel moved around Melina to stand by Hayden. She didn't miss the nasty glares shooting between them.

"You checked her out on Facebook," Gabriel whispered too loudly, "but did you happen to catch where she lives?"

Hayden shook his head.

"Haight-Ashbury."

Tension whipped through the air, so palpable, Melina and Laurie cut their conversation short. What was wrong with her neighborhood? Hipsters and hippies were everywhere, but they were harmless. She'd lived in her building five years. The neighbors were quiet, and the rent was controlled.

Hayden shot Gabriel a concerned look, his eyebrows pinching as if he was deep in concentration. And then the weirdest thing happened. Gabriel stared back, and nodded. It was a small move, the slightest bob, but Melina caught it.

Had these guys talked about this earlier?

Reaching into his jacket pocket, Gabriel pulled out his phone and stared at the screen. "This is the worst timing."

"What?" Melina asked.

"I just got called in to work. There's been a new development on this big case we're working on, and—"

"No need to go into detail," she said, setting down her glass. "It's all right. We can go."

"No, that's not necessary." He took her hand in his and the strangest sound—almost like a growl—came from somewhere beside them. Gabriel dropped her hand as if it was on fire, and shoved his hands in his pockets. "You stay here with Hayden. Drink up and enjoy your night. I'll call you."

Another growl. Deeper and louder.

"Are the speakers vibrating?" Melina searched the corners of the room behind them for subwoofers, though the room was so dark, it took time for her eyes to adjust. "Do you guys hear that? It's a deep, rumbling sound…"

When she faced forward once more, Gabriel and Laurie were gone.

"Where'd Gabriel go?" Melina asked.

"He left."

"Just like that?"

Hayden nodded. He'd moved closer. Right beside her.

"I didn't even get to say goodbye."

"He said he'd call you later." Hayden exhaled heavily. "And you can trust Gabriel to keep his word."

"Where'd Laurie disappear to?"

"She's at the front, meeting the director of the aquarium." Hayden pointed to the tank housing a vibrantly-colored coral reef. "She's the hostess tonight, so I'm sure they're going over last-minute things." He eyed her carefully. "Ready to see me work magic?"

Magic? With him? Hell yes.

"Depends what kind of magic you're talking about."

"You think I party all night. You read the slanted stories about drinks, fights, and late nights. I'm going to show you what most of my parties are really like." He took her arm and slipped it through his. "As the face of Dean, Hyde, & Hammer, I have to work the room. And tonight, you're coming with me."

He led her around the room, introducing her to everyone who crossed his path. He presented Melina as his business associate, someone who was writing an article on him. It was as if he wanted everyone to know, without a smidgeon of doubt, that they weren't personally involved.

At first, the thought stung. But by the tenth introduction, Melina was beating Hayden to the punch, talking about the article and how it was going to be a nearly-impossible feat to clean up his image.

It was a comical ice-breaker—one that even had Hayden chuckling.

He knew everyone's name. He smiled and laughed effortlessly, oozing the charm she'd come to know him for. But he wasn't cheesy, the way she'd totally expected. His laughter and conversations were genuine. He was a people person, she realized, shaking hands with San Francisco's mayor.

He didn't put off the vibe of a drunken partier, or a slick womanizer. An air of nobleness surrounded him, no matter who he talked with.

As he laughed with the mayor about the upcoming election, Hayden squeezed Melina's arm. He leaned in. "Remember when I asked you if you could improve my image enough to run for mayor?"

She nodded, watching the mayor whisper something to his elegant wife.

"No one could do as good a job as this guy. His ability to lead is remarkable. I should be taking notes."

"For what?"

He stared, his eyebrow giving a tell-tale twitch. She'd made him uncomfortable. "I don't know how you do it, but a few minutes with you and I forget we haven't known each other longer. I keep forgetting you don't know all my secrets."

"Maybe I should." She emptied the last of her Lemon Drop and snatched another off the tray of a passing waiter. "It's about time we should bulldoze those walls you've got up, don't you think?"

Without answering her question, Hayden bid farewell to

the mayor and his wife. He rested his hand on the small of her back as he guided Melina toward their table. Even from the smallest touch, her chest swelled with pride. She couldn't help it. Strolling around with the hottest guy in the room was a rush. Hayden was also the sweetest talker, the funniest, and the only one who heated her veins with uncontrollable lust.

Before they reached their table, a group of Hayden's friends signaled for them to come over. He exhaled heavily, and escorted her to them.

"Hayden!" A burly, thirty-something guy slapped Hayden on the back. "About time you introduce us to your lady friend."

He made the rounds, naming his friends, though there were too many for Melina to remember any one in particular. They all looked oddly similar. Shaved heads. Tuxedos stretching over their brawny shoulders. Dark eyes. She shook hands with each of them. A few winked. Others grinned. Hayden stood behind her, and although he didn't touch her, an umbrella of warmth covered her body.

"I was just telling Hayden that he needed to find a good woman who'd knock some sense into him," the burliest of the group said. If she remembered right, his name was Merrick. "When did you two start dating?"

"We're not dating," Hayden interrupted. A wave of heat flashed over her. "She's a business associate."

"Really?" Merrick said, bushy eyebrows doing an up-down dance.

"She's writing an article on me for *Celeb Crush* magazine."

"I'd never date him," Melina interjected. Her cheek heated where Hayden's gaze burned. "He's got poor taste in teams, for one. He's a 49er fan, and I can't lower my standards that far."

The group laughed, low and husky.

"Ouch." Merrick eyed her intently. "This one's got bite,

Hayden."

"You have no idea." His jaw clenched.

"Truth be told, I'm not much of a football fan in general." Merrick slid to the forefront of the group. "But I think you could convince me to jump on your sidelines."

Hayden took her elbow and gently guided her back toward him. "I think they're about to start, gentleman. We're going to take our seats."

"Where's Gabriel?" a shorter one asked. "We were hoping to talk about—"

"He left on official business," Hayden spat. "If you need him, I'm sure you still have his number. It hasn't changed."

The shorter friend nodded, his dark eyes focusing far over Hayden's shoulder. Something electric flickered in the space between them, but she couldn't put her finger on it. The vibe was tense and foreboding. Chilling.

"Come on, Melina." Hayden led her away from the group, and then glanced back over his shoulder. "Have a good night, gentleman."

Hayden's lips tightened as he watched them walk away, and then escorted Melina to her seat.

"Who were those guys?" she asked him once they were out of earshot. "And don't say your friends. I won't believe it."

"Before my dad died they were the most loyal friends I'd ever had. After… Well, let's just say they don't feel the same way about me."

Sadness tainted her lifted spirits. She'd thought maybe she'd just met his most inner circle of friends. It was depressing to think they'd turned on him after his father died. She wanted to press further, but thought twice about it. Wasn't the time, or the place to dive into family and friend issues.

"You sure aren't afraid to talk to anybody, are you?" he said, turning toward her. "I think you'd talk to the Devil, if he presented himself."

"If he wanted to go on record, abso-freaking-lutely. Can you imagine the press I'd get if I improved *his* image? We're talking Nobel Peace Prize honors."

They laughed, and his expression loosened once more.

The supporters circling around through the room had moved out of the foyer and made their way to their seats. The space buzzed with excitement, and on the far side of the room, Laurie stepped up to the podium.

"What's wrong with my neighborhood?" she asked, remembering Hayden's encounter with Gabriel.

His smile dropped. "Excuse me?"

"I heard Gabriel tell you where I live. You guys got all gargoyle-faced, right before he left. Is there a problem?"

"There've been some crimes there lately that have come to our attention." His gaze held hers. "Just be careful, okay?"

"Change my Facebook privacy setting, watch my back, what's next? Stick to a Paleo diet?"

"Hell no," he said, leaning in. "Your figure's flawless. No dieting for you."

"Stop," she flirted, pushing him back. "Your lines won't work on me. I'm immune to your charm."

"Is that so?" He palmed the small of her back, dragging her attention away from the guests. Chills spread up her spine as he whispered, "You look beautiful, Melina. The brightest star here."

"Thank you. Still not working." *Liar.* She took a drink to quench the fire burning in her middle, and sat in the chair he'd pulled out. "I knew Ruby would work wonders for you."

"She had more suits delivered to the office yesterday, though this one takes the cake." He slid into the seat next to her and tugged on his right lapel. "What do you think?"

She hid her smile. Of course she liked his tux; it was Armani. She hated to admit it, but she liked the way Hayden looked in it more.

"You must be a Leo," she said. "You need constant validation."

He flinched, then laughed, sliding into the seat beside her. "I do not."

"I take it you are a Leo, then?"

"I am, actually. My birthday's August 15th." He folded his arms over his chest and leaned back. "What are you?"

"I'm a Sagittarius." She took another drink, emptying her second Lemon Drop of the night. "You know I'm a perfect fit for a Leo. Horoscopically speaking." She frowned. "Horo—Horiscopically?"

"Do you mean astrologically?"

She laughed so hard at her mistake, she held on to the edge of the table to keep from bowling over. "That's it. Horoscopically." She shook her head and then snorted, covering her hand over her mouth. "You'd think I'd have a better way with words, seeing as how it's my job…"

"I've never read your column, so I can't attest to your way with words…" He rested his arm the back of her chair. "But I can definitely say you have a way with your mouth."

The air ripped from her lungs. He was a player, toying with her emotions. But if she wasn't mistaken, he'd also brought over her drink, pulled out her chair, and had kindly introduced her to just about everyone at the event.

She didn't have a calendar full of dates to compare this one against, but he'd been a complete gentleman. A surprise.

"I've never bought much into horoscopes before, but I'm interested," he whispered, scooting closer. "What do they say about us?"

Us.

Fireworks of tension and desire soared through Melina's limbs, and then exploded, leaving her tingly and warm.

"They're—we're—both fire signs," she said, as he completely turned her way. "So a relationship between the

two—between us—is supposed to be fiercely passionate."
Like fireworks. She willed the blush in her cheeks to return to their natural color before continuing on. "We're loyal, powerhouses, full of energy, and work perfectly as a team."

"Very interesting." He eyed her intently. "Perfect together, huh?"

Heat radiated through the space between them, nailing her in place. Her breath came out in pants as his gaze raked over her face, her neck, down to her breasts. Desire licked up and down her body as if it were his tongue. She trembled, sensing the need building inside him.

She'd never been more in tune with a man in all her life.

This had to be an expertly-timed facade.

Hayden couldn't be the kind of man she'd witnessed this week, could he?

Had she been wrong about everything?

"What do you say we get out of here? This tux is strangling me," he said, loosening his tie, "and I've been to a thousand of these before. I already bought the seats, which means I've already made my donation."

And she'd already witnessed how Hayden networked, which would absolutely go into her article.

"Ladies and gentleman," Laurie announced near the coral reef tank. "If you'd take your seats, we'd like to thank our gracious sponsors for their warm hearts…and deep pockets."

Laughter spread through the room as the last of the guests took their seats.

"What about dinner?" Melina asked, heart drumming overtime.

"If you're hungry, I know a place not far from here that serves amazing seafood." He took out his phone and tapped a text. "If you're worried about wasting the food here, I'll have the plates served to empty seats sent to homeless shelters."

There it was. Another glimpse into the hidden part

of Hayden's soul. She could put this in the article. *Multi-millionaire donates money to aquarium, extra food to shelters for hungry and homeless.* She didn't have to change a thing.

He truly was generous, wasn't he?

In the dark, Hayden's features shifted. His grin wasn't sly, and not one ulterior motive burned behind his sultry eyes.

"Honestly," he whispered, "I feel like there are thousands of eyes on us in this place. After all the schmoozing we just did, I'm craving some peace and quiet. What do you think?"

"Okay." Something inside her cracked like a twig. "Let's go."

If this was the real Hayden Dean, she wanted more of it.

As Hayden pulled out her chair, the way a gentleman would, and led her across the floor, Laurie thanked the sponsors by name. The guests clapped wildly for each one. When they got to the platinum sponsor, the one person responsible for donating more than five million dollars each year to the growth of the program, Hayden pushed open the outside door and escorted her through. But not before Laurie announced his name.

The aquarium went wild with applause and cheers.

Hayden didn't even flinch as he grabbed Melina by the hand and escorted her out the doors to his sports car parked at the curb.

Chapter Thirteen

After seeing Merrick and his groupies at the aquarium benefit, Hayden knew he and Melina couldn't stay. Those guys weren't rogues—they hadn't made their loyalty known yet—but they weren't happy with the change of leadership in the pack.

And they'd taken a keen interest in Melina.

They had to get out of there.

He was just happy she'd gone along with him. Since they were dressed up and starving, he didn't want to drop her off at home, and the only thing waiting for him at his place was a microwave meal. He could've called up for food, but why bother the staff?

No, a quaint, quiet restaurant on the end of Pier 39 would do fine.

It'd started raining shortly after they arrived, driving away most of the tourists.

They were alone.

"I have to admit, I've lived in San Francisco my entire life, and I've never eaten here." Melina popped a piece of calamari into her mouth, and then worked on emptying her second glass of Chardonnay. "I thought tourism would've made this place go straight to the dogs. I'm happy to say I was wrong."

To the dogs. Hayden laughed mid-drink and snorted wine through his nostrils. Tannins burned like a son of a bitch.

He toasted her glass. "Being wrong isn't something every woman will admit."

"Well I'm not like every woman," she rebutted, grinning.

She was absolutely right. She was unlike any other woman Hayden had ever met. The women who crossed his path were usually offering themselves on silver platters by now.

But not Melina.

She challenged him in every way, and it was incredibly refreshing. Not only was she irritatingly stubborn, but he couldn't seem to keep his distance from her. He wanted to pick her brain, ask her what she thought about the pack and the problems he'd been having there. She left out the bullshit because she wasn't intimidated by him.

Given all that, she was surprisingly tender. And soft. When she smiled, it illuminated something inside him. Happiness bloomed through his chest when she laughed, and he couldn't help but laugh with her.

She was quite possibly the most perfect person in the world for him.

She stole another piece of calamari and leveled him with a curious stare. "What drew you to donate to the aquarium? Five million a year is really generous."

"I tried to get you out of there before you heard that."

"You don't have to hide," she said. "I still don't understand why you do."

Letting people in meant people were closer to the truth. He was a wolf. Future Alpha of one of the strongest packs in the country. He'd learned to survive by closing out the world and letting them think what they wanted to think. As long as he did right by his family, friends, and the pack, he was solid.

As he chewed over how to answer her question, the rain ceased and the clouds parted, offering a glimpse of the full moon. Its shifting energy pierced through the window, and hummed through Hayden's gut.

As a turned wolf, he could only shift during the full moon. Controlling the urge was difficult, but he'd learned to manage it. That didn't mean he didn't ache to blow through this form and embrace the power of his other.

He took a bite of lemon-crusted salmon before saying, "My mother was a fan of the arts. She worked closely with Serephina Vanguard—one of the city's brightest visionaries—to keep the arts protected and treasured. While Serephina preferred the museums and opera houses, my mother loved animals. The aquarium was her favorite. She liked the rays, especially."

"That explains a lot." Melina stared through him, her gaze burning deep. "Does your mother still live in the city?"

"No, she's long gone now." His biological mother had been a non-shifter, though he wasn't about to tell Melina that. And there'd be no record of Cara Dean, Angus's late wife, if Melina wanted to go searching. "She died when I was thirteen."

"I'm so sorry." She averted her eyes to the street behind him, and her shoulders rolled forward. "That's terrible. You were at such an impressionable age."

He nodded, the memories of her death slicing through him. "She was killed in a car accident."

Unable to finish the thought, Hayden drank to soothe the ache in his chest. It didn't work. If Hayden hadn't been attacked and left for dead on the streets…if Angus hadn't found him and finished the transition himself, Hayden would've died. Angus had a heart of gold, a soft spot for helping wolves in trouble.

"It's a blessing you had your father. Angus worked hard

to build an empire for you."

"His whole life was dedicated to it." He chased a bite of salmon with a gulp of wine. "But I'd rather not talk anymore about my family, if that's all right with you."

She shook her head slowly, taking him in with those mesmerizingly beautiful eyes.

"You're so different than you were before." She leaned over the table, clasping her hands in front of her. "Can I ask you something before you close off completely?"

"What makes you think I'll do that?"

She *tsk'd* her tongue against the roof of her mouth. "Come on. I think I know your games by now."

"All right, then." He pushed his hips out and leaned back in the chair. "Go on."

"Who's the real Hayden Dean?" Her voice was soft. Hesitant. "The one from the shelter, and the aquarium…the one sitting in front of me right now? Or are you the Hayden Dean on the covers of the magazines?"

"You want to know the real me? Ask away." He swiped the napkin over his mouth. "But is this for you, or the article?"

"This is for me. Off the record."

He wasn't sure, and something told him she wasn't either. Better to give her a boundary.

"Five questions," he said. "But the trade-off is I don't want you following me to the office anymore."

"Why?"

Too risky. She'd already been seen there once. It'd be safer if they didn't make their behavior a pattern. If the rogue wolves caught on to the fact that Hayden had taken a liking to Melina, she'd have a huge target pinned to her back.

"I have my reasons," he said. "That's the deal. Take it or leave it."

"Fine." She motioned for the waitress to refill her wine glass. "I've already seen all I need to see there, anyway. Don't you ever feel the need to get a law degree to join the ranks of the others in the building?"

"Already have one." He finished off his salmon. "Stanford Law. That's one down."

"No, wait." She pointed across the table. "That wasn't one of my questions."

"It was phrased as one. You've got four left. I'd suggest making them count."

She fumed, her eyes narrowing.

Damn, she was cute.

"Why bother getting a degree," she said, each word deliberate, "if you don't have plans to practice law?"

"Because once upon a time, my father had hopes I'd take over every part of his empire." He sighed, resting his fork on the edge of his plate. "My family tried hard to push me into the courtroom for years, but it's not my thing. I'm much more interested in…organizing movement within the company, I guess you could say." *The movement of the werewolf guards in the city, to be specific.* "I make my own hours, and take on projects as they come to me."

"And you feel like that's enough? You don't have any desire to be a lawyer? To follow in your father's footsteps?"

"I'll take that as one really long question." He smirked as she shot daggers from her eyes. "I don't have to shadow my father's path in life to honor him in death." It was the simplest way to put it. Hayden wanted to rule the wolf pack, but law wasn't for him. Never had been. "I will work closely with certain groups within his business structure. That satisfies my needs. For now."

He had other needs, though, and they wouldn't be appeased as easily. Being close to Melina this way, alone in the corner of the restaurant, made him wild with want. Tension coiled through his body, hardening his muscles to the point of pain. Restricting himself was becoming an impossible feat.

How much longer would he be able to go without touching her, kissing her?

What he wouldn't give for one taste of her succulent flesh...

He'd heard the Luminary bond was undeniable and maddening, but this—this feeling never eased. He was ravenous. Hungry to taste her, feel her heart beat against him as he held her close.

"Hayden?" She placed her hand over his and shook. "Are you okay?"

Her touch awakened something inside him. The lust clouding his brain cleared. Melina stared, her eyebrows raised and her forehead crinkled.

"I will be." He had to claim Melina as his own and drive deep into her warmth, or get the hell away from her before he combusted. "That's another question by the way." He laughed when she growled in frustration. "You've got one left."

As the waitress arrived at their table, Melina ordered the chocolate mousse cake. Rather than disappear to the back to retrieve desert, the waitress hesitated, her gaze bouncing between them.

"I have to ask..." The waitress fiddled with her pen. "...is this your first date? The staff has bets going."

"No," Hayden blurted, reciting the lines he'd said a hundred times over. "We're here on business. She's writing an article on me for *Celeb Crush*."

The waitress smiled, cocking her hip to the side. "That's what I thought," she talked so quietly, she nearly purred. "I'll be right back with that cake."

As Hayden brought his attention back to Melina, she smiled tightly.

"If what's happening here is only business," she said, swiping her finger round and round her empty wine glass, "then why'd you kiss me in your office?"

She sensed their connection.

The blood drained from his face. "I think you've fired off enough rounds of questions."

"Oh, no, no, no, Mr. I'm-Going-To-Count-Every-Damn-Question." She pointed a finger at his chest. "I've used four. I have one left."

As Hayden fought to find the words, his mouth dried. He licked his lips to return the moisture, but it didn't work. Suppressing the desire to kiss her again, to show her how much he wanted her, Hayden folded his arms over his chest.

The waitress brought the cake, set it between them, and hovered longer than usual. If she said something to either of them, he didn't hear it over the buzzing in his ears. When she left them alone once more, Hayden picked up the fork and slid it through the center of the cake. As he lifted it to his mouth, he realized there was more than one way to answer her final question.

"If this was the most delicious cake in the world, smelling like heaven and tasting like ecstasy, and you knew one taste would ruin every other cake in the world for you, would you sample it?"

Her lips fell apart, and he could hear her heart begin to race.

She bit her lower lip. "Are you asking me if I want some?"

"No, I'm answering your final question." He shoved the cake in his mouth and savored the rich chocolate tang as it hit his tongue. "I couldn't resist sampling you." He set the fork on the edge of the plate and licked the flavors from his lips. Her gaze landed on his tongue and her breathing quickened. "As much as I enjoyed it, kissing you was a mistake. One forbidden bite, one luscious taste, will have to be enough."

As the words hit him as truth, a pang of regret jolted him like a thunderbolt. He felt sick. Either the cake was bad, or Melina had gotten under his skin. He couldn't breathe without picking up her scent. Couldn't think without seeing her face in his mind. If he sat across from her much longer, he was liable to haul her against him. The waitress wouldn't believe their relationship was strictly business once Hayden's face was buried in Melina's neck.

"Excuse me." He pushed back from the table and stood before she could answer. "I need some air."

He paid for the bill before pushing out the doors and striding down the street. The air was cool and crisp, smelling of salty sea spray and seafood from the restaurants on the pier. He didn't look back to see if Melina had followed, but when a draft of cool air whipped through the pier and smacked into him, hints of her aroma were carried with it.

"Damn it." He spun, and watched her charge at him. He blew out a breath and lifted his arms from his sides. "Go back inside."

"I don't know why you haven't received the memo by now, but I don't take orders from anyone." She stood her ground, inches from him. "Why does it feel like you are constantly fighting a battle between who you are and who you want to be?"

"What do you want from me, Melina?"

"You." Her eyes went wide, as if she hadn't meant to say it. "I mean, I want to know what motivates you to act the way you do. I want to know what you want. Truly, deep down inside. Is it fame? Money? Prestige? Women falling all over you?"

"Not all women." He closed the space between them. "Just one."

As waves of desire flashed through him, he gripped the back of her neck and smashed his mouth to hers. She whimpered, throwing her arms around him. Blinding heat exploded through his body as she thrust her tongue into his mouth. The tantalizing scent of her arousal hit him hard, nearly buckling his knees. He hauled her against him, lifted her off her feet, and swallowed her whimpers of delight. Nothing existed but her taste, her smell, her lips, and warm, cavernous mouth.

And then, a familiar scent melded with hers, hitting Hayden's nostrils and stopping him short. He set Melina back on her feet and pushed her away from him. She stared, a mix of shock and desire glossing her dark eyes.

Fear hardened into a knot and lodged in Hayden's chest.

There was someone—something—lurking on the second floor of the parking garage across the street, watching them with beady onyx eyes.

Wolf.

Chapter Fourteen

"I need you to go back inside." Hayden gripped Melina by the shoulders. "Now. Run."

"Why, I don't—"

"I'll explain later," he said, the urge to shift lurching through his veins. "Just go. Please. Choose a table away from the windows and wait for me. If I don't come back in ten minutes, take a cab home and lock yourself inside. Don't answer the door to anyone but me. I'll meet you there as soon as I can."

"You're scaring me." She trembled in his grasp. The need to protect her, at all costs, clawed its way through him. "Hayden? What's happening?"

Adrenaline pulsed hot and fast through him. "Go."

She took off toward the pier, faster than he would've expected given the height and spike of her heels. Keeping his attention locked on the parking garage and the wolf hunkering there, Hayden waited until Melina's scent was gone from the wind before stalking toward the garage.

He searched north and south down Embarcadero, and

seeing the coast clear, bounded into the shadows. Another few seconds and he'd be able to shift without being seen.

Striking the ground hard, Hayden focused on the shifting power rushing through him. He gritted his teeth, let the energy gather into a ball in his gut, and then exploded into wolf form as he leaped into the shadows of the garage. The tuxedo fell away to shreds. His muscles elongated and strengthened, expanding to their robust size, and a coat of thick gray fur blanketed his body. He gave one final shake, hardening into wolf form, and then let the aggression flow freely through him.

Being in this form felt right and good, and damn he was ready to kick some ass.

He took off into the garage, using the stench of the wolf to guide him.

Who are you? What are you doing here? He projected through the cement jungle using the werewolf's process of mind-speak. The wolf would be able to hear Hayden's projected thoughts, even if he was no longer a member of their pack. Whether or not he would communicate, or obey, was a different matter entirely.

No response.

Just as Hayden thought.

Fine. He threw the thought out there. *We can do this the hard way.*

As his strides widened, he rounded the ramp and used his heightened sense of sight to scan the second level of the garage. He padded slowly, cautiously, around row upon row of cars.

Might as well show yourself, Hayden sneered. *You've got nowhere to run, and I've got nothing but time to hunt you down.*

From the corner of his eye, Hayden caught movement. But it was too late. The wolf was pitch black, blending with the shadows. He used the dark to his advantage and attacked, leaping onto Hayden's back. Before he could bite, Hayden shook violently, slinging his enemy to the floor.

With a hideous snarl, the wolf rose up on his haunches and pulled back his gums in defiance. The rogue had a sharp ridge on his back, and thick paws, though he'd be no match for Hayden muzzle to muzzle.

Identify yourself. Hayden paced round and round the wolf, eyeing him carefully.

You can call me Rogue.

Wasn't that fitting…

You don't belong here, Rogue. Not in that form, anyway. Explain yourself.

Until you take your place as Alpha of the pack, you don't own the city, and you certainly don't own me. Rogue matched Hayden's path, round and round. His muzzle remained tilted high, challenging. *I haven't broken any laws. Not a single non-shifter has seen me in this form.*

I asked you to explain yourself. Your presence here is unwanted and unwarranted. Hayden growled, showing his incisors. *Are you following me for your new Alpha or for you own foolish reasons?*

If the rogues had assigned a new Alpha, things were only going to get worse for the San Francisco Wolf Pack. Wandering rogues who refused to join a pack were tolerated, as not every wolf could be expected to accept a unified set of laws. But if they joined together to form a new pack, that was a different situation entirely. Resources and territories would be challenged day and night as the two packs fought for ground. Packmates would be injured or worse in the battle. Families could be split by boundary lines.

Disaster.

We don't have an Alpha yet, but soon, Rogue answered. *We're waiting to make sure a mutt like you doesn't take control over the city's pack. How can you possibly think you can slide into a position like Alpha wolf, without even a drop of royal blood in your veins?*

Hayden stilled, his own fears erupting inside him.

He wasn't worthy.

Never would be.

The pack wouldn't follow him. Not without Dean blood in his veins.

You're brave, Rogue, but you're also incredibly stupid. Hayden pushed out the thoughts. *You must have a death wish if you think you can come here and throw a challenge like that in my face.*

Even though Rogue stood strong and stoic, the rancid scent of fear burned Hayden's nostrils. Alpha or not, Hayden had always had a dominant presence. It was undeniable. He was a fighter, a scrapper, through and through.

And Rogue was afraid.

Hayden took the chance and sprang, lunging for his neck. Rogue ducked, and rolled out of the way, popping to his feet as if he'd performed the maneuver a thousand times before.

The wolf must've been a former guard for the pack.

He knew how to move.

Hayden growled low in his throat and stalked closer, slowly, channeling all the power he could into his back legs. The hair on the back of his neck stood on end. His vision blurred red. Then, when Rogue took a small step back, Hayden advanced, shooting forward, ramming into Rogue full force. The hit jolted Rogue hard. He staggered back. Hayden pushed forward, slamming Rogue into a Volvo in the nearest parking stall. Its alarm went off, bleeping and honking into the garage. The pitch was achingly high, piercing Hayden's ears.

Rogue howled, his ears falling back as his head thrashed side to side.

Sensitive hearing, Rogue? Hayden projected, as a laugh bubbled deep in his belly. *That's one of the benefits of being turned. My hearing's not as sensitive as yours.*

With Rogue distracted and his eardrums most likely ready to burst, Hayden nipped at his neck, smashed his body against his, and drove him to the ground. He pinned him to the concrete, one paw on either side of Rogue's muscular body.

Howling, Rogue whipped his body beneath Hayden's.

I'm only going to ask one more time, Hayden said with his mind. *Why were you spying on me?*

No answer.

Desperate to end the fight and get back to Melina, Hayden reared up, and then hammered his muzzle into the side of Rogue's neck. He didn't bite—if he severed his artery, he'd kill his enemy, which wasn't what he wanted. Not exactly.

Why are you here? Hayden growled, gearing up for the inevitable.

You're incredibly brave, but you're also incredibly stupid, Rogue answered, repeating Hayden's earlier words. *We were counting on that.*

Counting on what?

Rogue's gums pulled back over his wretched canines in a twisted sort of smile. *You were right earlier. Your hearing isn't as good as ours. We were counting on that, too.*

What should he have been hearing?

Melina.

Moving with lightning-quick reflexes, Rogue swiped his paw across Hayden's face, raking his nails through the flesh over his eyes. Hayden recoiled as blood squirted from his brow and oozed into his eyes. Rogue slipped from beneath his hold and darted away. Hayden scrubbed his eyes with his paw, but his vision was too blurred. The blood dripped thick, stinging him.

Melina.

He tried to stand and stumbled, smacking into the Volvo when his eyesight doubled. He strained, listening for any hint of Melina's voice.

Nothing.

Shifting back to human form would heal the wound instantly, but it would also leave him vulnerable if Rogue wanted to return to kick his ass. And if he went to meet up with his disobedient friends to rope them into the fight, Hayden would be screwed.

One wolf, he could handle. A pack full of rogues? Not so much.

By the time he reached the first level and padded through the entrance, he was nearly blind. He sniffed, picking up hints of the city. Not a trace of Rogue, or Melina.

Pulling the shifting energy into his middle, Hayden knelt and bowed his head. He shook violently as his fur flattened and smoothed to skin, and his muscles returned to their normal size. His head ached like a son of a bitch, right across the forehead, but he'd been clawed to the face. He expected nothing less than the migraine from hell.

"Melina!" he called out, striding through the shadows.

He covered his genitals with his hands, and ran behind parked cars until he could cross the street to the pier. People walked down the long walk of the Embarcadero, some couples holding hands, others biking, running. He wasn't going to be able to go far before someone spotted him and made a scene.

Thank God there weren't children around at this hour.

A Civic sped by, and then there was a break before the next light flashed green. Hayden took his shot. He sprinted across the street, stepping on broken glass and garbage, and kneeled behind a cement bench. A few people turned, and laughed, pointing. A twenty-something woman standing near a flowerbed took a picture with her phone.

Effing spectacular.

He could draft the headline himself: *Hayden Dean: Nudist, Terrorizes City.*

The homeless man sprawled across the bench in front of him craned his neck around and stared. As if Hayden were the strange one.

"If you don't mind, I'm going to borrow this," Hayden said, sliding the greasy coat off the bum's body. "Two minutes, and I'll bring it right back."

"Hell you are!" The bum ripped the coat out of Hayden's hands. "Help! Police!"

"Shhhh!" Hayden dropped the coat and hid, covering his family jewels. "Never mind, just be quiet, okay?"

"Help! I'm being assaulted! Sexually!" His voice boomed, echoing down the street. "Help! The pervert stole my pants!"

His...*pants*?

Turned out Hayden had been wrong. The coat wasn't a coat at all.

Oh yeah, add to the humiliation.

Sirens whoop-whooped from the street behind him, and those unmistakable red and blue lights reflected off the buildings.

It hadn't been more than ten minutes since he'd left Melina at the pier. She had to be safe. Had to be. Rogue had been trying to spook him...hadn't he?

Desperation and fear streaking through him, Hayden took off like a bolt, jumping over the bench and high-tailing it toward the restaurant. Orders were shouted behind him, but he couldn't hear over the pounding in his head. He pushed around an older man on roller blades and shoved a runner aside. Leapt over a planter box. Weaved between a group of tourists. He nearly rammed into a woman pushing a stroller, but stopped himself short. His hesitation allowed the officer to catch up. Hayden took off, but only made it a few steps before he was dragged to the ground from behind.

Face down on the concrete, the officer put a knee in Hayden's back and ripped his arms behind him.

More laughter, more phones held up and pointed his direction.

He arched up, searching for Melina, breathing in deeply to pick up even a single hint of her aroma.

There.

Faint. On the sea breeze. Fading.

As the officer lifted Hayden off the ground, his gaze landed on a blacked-out Lincoln parked at the curb, a few car lengths ahead of the police cruiser. Hayden's eyes might've been playing tricks on him and he might've been hit in the head one too many times, but he couldn't mistake the blue peacock feather caught in the rear passenger door. A peacock feather that looked like it'd come from the bottom of Melina's dress.

He fought against the officer's hold. Hayden was stronger. He could burst through the officer's grip…

As he tugged, slipping one of his hands out, the officer said, "Oh no, you don't," before clamping a cold rod of steel around his wrists and jerking him backward.

"Melina!" Hayden's insides soured and boiled with unadulterated hatred. He lurched to be set free, straining against the officer's hold. He could run with cuffs—the physical aspect wouldn't be a problem. He could shift and break free, once he was out of sight. But running from the police was a line he couldn't cross. "It'll be okay. I'll find you. I promise."

She was in danger. Because of him, an innocent woman, the most beautiful woman he'd ever met in his entire life, *his fated mate*, was gone.

He'd never felt more alone.

"Easy there. I'll let you go and you can go get her," the officer said over Hayden's shoulder. "As soon as you get some clothes on, and answer a few questions. First, you're going to explain to me what you were doing with that guy over there."

Hayden's vision blurred. Knives stabbed through his temples. He staggered. And threw up his dinner into the gutter.

That got immortalized on video, too.

He didn't care. Not for one second.

All that mattered was getting Melina back unharmed.

Lord help them if they touched a single hair on her head.

Chapter Fifteen

Melina awoke from the deepest sleep of her life, tilted her head to the side—damn, it ached something fierce—and felt a yawn coming on. Her mouth wouldn't open. It felt like something had taped her lips together.

Her system spiked into panic mode. She gasped, breathing heavy through her nose. Tugging against the binding on her hands and ankles, she took frantic inventory. The room was dark and damp, and the musky smell of grime burned her nose. Duct tape covered her mouth. Bound to a chair, she forced the fog from her brain.

Where the hell am I? Why am I so weak?

"It was an anesthetic," a gruff voice said from somewhere in the corner. "It's mostly harmless. Just enough to knock you unconscious and get you here. You'll probably be groggy for a while."

Tears burned her throat. She screamed, though the sound came out strained and muffled against the tape. No one would hear her.

"You might as well save your energy," her captor said

again. "We own this lot and the ones around it. The only wolves who can hear you are the ones who work for us."

Wolves?

Where the hell was she? Alaska? She couldn't have been knocked out *that* long.

Heart racing, Melina peered through the dark, and tried to make out the man's shape. He was burly, but not overweight. Built like a bear. She worked on her wrists, sliding them against the rope. Her right one slipped, and then caught once more.

"There's no reason to scream or try to get free, so wipe that from your pretty head right now. We're not going to hurt you." Her captor stood from the chair and stalked closer. "You're insurance for us. As long as Hayden steps down from the running, we'll let you go. We don't want you involved any more than you have to be. That's all we want. No more, no less." He stood over her, a looming shadow in the dark, and brushed his hand across her cheek. "Though if it were up to me, I'd want a lot more. It's too bad you weren't born, like us."

Born?

Umm…she was *here*, wasn't she? Of course she was *born*.

Disgusted and confused, Melina leaned away from his grimy touch. She tugged at her wrists harder, sliding and pulling, gaining fragments of space in the rope with each wiggle.

"Aww, I'm not so bad," he said, chuckling with a sick husk. "I may not have a face like your boyfriend Hayden, but I'm not Quasimodo."

Boyfriend? Did they really think she'd hooked up with Hayden? Yeah. Like he would want something long-term… with her, no less.

Not likely.

What was her problem? She had serious issues here. Hayden wasn't one of them.

As she yanked her hands apart from one another, jerked them together, and then gave them a solid tug once more, the rope slackened. She slipped her right hand free.

Swallowing down a happy squeal, Melina stared straight forward so Quasimodo wouldn't know what'd happened.

"I'm going to check on the status," he said, turning for the door on the far wall. "See if they've reached Hayden yet."

Strength she didn't know she had reared up in her heart and soared through her. The moment Quasimodo exited into a dimly lit hall and shut the door behind him, Melina broke her wrists free. As quickly as she could, she untied the ropes on her ankles and kicked loose.

She slipped off her Jimmy Choos and clutched them in her hands with the spikes pointing outward.

Oh yeah. Armed with fashion.

Tiptoeing across the room, Melina tried the handle. It turned. They were either the worst kidnappers in the history of ever, or they'd seriously underestimated her.

She cracked the door open and peered down the hall, first one way and then the other.

Better look out for those wolves Quasimodo had mentioned.

The coast was clear. Not a paw print on the dusty floor. She rounded the corner and turned right, down another hall that sounded quiet. Out of the shadows ahead, something shook like a big fluffy dog…and then moved slowly her direction.

Shit.

The gigantic canine stalking her way wasn't a dog at all.

It was a *wolf.*

She froze, and then forced her feet into a quick and sudden retreat.

A growl vibrated the very air she breathed.

"Easy, boy," she whispered, not wanting to bring Quasimodo back into the picture. "I'm going back, okay?

Eeeasssyyy."

He padded forward, as deep snarls echoed from all around her.

More wolves.

Clutching her heels tightly against her, Melina turned and bolted down the hall in the opposite direction. Something hit her hard from behind, knocking her to the floor. A heavy weight settled over the top of her. She spun, and faced the most gruesome canine she'd ever seen in her life.

Big, gnarly snout. Jagged teeth in need of a clean. Round eyes that looked oddly human.

Shuddering, she pinched her eyes tight, and then shoved the heel of her shoe into the flesh of the wolf's neck.

She screamed, cowering from the stream of blood. "Take that!"

Death by Jimmy Choo!

Killer fashion sense totally had new meaning...

The wolf howled and reared up, pinning her within the cage of his powerful body. As she tried to shimmy out from underneath it, the wolf's gums peeled back over its fangs. It was pissed off and going to bite.

She froze. "I'm...sorry?"

Fury churned in the wolf's eyes, and as she flattened herself to the floor, shrinking away, it hammered its head against her neck and sank its teeth deep.

She screamed for the heavens as fire and lightning erupted inside her. Without thinking, she roped her fingers through the strap on the other shoe, slung it around, and stabbed it through the wolf's neck on the opposite side. It thrashed and howled as two spike heels knifed their way through its fur.

Time slowed to a painful halt.

As the wolf unsheathed its teeth from of her neck, Melina scooted from beneath its wavering body. She took off running without looking back, even as a thunderous roar of footsteps pounded behind her. She turned the corner, sprinting hard toward an emergency exit. Shouts and screams came from behind her, followed by the most hideous howls she'd ever heard.

How many wolves were there?

Holding her hand to her neck to stop the bleeding, Melina pushed out the doors onto the street, turned right, and took off running. She tripped and fumbled, dizzy from the loss of blood.

Spinning around to gain her bearings, Melina gasped. She was still in San Francisco. Right in its heart. South of the Mission in Bernal Heights, to be exact. She knew the area well. One of her first apartments in the city wasn't far from here. And if she wasn't completely disoriented, she'd just stumbled out an old cathedral.

Holy Mary Mother of Cujo? That couldn't be right.

The streets were surprisingly empty for the city that never slept. Mustering her strength, Melina ran toward lights of a few shops on the next block.

"Help!" she squeaked, but her words were quiet and hoarse, straining her throat as they were spoken. "Help!"

Quasimodo's words rang through her ears: *We own this lot and the ones around it. The only wolves who can hear you are the ones who work for us.*

She had to make it a block, maybe two, before she could trust anyone to help her. Her luck, she'd run into someone who'd take her right back where she came from.

Passing a liquor store and a pediatrics drug store, Melina ran until her legs gave out. She fell against a railing for the bus stop, fighting for air. Strength leached from her muscles and needles of pain stabbed their way through her body. She was going to pass out. Right there against the glass. She'd look like a druggie, an alcoholic, a bum looking to sleep on the MUNI, or all three rolled into one dysfunctional ball. No one would know how she'd been kidnapped by some crazy circus freaks toting around wolves. No one would know how she'd fought her way free.

Were they following her?

She couldn't even muster the power to check. Her eyes fluttered closed as she clutched her shoes in her hand. Just in case she had to fight her way through round two.

Sleep sounded good right about now. A few minutes of sleep and she could run again. The world faded away beneath her.

"Melina, thank God," someone said from beside her. A shadow. A deep, familiar voice. It sounded like Hayden, but it couldn't be. "You're going to come with me now." Two fingers brushed her neck. Shivers coated her body. "Oh shit." Gut-wrenching silence. "You were bitten. We don't have long." Hands beneath her knees. Big, strong hands. "They're coming, sweetheart. We have to get you out of here. You ready?"

Reality came crashing down as the stranger tried to move her. Quasimodo had found her! He was taking her back to feed her to the wolves.

"I won't be thrown to the wolves." With the last ounce of strength pulsing through her body, she flung one of her shoes at the stranger and swung the other shoe for his face. "Back off jerk. I've got Choos—*shoes*!"

Chapter Sixteen

Hayden dodged the first flying shoe, but the second one got him square in the nose. Starbursts went off behind his eyes.

He wasn't expecting Melina to fight back. She looked worn and winded, slumped against the bus stop glass. He wasn't expecting her here at all, actually. Gabriel had tracked her scent to Bernal Heights, but lost it once they got on Church Street. After doing a quick search for buildings purchased by packmates within the last year, Hayden noticed a clump of them in this area and thought it couldn't hurt to check.

"It's me," he said, lifting her off the ground. "It's Hayden. I've got you now."

She stopped striking her shoe against his jaw. Momentarily. "Hayden? It's really you?"

Her eyes remained closed, but he nodded. "Yeah, it's me. You're going to be okay, but we've got to move fast."

He'd left the door of his Bugatti open. He laid her inside as the door to the cathedral on the corner flew open and a group of rogue wolves flew out. They pointed and hollered, and took off at a dead sprint. Tucking Melina's dress in the door, he shut it tight, slid over the hood, and hopped inside.

"Hayden?" she asked, as he peeled away from the curb.

The car gripped second gear as he floored it around the corner, leaving the packmates in his exhaust.

"Yeah?"

He downshifted up a hill, checking his rearview for lights.

"You're not so mean," she whispered. "I'm sorry I didn't believe it before."

His heart pinched. "You don't have to talk about that now. I'm sorry I got you into this mess."

As they approached a crowded intersection, Hayden stopped at the line and did a quick check for injuries. He brushed dark strands of hair out of her face, revealing a bruise under her eye. A demonic growl burned inside his chest—he gritted his teeth until they nearly cracked under the pressure. He didn't want to growl and scare her, but those bastards had bit her.

He'd break every bone in each one of their bodies, and then watch them crawl their mangled way out of his city.

He eyed the bite on her neck. Tendon and ripped flesh jumbled together into a bloodied mess on her neck.

"Does the wound on your neck hurt?" The words were hard for him to say. He remembered how much the bite had hurt him when he'd been attacked. He was hoping against hope that Melina was in shock. If her system overloaded, it'd shut off her pain receptors.

"It was a wolf, Hayden. A freaking wolf bit me! Do you think I need a rabies shot?" She laughed sickly as the color drained from her face. "It's going to leave a scar, huh? I'm not even going to be able to hide it. It's going to have to be scarf season year-round in my house."

"The scar will heal, Melina, but right now we have to worry about loss of blood and…"

…*biting you again.*

Being bitten by a wolf on one pulse point was deadly. The only way to survive the bite was to be bitten on another pulse point. It'd start the transition process, and she'd shift into a wolf for the first time during the next full moon, starting her new life as a werewolf.

But if he could get her to Howlands, maybe he could plead with the doctors and they could find a way to stop the poison from the wolf bite and she could live as a non-shifter again.

There had to be another way.

Melina didn't belong in their world. She was too special, too fiery, and *much* too independent. She didn't take orders well, and as her Alpha, he'd have to dish them. And she'd have to obey him.

He'd only known Melina for a short time, but there was no way in hell *that* was happening.

"Where are you taking me?" she asked, as he put the pedal to the metal.

"To the hospital." He gunned it, running the next red light. "You're losing too much blood."

It had gushed down her neck and soaked her dress. She coughed, and tried to cover it with her hand. Blood squirted onto his dash.

"I'm sorry," she said, leaning back into the seat. "I can clean it."

"I'm not worried about my car." *Not in the least.* "I'm worried about you. How are you holding up? Talk to me, okay?"

Her head lolled to her opposite shoulder. "What about?" Her words were weak, and fading away.

"Tell me about the first time we met. Did you think I was a tool?"

"No, not that." Her words sloshed together so badly, Hayden could barely make them out. "You-were-Prada."

He had to have misheard. "Prada?"

"You know…" she sighed heavily. "…Perfection."

Nerves tightened in his stomach. He'd thought she was perfect, too. Keeping one hand on the wheel, he placed the other on her thigh and gave it a reassuring squeeze. He knew exactly what she was going through, and what she'd need. The tremors wracking her body, and the disorientation in her brain would soon be followed by chills.

This was his fault. He shouldn't have spent so much time with her. They could've Skyped for crying out loud and kept physical contact to a minimum. But then he wouldn't have known his Luminary was out there. He wouldn't have known the pull he had to her, to protect her.

"But then I saw you wit—with the girls—the two girls on the red carpet, I saw you." She coughed up more blood. "That hurt."

"Melina," he said, a hole forming in his chest, "I wanted you to be at my side, but something happened in my family, and when it came time to pick you up, my father told me to take someone who was more like us. Someone closer to the family. I couldn't betray him, not when he gave a direct order that way. I wish you could understand our family dynamic."

Silence.

"Melina?" He shook her leg. "Melina, wake up. I know you're tired, but you have to stay awake. We're almost there."

"Damn it!" He slammed his fists against the wheel. "Fastest fucking vehicle in production and I still can't get to Howlands in time."

The engine roared, jerking the car as it gripped each turn.

"Melina, say something." He glanced at her once more. "Come on, we've got about ten minutes left. Stay with me."

"Willyoukissme?" she mumbled. "Iwanna…feelheaven… beforeIseeit."

Sweetest words ever spoken.

Using two fingers, he brought her face around to his. Her

lips were pale and parted. Her eyes were closed, the color of her face a sickly shade of gray. He planted the softest of kisses on her lips, and had the strangest feeling he'd stolen her last breath.

Panicked, he lifted her wrist to his ear.

Fading pulse.

"No!"

Desperation bellowed through him as he swerved against the curb and killed the engine.

"Melina." He gripped her by the shoulders and turned her to face him.

It'd be so easy to save her. With one bite on her radial artery, she'd wake up a few hours later, have a killer headache, and a hearty appetite. She'd get to smile, and write her column, and live a happy, healthy life.

But turning into a werewolf wasn't the natural way of things.

She didn't choose their way of life.

Damn it, she was *dying.*

Another few seconds and her heart would beat for the last time. No more sly grins or cheap shots against him, no more faux fur coats, crazy dresses, or funky hair-dos. Never again would he get to see her radiate with happiness, or watch those luscious lips pull back into a satisfied smile. He'd never know the warmth of her body, or the full power of her mind.

She was special, a gem in his world. Not *only* his world, he realized, but the big blue one that spun 'round and 'round.

"I can't let you go." He shook with fear. "Please forgive me."

Letting the power of the full moon tug on the deepest part of him, Hayden resisted the urge to burst through human form completely. Channeling only the shifting energy he needed to perform the act, Hayden's fangs dropped. His snout began to stretch.

He hesitated, listening to her heartbeat stutter and slow. And then, with the final resounding pump of Melina's heart, Hayden lowered his mouth to her wrist and sank his teeth deep.

Chapter Seventeen

Melina rolled over, clutching the satin sheets to her chest. Yawning, she kicked her feet, swishing them over the fancy fabric.

She *loved* satin sheets.

One teeny tiny problem: she didn't have them on her bed.

She shot up, taking a mental snapshot of her surroundings. She was in a small bedroom. Steel-gray walls. Dark hardwood floors. Gigantic bed that dwarfed the space. Ficus tree by the window, and floral arrangements on the dresser. Large cabinet built into the wall to her left. Huge windows and French doors latched tightly on the opposite wall. Through the glass, ocean waves rolled toward the bright-blue horizon. Large trees—were those redwoods—towered across the way. The room smelled like an exotic combination of sea, salt, and wood-smoke.

Where the hell was she?

And what happened last night?

She rubbed her head, and absentmindedly removed the bobby pins from her hair. Hooking them together, she threw them to the foot of the bed. She glanced at her clothes: glittery tank top and black booty shorts.

Did she go to a rave while she slept?

Sliding off the bed, Melina set her feet on the cool floor and shuffled toward the windows. The house—whichever house this was—was perched on a slight hill that faced the ocean. A wooden staircase off the back deck zig-zagged down to a sandy beach. The foggy marine layer plumed over the waves and ghosted over the hill, coating the windows in a light, airy mist.

She took a deep breath and willed her memories of last night to return.

Movement down the beach caught her eye. Someone was running along the shore, a black hood pulled over his head. The jogger had a strong pace and didn't appear labored from it. His steps were hard and powerful, eating up the ground as he weaved around waves lapping against the sand. When he neared the bottom of the stairs to the house, he stopped to stretch.

As he twisted his torso this way and that, Melina caught sight of a shadow of stubble. Wide jaw. Dark, unforgettable eyes.

Hayden.

Crap.

With a loud *meeping* sound, Melina backed away from the window, but not before she saw him see her. She was in his house, which could only mean one thing: they'd slept together. *Oh, peachy.*

They'd hooked up and she didn't even *remember* it.

"Melina?" he called from somewhere inside the house.

Crappity-crap.

Her insides squirmed. Panicked. Melina scanned the room, looking for a way out.

Two knocks on the door.

"Umm…" The scent of freshly brewed coffee hit Melina hard, making her mouth water. "Come back in a few minutes?"

"I'm not housekeeping." He laughed softly. The sound soothed her. "If you want to be alone in there, I can talk to you through the door."

Persistent sucker.

"Give me a minute. I'll be right out." How was she going to get out of this mess? What was she going to say? Should she pretend to remember? Be honest and say she couldn't remember a thing? Absentmindedly, Melina clutched at her chest and hit a tender spot. Flinching, she brushed her fingers over the sensitive skin. "I think"—she searched for a mirror in the room and came up empty—"I think I might have a bruise on my neck."

Officially the worst one-night-stand in history.

No memory of the sex. Bruises. Gaudy morning-after outfit.

"I can explain that." Slowly, Hayden pushed the door open, and leaned against the frame, crossing his arms over his barrel of a chest. Sweat coated his face and ran down his neck in beads. Damp hair fell over his face, nearly reaching his brow.

She squelched down the urge to push him against the doorframe and start his second workout…with her.

She'd never had a thing for jocks before, but the sight of Hayden in his workout gear had Melina changing her tune. He was built like a hardcore athlete, tall and strong, with ripples of bulky muscle. But he didn't look stiff, as if his workouts were restricted to dumbbells and squat racks. No, quite the opposite. He had the look of a fighter, of someone who could move in a pinch and use his strength to his advantage.

How had she not known he was athletic? When she'd suggested he try yoga, meditation, or acupuncture on his image-improvement plan, she hadn't realized Hayden already had something to keep him active in the off-hours.

Why hadn't he said something?

His workout gear only added to his sexual appeal. Black shorts dropped low on his waist. White cotton T-shirt beneath an unzipped black sweatshirt with the hood dropped back.

The room was much smaller with him in it.

"How do you feel?" he asked.

"I'm not sure." She rubbed the sore spot on her neck. "Am I bruised? Right here?"

"Your skin might feel tender for a while, but it's perfect. Unblemished." He eyed her neck, her face. Heat trailed his gaze. "Like porcelain."

"Oh, I—" She hadn't been prepared for that. Her mouth went dry, and she dropped her hand from her neck. "Where am I?"

"You're in my home, in my spare bedroom."

The question of the hour pressed at her lips. "We didn't— did we—you know?

"No, nothing like that." A hint of sadness coated his tone, and if she wasn't mistaken, a blush crept into his cheeks. "How do you feel?"

"Fine, I guess." She brushed her hand over her hair. It was tousled and frizzy, as if she'd fought a lion during her sleep. "Never slept so hard in my life."

He nodded slowly. "Do you remember…anything?"

"Yeah, I remember having dinner with you, and you racing off toward the parking garage." Pickaxes stabbed through her brain as she fought to remember the rest of the night. "I remember a black car pulling up to the curb and someone calling my name…and that's it." Everything else was blank. "How'd I get here?"

"I'm sure you have a lot of questions and I'll tell you everything you need to know, but how about we do this downstairs." He motioned toward the hall. "If you're feeling up for it, I made coffee. And pancakes. Secret family recipe."

The Adonis cooked, too?

That must've been how he swept all the ladies off their feet.

"I love pancakes. To be honest, I'd eat anything right now. I'm starving."

"That's normal," he said, and backed into the hall.

Normal for what?

"There's a robe on the back of the door if you'd feel more comfortable," he said. "Meet me when you're ready."

Food was more important than a robe, so she followed him down.

The colors of his home were cool and calming, grays and light blues and off-whites. Plants were everywhere—to her surprise—leafy and green and lush. With the ocean and forest outside the lengthy windows, the décor inside made the place the ultimate beach home.

Except it was small. No bigger than her apartment.

Not what she expected from someone like Hayden, who made it a point to be over-the-top in every aspect of his life.

When they reached the first floor, Hayden disappeared into a room off the kitchen, and a faucet started. A few seconds later he reemerged, looking cool and refreshed. As she took a seat at a table near the window, he jumped into the role of chef seamlessly, flipping pancakes from a warming container onto a plate. He dropped a heaping plate of heaven in front of her, along with a steaming cup of coffee.

"If this is the treatment you give every woman who comes here, it's no wonder you're such a heartbreaker." She stabbed a chunk of pancake and shoved it into her mouth. It was rich and warm and syrupy and—ZOMG, there were blueberries mixed in. Her favorite treat from childhood. "I bet every woman falls in love with you after this."

It'd be easy to, if she'd let herself. Which she wouldn't.

"You're the first woman I've ever brought here, actually," he said, sliding back behind the island.

She nearly choked. "Really? Why's that?"

"This is the only place that's truly mine. The one place I can go to be alone…to be me. The *real* me, not the one everyone thinks they know. I bought it using my mother's maiden name so no one even knows I own it. I've got the relaxing sound of the ocean with the privacy of the trees if I ever want to shift—" He cleared his throat again. Did he have allergies or something? "—gears," he finished quickly. "If I ever want to shift gears and head off into the mountains to hike, it's there."

"Where is here, exactly?" she asked between bites.

"Moss Beach. About forty-five minutes south of the city."

She'd never been in this area before, but from the current view, she'd say it was downright blissful. If this was the real Hayden, she had to admit she liked it better. And it fit him, too.

As she continued to quench the fire in her middle with the best pancakes she'd ever tasted, she said, "If this place is so special that you've never brought anyone before now, why me?"

"Under the circumstances, your place wasn't safe. I couldn't let you go back there." He poured his own cup and sat across from her. "And I know what you're going through. I've been there before, and I know you wouldn't want to be in the city right now."

Something wasn't adding up. He was answering her questions, but in a roundabout way, without actually answering anything.

She did the mental math. *Her place wasn't safe. Unexplainable memory loss. Tender spots on her neck. Hayden bringing her to his private sanctuary because "he'd been there before."*

"What happened after you left me at the pier?" she blurted, chasing the pancake with steaming coffee. "Did I get hit over the head?"

He frowned as if he didn't understand.

"It would explain the amnesia," she said, rubbing her temples. "Isn't that usually the cause when someone can't remember something? Unless you roofied my drink at the restaurant."

"I didn't roofie you, and you don't have amnesia." He swallowed hard. "Your body is adjusting to the transition."

"Transition?"

"Whatever happens, you need to know you're safe here." He leaned over the table, and for a second, Melina thought he was reaching for her. But then he clasped his hands together and sighed. "You're the same person now that you were last week. Whatever happens, remember that. You're Melina Rae, pain in my ass and columnist for *Celeb Crush*. You're no different than you were yesterday."

"Okkaaay. Do me a favor, would you?" Her heart raced as disorientation rooted deep. "Take a deep breath and spit out the truth. I don't digest bullshit well, and I know when someone's softening me up for the big blow. Why am I here? What's with the big mystery and—"

"You were kidnapped by a pack of rogue wolves who've split from the San Francisco Wolf Pack," he said on a single exhale. "They were trying to use you to get to me. I don't know how you managed to do it, but you escaped. You only had one bite here"—he reached out for her neck, and then pulled back his hand— "but I had to bite you again to save your life. Good news is you're alive and well. Bad news is the two bites will force you into transition and you'll become one of us. I brought you here to walk you through the basics. Rest assured, you'll be safer with me than anyone else."

The clock on the kitchen wall ticked loudly, matching the

pulsing of Melina's heart.

"Wow, that's quite the mouthful. No wonder you were dancing around it," she said, swallowing down a hysteric laugh. "So let me see if I have the basics here. There are wolves roaming around the streets of San Francisco."

"Not just wolves." He nodded as if to drive the point home. "Werewolves."

"And you're one of them."

He drank his coffee, eyeing her over the rim of his mug. When he set it down, he paused, wringing his hands together. "Yes," he said, his voice shaking with uncertainty. "I'm a werewolf."

Actually sounded as if he believed it to be true.

"But you're not like the *rogues* who kidnapped me." Her lips twitched. Damn, she loved teasing him. "You're different."

"I am, yes, but there are many others like me. The rogue wolves who kidnapped you are the minority. There aren't many roaming around the city. Most of the werewolves are governed by a single Alpha and follow a set of pack rules. We're not monsters. The werewolves in the city are...civilized."

"Of course they are." She shrugged. "Why wouldn't they be? I mean, how would werewolves be expected to make a decent living otherwise?" She giggled into a snort. "I suppose they could sell their fur online. There must be werewolf online retailers for that. I'd certainly buy a fur coat from a werewolf if they were open to selling it."

"You're taking this remarkably well," he said, refilling her cup. "Better than any turned wolf I've ever met."

And he was taking the joke far. He didn't break from the role easily, and he spoke as if he wholeheartedly believed what he was saying. He must've been a comedian who was deeply rooted in his story.

That'd definitely be a new and interesting spin for her article...

Hayden Dean: Comedian Behind the Scenes.

"Keep the pancakes stackin'," she said, swirling her fork around, "and tell me more about this secret society of werewolves. You said there are 'turned' wolves. Are there other varieties?

"Werewolves can be born or turned." Straight-faced, Hayden heaped additional pancakes on her plate and continued on. "Born wolves are shifters born from werewolf parents, and usually experience their first shift during adolescence. They're rumored to be stronger and faster, much like thoroughbreds in horse racing, though there are exceptions to every rule. Born wolves can shift at whim, and have more control over their primal reactions. Turned wolves, like you and me, are non-shifters who were bitten by werewolves. We can only shift during the full moon. We have control over it, but if we deny the urges too long, we start to go a little crazy. That last part is true for both turned and born wolves."

"Boy, you've really thought this through."

Her mind went wild with possibilities. Forget the comedic act. Hayden could sell this story to Hollywood. Become a writer and publish his paranormal work online.

Future headlines shifted and melted together in her head: *From Comedian to Creative Genius…Hayden Dean's Werewolf Tales.*

She'd been searching for something different. A new slant to recreate his image. Who knew he'd have this kind of depth? Changing the public's perception of him might've been easier than she thought.

"So because I was bitten twice," she said, going along with the tale, "I'll be able to shift into a wolf at the full moon?"

"That's right. You were bitten on two pulse points, which kick-starts transition. One bite and you would've died. Two bites on the same pulse point, and you would've met the same fate. The wolf who attacked you bit your carotid artery, and I bit your radial." He paused. "Melina, are you sure you're okay?" His hand found hers. "Do you feel faint? Tired? Insanely hungry? That's what you should be feeling right now."

Seconds ago, she *had* felt faint and tired and hungry, but the moment his hand touched hers, everything disappeared. The confusion, the humor in his tale, and the wall she'd put up to defend herself against his charm evaporated with his touch.

His hand enveloped hers in a warm, comforting grip, yet there was raw, scorching heat in his palm. She shuddered long and deep, relishing the sizzle and desire flooding her middle. Hayden took back his hand, though the heat remained in her chest.

"Sorry," he said, rubbing his thumb in circles over his palm. "I guess that was a bit much. We can dive into that later."

"Dive into what, exactly?"

"Our connection."

Now they were getting somewhere.

Maybe this was how Hayden sweet-talked all the women in his little black book—not that she'd ever seen it. He was into role-playing...sexual fantasies about werewolves, to be specific.

Intriguing.

Under normal circumstances, she might've told Hayden to go fetch a bone and find another woman to play his little game. But nothing about the way her body was reacting to Hayden or his fantasy was normal. Her thighs quivered, her mouth watered, and her toes curled from the dirty thoughts saturating her mind.

She'd do anything to satiate the ravenous craving in her middle.

"Our *connection*...I like the sound of that." She leaned over the table, and couldn't help but brush her thighs together.

She trembled deep inside, right down to the bone. If she wasn't mistaken, he shuddered, too. "Tell me more."

His Adam's apple jumped and a thin sheen of sweat appeared on his forehead. "You're amazing, you know that? You're handling this as if you've been prepped for it your entire life. But we need to slow down." He opened the window next to the table and sat back in the chair as a cool draft of ocean breeze swept into the kitchen. "Your senses will be heightened during transition. Your system should fluctuate between hot and cold on a whim. You'll have insatiable hunger for, well, everything, for at least a month. Sex, food, and violence, specifically. You'll want it all. And you'll have it."

As he stretched his arms behind his head and leaned the chair on its two back legs, an image popped into her mind. Hayden in the chair, the way he was now. Her legs straddling his lap. Her tank top pulled down beneath her breasts. The breeze in her hair, cooling their bodies as they pounded against one another.

Did Hayden kick up the thermostat?

"Are you offering?" she asked, nearly panting the words.

He shook his head. "I'm sorry, what?"

"Sex. Are you in or out?" She purred. "Please say both."

"Good God." His pupils widened. "You're a vixen."

Oh yeah, she had him right where she wanted him.

He could pretend to be a werewolf, vampire, ghost, witch, or the freaking Dalai Lama, if that's what rocked his socks. All that mattered was getting up close and personal with the sex god on the other side of the table.

Flames of lust licked through Melina's body, from the juncture between her legs to the crease in her breasts. She squirmed in her seat, going damp as her gaze honed on Hayden's supple mouth.

If she didn't kiss him, she'd burst through her skin.

The lights in the kitchen dimmed, the sounds of the

ocean quieted, and the sugary-sweet smell of the pancakes dwindled. Suddenly and unexplainably, Melina picked up the chestnut highlights streaking through Hayden's hair. His heart thumped in his chest, wild and hurried, and the smell of his aftershave, fresh and crisp, hit her nose.

Every nerve seemed heightened. Frayed and jittery. She'd never done drugs, but she'd bought Chanel at auction, and thought at the time, that the occasion probably came close to getting high. Nothing could have prepared her for this.

Nothing.

She was so in tune with him, paired to his frequency, linked to his every intake and exhale of breath. She wanted that mouth on her, sliding up her body, his tongue darting in and out of her warmth.

"Melina, you have to calm down," Hayden said, breathing hard. "I can feel what's going on inside you right now and I'm barely holding on to a thread here myself. Believe me, there's nothing I want more than to give you what you need, but with the connection between us, we have to be careful not to—"

A shockwave of delicious ecstasy rocked Melina out of her seat, cutting his words short. All that mattered was the insatiable need clawing at her insides and the desire to lick his rock-hard body until her mouth went numb. She had to touch him and feel the pressure of his body over hers.

She'd never been this hot over a guy. Not ever.

If he wanted a werewolf fantasy, she'd give it to him.

Bow-chica.

Bow-wow.

Chapter Eighteen

Easy. Take it slow.

He'd meant to say the words, he really had. Really.

But the words "easy" and "slow" disappeared from his vocab. He'd been holding back from her since they arrived here last night, since he had to strip the blood-stained peacock dress from her glorious body. He hadn't peeked. Other than what was necessary to dress her, of course. She was officially the sexiest thing he'd ever seen in booty shorts and a shimmery top.

It was a miracle and true testament to his willpower that he'd stayed away from her this long.

As she rounded the corner of the table, he could *feel* her desire—it fed his own. The scent of her arousal, fragrant and sweet, beckoned him closer. He wanted Melina like he'd never wanted anyone before.

He caught her in his arms and pulled her over his lap. *Finally.* He groaned as their lips met, and her arms flew around his neck. The kiss was fierce and wild, awakening his hunger to claim her as his own. As her tongue shot past his lips, every muscle in his body went on edge. He pulled her against him, closer, couldn't be close enough. She clung to his shoulders and tilted her head to deepen the kiss.

"I've wanted you from the moment I met you," she said, flicking her tongue out over his lips. "But what I feel for you now is beyond want. It's *thirst*—no that's not it either." She swirled her hips over his lap, searching out her own pleasure. "It's starvation. I feel like I'll die if I don't get you inside me."

Holy shit.

His cock twitched under his shorts, giving its own eager response. Hayden knew Melina would be crazed with need—newly transitioned werewolves usually were—but this was beyond his wildest fantasy. Hearing the naughty words escape those succulent lips nearly did him in. And he hadn't even touched her flesh to flesh.

Yet.

She opened her mouth to say more, but he swallowed her words with a crushing kiss. He had to taste, consume, and pleasure her until she was dizzy and exhausted. Her shirt crept up. He grasped the bottom and fisted the springy material.

"Get it off," she breathed.

Gone were the issues awaiting them on the horizon—the problems with the rogues could wait. All that mattered was getting her clothes off and burying himself deep, so deep, inside her.

With a swipe of his arm, the breakfast spread crashed to the floor. Dishes and mugs scattered over the tile, making a mess he didn't give a rip about. Frantic with his own rising lust, he gripped Melina by the waist and lifted her onto the table. She clawed at his shoulders, lunged for his mouth, and moaned when their lips collided. Jerking her to the very edge of the table, he skated a greedy hand up her thigh and used it to coil her legs around his waist.

He devoured her, sweeping his tongue along hers with

fevered strokes, as he peeled her shirt from her body. Her breasts were a staggering vision. Tight and round with pink temples he longed to tease with his tongue. He wanted to skate his hands over her body, study every soft curve and every delicious flavor on her skin.

As lust stirred in his belly, Hayden stripped out of his sweatshirt, his T-shirt, and then had the realization he'd recently finished a five-mile run. He should shower, clean up, and dab on some aftershave or cologne. He should pull back the sheets on the bed, light some candles, and turn on some mood music. At least that's what he usually did. Wasn't that the image of romance every woman had painted in her mind?

"I should clean up," he said, pulling back. "Give me five."

"Nuh-uh." She shook her head, her hands sliding up and down his bare back. Her eyes hazed with lust. "You're not going anywhere."

"But—"

It was all he got out before she snatched his hand and shoved it down the rim of her shorts. A moan erupted from his throat, low and raspy, as he plunged his fingers through her heat. He claimed her mouth, worked her sensitive flesh, and groaned as she began to tremble.

She was so hot and wet, and he was already so close to his own release.

"Hayden," she rasped, rolling her body over the table and writhing against him. "I'm going to—oh my God!"

He rubbed her clit, teasing the orgasm out of her. She bucked and gasped, her breasts rising and falling as ecstasy danced its way through her. When she stilled, her lips parting in supple invitation, Hayden kissed her open-mouthed and unhurried. Languid strokes of his tongue against her cheek had her mewling for more.

He caressed her breasts, and cradled them in his hands. Drawing the right one into his mouth, he teased her nipple with his tongue. She arched back in pleasure, digging her hands into his hair. When he moved to the left creamy breast—had to be even in his attention—she clutched at his hair and yanked his head back.

"Just so you know," she said, nipping at his bottom lip, "this is off the record. None of this"—grinning, she raked her hands down his chest and left a scorching trail behind—"is going in the article."

"That's too bad." He rubbed his hand along her inner thigh. "This is going to be quite the spread."

He palmed her stomach and gently pushed her back onto the table, and then splayed her legs wider.

"Wha—ooh…"

Kneeling, he stripped her shorts from her lean legs. She was soft and silky smooth—he'd always been a leg man—clean-shaven and tidy. Her knees met, and her thighs brushed together.

"Oh no," he said, lifting her rear off the table with both hands. "I won't let you pretend to be modest. Not now." He licked a slow, dragging line up her center. "We're beyond that."

Her legs dropped open with a shudder, and her head hit the table. Slowly, he spread her slit and dove into her wetness. Once he tasted her, he couldn't stop. He kissed her open-mouthed, savoring her tart sweetness. He plunged his tongue into her heat. Kneaded the tight flesh of her rear. Devoured her arousal and stoked his own. And when she tightened, crying out his name, Hayden swirled his tongue around her pleasure spot, drawing the orgasm out of her.

Staring at the ceiling, Melina hit her head with her hand. "You're going to kill me."

"Does that mean you want me to stop?"

"Hell no." She sat up, cheeks flushed, desire still lingering in her honey-brown eyes. "Do you have a condom?"

"No, but werewolves don't carry diseases." From the ground, he had the perfect view of her dainty figure. She was the perfect mix of lean and soft, strong lines and graceful beauty. Studying her, Hayden's hands skimmed up the dainty curve of her waist. There was no telling how many times he'd get to see her this way. Not many—he was sure of that. "And werewolves can't get pregnant unless they're in heat." He rubbed his thumb over her nipple, eliciting a moan that spoke to him on the deepest level. "You have nothing to worry about."

"Back to the wolf thing, huh?" She raked her fingers through his hair. "That's fine, but if you don't put a muzzle on your dog, he's not coming out of the doghouse. And believe me when I say, I really"—she leaned over and stroked him outside of his shorts, ripping a hiss from the back of his throat—"*really* want him to come out and play."

Laughter ripped through his chest. She was comparing him to a dog. "You're downright irresistible. Anyone ever tell you that?"

"Yes." She kinked her head to the side. "Still, no muzzle, no bone. I have a few condoms in my purse, if you can't find one here somewhere."

If she had condoms with her, that meant she'd taken one to the charity event. She'd been hoping to get lucky, apparently.

But she hadn't gone with him; she'd gone with Gabriel.

The realization rumbled through him like thunder.

As if she read his mind, Melina roped her arms around his neck. "I always carry them," she said, "for unexpected times like these. You can never be too safe, right?"

Possessiveness shook Hayden to the core. Rising to his feet, he hauled her against him and planted a scorching kiss on her mouth. He tried to communicate with the most intimate part of her, to say the things he couldn't speak aloud. He wanted only her, and he wanted to be the only one she wanted, too.

The thought scared the shit out of him, but there it was. He didn't want to complete the Luminary bond with her—that would require a promise of forever while they were making love. He definitely didn't want that.

He simply wanted *her*. Right here. Right now.

It was all he could think about.

"Wow," she said, when they came up for air. She breathed heavily and rested her forehead on his. "I'm dizzy."

"Me too."

"I've never had two orgasms in a row," she said, plunging her tongue past his lips. "You truly are amazing. But you've probably heard that before."

"Not from you." His lips quirked. "If you let me, I'll take you there again."

"I think my legs will turn to jelly." She stroked his bare chest, grinned, and then shrugged. "I don't need to walk for the next day or so anyway."

Glad she had her priorities straight.

She smacked him in the backside playfully. "Now how about that muzzle?"

Not wasting any more time, Hayden strode into the living room, pulled her purse from beside the couch and brought it to her. As she dug around for protection, a cool breeze swept through the kitchen windows and blew through Melina's hair. The fragrant scent of her arousal invaded his senses. It was a mixture of sugar and warm spice, an enticing scent that had him salivating to taste her again, and again.

Yanking down his shorts, he stepped out of them and stood before her. Her gaze dipped to his manhood. She gulped.

"The rumors were true," she whispered.

"Rumors?"

"Tabloids and online gossip articles. I still don't know

which ones to believe." She licked her lips and wiggled off the table. "I assume all werewolves are well endowed?"

Both his dick and his ego swelled with pride. "I can't speak for all the werewolves in the city, but I'd like to think I'm one of a kind."

Blush tinged her cheeks as she shoved a foil wrapper into his hand.

As he rolled on the condom, she slowly traipsed around him, ghosting her fingers over his shoulders, his back. "What do werewolves like?" she asked, moving around to his abs. "I might need direction."

He nearly laughed. "Believe me, you won't need any help. I'm barely hanging on to a thread of control here, and we haven't even started."

Her lips curled into a devious grin. "Is that so?"

He'd issued a challenge, and suddenly felt the reins pass hands.

She pushed him back against the granite island and assaulted him with her mouth. Ghosted her hands over the grooves of his abs. Nipped at his shoulder and reached low to stroke his thick length. The instant her hand touched his cock, he hissed. Every muscle in his body tightened into a fist.

She was everywhere. Her scent in the air. Her breasts brushing against his chest. Her hand stroking him closer to climax. He could still taste her on his lips.

Wiggling out of his arms, she backed away, spun, and bent over the table. She gave a little shake and glanced at him over her shoulder. "Is this what wolves want?" The innocence in her voice made his toes curl. "Come and get it."

He bit into his bottom lip so hard, he drew blood. He growled, and the wolf in him howled to slip into her heat from behind.

In a flurry of movement, he snatched her around the waist, and twirled her around. She cried out in shock, grinning as he pinned her to the wall.

"I want to see you when you come," he said, sliding his hand between her legs.

She stamped a white-hot kiss on his mouth, and melted into him. Arms wrapped around his back, she propped her foot up on a rung of the nearest stool and rocked her hips upward.

Damn, he loved the way her mind worked.

As gently as he could, he eased inside her. Their lips parted and he met her eyes. They were heavy-lidded and dreamy, shimmering with the promise of sweet release. His spine tingled. His balls seized. He claimed her, crying out as their hips met. She clutched at him, holding onto his shoulders to pound against him. She was tighter and hotter than he'd expected. Flawless and scorching.

Mine.

The urge to claim her sparked in his gut. He bit it back and plunged into her slick wetness. He pounded against her hips, right up to the hilt. She cried out over and over again—music to his ears. She slid along the wall, her mouth falling open, her gaze caught on his.

Could she see his desire to bond with her? To claim her as his own?

He pinched his eyes shut and thrust harder. Angled her hips up and dove deep. Her core pulsed around him, minute vibrations that milked his shaft to the very brink. Their rhythm sped.

Mine.

"Oh, Hayden," she moaned, her voice faint. "Faster."

His name on her lips fueled the frenzy. Delicious want snaked through him. Explosive surges of heat scorched the skin over his bones. He needed to slow down, to focus, to make sure this lasted in case it was the only time they'd get to do this. He wanted to savor this, and treasure her. But as she rocked against him, speeding the pace, he clenched. Grasped her rear. Thrust his tongue into her mouth. And when she erupted beneath him, writhing in the grips of passion, he held her tight, supporting her weight. Starbursts went off behind his eyes. She sucked on his tongue, sending him over the edge. He emptied himself into her depths, and squeezed his eyes shut as the sensations overtook him. Over and over again, her name erupted from the depths of him. It was a cry, and then an agonizingly sweet moan. Her name faded into a whisper. A wish. A promise he couldn't keep.

Melina.

They hadn't completed the Luminary bond, but his pull to her was tangible. He wanted to claim her so badly, he physically hurt. He couldn't remove himself from her center… he'd be empty and incomplete. He didn't even have to test the theory. He knew the truth as he knew himself.

Fear coiled around his heart, and gripped tight.

If he felt this way now, their connection would only increase as time passed.

If something happened to Melina, which it inevitably would as an Alpha's mate, he'd be devastated. Ruined. He'd be like his father, a shell of what he used to be.

As he unsheathed himself from her core, Hayden made a vow to himself, to her. No matter what, he couldn't let their connection grow any further.

But for now, for today and tonight, she was his.

He lifted his angel into his arms and carried her into the bedroom where he laid her down and tucked her against him. Somewhere between her gentle intake of breath and the drumming sound of her heartbeat, Hayden's eyes closed and he drifted to sleep.

He'd never slept so sound.

Chapter Nineteen

Melina awoke to the muffled hush of a shower, and a deep, husky whistle. The tune was familiar and upbeat. Was it Sinatra? She'd always loved the smooth melody of the classics. It was dark as pitch outside, which meant it was late Sunday night and she had another few hours with Hayden before thinking about Monday morning and all the worry it'd bring.

With a long, relaxed sigh, she rolled over and spread-eagled over the bed.

If only every night could be this way. After their first interlude in the kitchen, he'd brought her to his master suite. They hadn't slept more than thirty minutes before she rolled over, felt him beside her, and pounced on him. Sexcapade number two quickly turned to number three…and then four. They'd wasted Sunday morning and afternoon tangled in his sheets, though wasted was the wrong word to use.

She couldn't get enough of him.

Her body felt as if it'd gone into some sort of sexual overdrive. She flipped from hot to cold—the way he'd said she would, oddly enough—and couldn't look at him for more than a few seconds without having the insatiable need to jump his bones.

He didn't seem to mind, she thought with a grin.

Sighing, she rolled over and tucked her arms beneath the pillow. This place was nothing like what she'd expected it to be. His beach home was understated. No grand piano and no bar. No original pieces of art, and no secretaries or butlers. It was a refreshing getaway far removed from the hustle and bustle of the city. The whole place gave Melina the feeling Hayden only bought the things he absolutely needed, rather than what money could buy him.

She could breathe here, she realized, staring at the closed door to the master bathroom. She hadn't thought about work or the article since the event at the aquarium, actually.

She'd have to get back to work mode bright and early tomorrow morning when she clocked in.

A hint of the blues struck her as she thought about this weekend coming to an end. Couldn't they stay here? Just the two of them? Somehow, in such a short amount of time, Hayden had become a completely different person. In this place, he wasn't the playboy millionaire who smiled for the cameras, partied too hard, and slept around too much. He wasn't rude or pretentious. He wasn't cocky or arrogant.

He was exactly the person she'd thought he was when she first met him at Starbucks last year—the man she'd spent the last week with.

It was going to be easier to write the article for *Celeb Crush* than she thought.

As the sound of water hitting tile echoed into the bedroom, Melina slid to the edge of the bed and let her feet dangle over the side. The bed was huge, she realized. The biggest one she'd ever seen. It was fit for a king.

How surprised would the "king" be if she joined him in the shower? Merely thinking about water sluicing down

Hayden's rippling muscles made butterflies dance through her belly.

She grinned as her mind went ravenous with ideas.

Ping!

The bleep came from the nightstand beside her. Besides a lamp, an alarm clock, and a bottle of Dasani, the table was empty.

Ping! Ping!

Opening the top drawer, she pulled out an iPad and set it on her lap. The screen was alive with snippets of emails, but one in particular caught her eye.

Rogue Wolves: the information you requested.

Email sender: Gabriel Park.

The breath whooshed out of Melina's lungs as she read the snippet over and over again. She'd figured the wolf thing was a stupid fantasy, or a joke of some sort Hayden liked to play on the women he dated. Unless Hayden had told Gabriel to email him, and had planned on Melina digging through his bedside table to find the message, the email had to have been legit.

But that couldn't be right.

Tingles of awareness pricked the back of Melina's neck. Suddenly cold, she ripped a fuzzy blanket off the back of the bed and wrapped it around her. A shiver rolled through her as she swiped her finger across the bottom of the iPad. Gabriel's email filled the screen. Melina skimmed quickly, picking up bits and pieces she didn't understand. She bit her lip so hard it hurt, but she had to feel *something*. She'd gone numb. Her heart rate skyrocketed, thumping wild in her ears.

Multiple attacks.

Rogues forming a pack on Church Street.

Asher has claimed responsibility. New intel suggests he's working for someone higher up in the pack.

Melina…

She let out a yelp when she spotted her name.

"Melina?" Hayden shouted. The shower turned off. "Are you okay?"

"Yeah, I'm fine!" But she didn't sound fine. Her voice was strained.

She read quickly.

Melina will need to be inducted into the pack immediately if she wants our protection. I'm sorry this happened. I know it's not the way you wanted things to go down between you.

The bathroom door swung open.

"What are you doing?" Hayden stood in the doorway, soaking wet, holding a towel over his groin. Even when she was pissed at him, and confused beyond belief, his hotness permeated her thoughts. "What's going on?"

God, she didn't know.

"I'm, uh...reading." She swallowed down the desire to shoot a gazillion questions at him. "It went off, and I found it."

How stupid could she sound? She was having problems finding the words, and feared she never would.

He nodded, his dark eyes giving away nothing. "Anything interesting?"

"Gabriel emailed you."

His lips went white as he ate up the room in a few solid strides and removed the iPad from her grasp. He scanned quickly, and then met her gaze.

"I've asked him to follow up on the rogues who attacked you." As he dried off, the sound of water splattering on the tile hit her ears. "I've also put in a request to the council to have the guards move toward the Mission and scour the streets for any sign of the rogues. They'll be regrouping soon to reevaluate their strategy. I don't think they'd planned for you to escape. Heads will roll and plans will change."

Rogues and attacks had been mentioned before, but suddenly, with the weight of a thousand bricks, reality set in. She couldn't be the brunt of the longest running prank in history, could she? When he spoke about werewolves, a hard truth burned in his eyes. There was no hint of laughter, no teasing undercurrent.

"You're, ah…" She swallowed hard, fearing the words. "…not joking?"

"This isn't a joke to me, Melina." He sat beside her, the towel creeping up his thighs. "Your safety is *far* from a joke."

"And I'm…" Panic tightened her throat, cutting off her air supply. "I'm a—I've been bitten and there are—and I'm going to be a—"

"Werewolf. We went over this earlier, remember?" His hand found her shoulder. Chills spread from his palm, down into her chest. "I know transition can be disorientating, but what happened wasn't a dream. Is that what you thought?"

Shrinking away from his touch, she leaped off the bed and cinched the blanket around her. "Stay away from me."

His lips quirked in that sexy way that curled her toes. Even in the face of fear, her body responded to his on a primal level.

"I'm not going to hurt you," he said. He sounded as though he meant it. "I brought you here so you'd be safe. The last thing I want is for this to be hard for you. Why don't you sit?"

She didn't fear him. Not really. If he'd wanted to hurt her, he would've done it already. What she feared was much worse…

"Why don't you tell me who the hell you are? No more bullshit."

"I'm Hayden Dean, the same man I was yesterday."

"Okay then," she said, skepticism setting in, "*what* are you?"

Exhaling heavily, he leaned forward and rested his hands on his knees. "I'm a two-hundred-year-old werewolf. I was born to non-shifter parents, who died when I was young. I lived on the streets, was attacked by a werewolf, and transitioned during the next full moon. Angus Dean saved me from the streets, accepted me into his pack, and adopted me as his only son. Your path to this point isn't much different, but if you look at how much I've done with my life from then to now, you'll realize everything's going to be fine."

Her breathing became shallow and little pinpricks of starbursts swirled in her line of vision. She shuffled to the end of the bed, stared out the window at the crashing waves, and used the bedpost at the foot of the bed to support her weight. She seemed to sway with the ocean swell, her ears filled with the same muffled hush and boom.

She couldn't wrap her head around the reality Hayden had painted. It might as well have been the script from a movie.

"I was kidnapped…" she fought out, strangling the end of the blanket in her grasp. "By werewolves."

Wouldn't she have remembered something like that?

"They took you from somewhere on the Embarcadero, probably before you reached the place we had dinner." There was truth in Hayden's voice. Remorse, too. "The transition from non-shifter to werewolf can make your memory patchy. That might explain why you have blank parts when you try to recall what happened, but if you try to piece it together, it'll come back."

A blacked-out car parked at the curb on Pier 39 streamed into her mind. Someone had emerged from the back of the car, chased her down, and stabbed her with something in the neck.

Touching the spot under her jaw unleashed an onslaught of horrific memories.

Quasimodo. The horror of the first bite. Hayden finding her. He'd saved her.

"And then…" She couldn't speak the awful words.

"You fought one of them." He shook his head and lowered his gaze. "You were so brave, Melina. There are wolves in my pack who wouldn't fight a rogue head to head. They don't have honor or live by codes the way we do, which is why they split off to begin with."

"I just want to clarify something." *One breath. Two.* "We're talking about werewolves." Her head spun as she tried to get the details right. Air *whooshed* in and out of her lungs, deep and labored. "As in, men who turn into hairy, snarling, beastly wolves."

"We're not snarling or beastly, but the hairy part would depend on the man, I suppose." He cracked a smile, but recovered quickly. "And it's not only men. Women, too."

Her hands and feet tingled. "This isn't real. This can't be happening."

Hayden rose and stood behind her She could feel his presence against her back, though he didn't touch her. "We went over the details yesterday, remember?"

"Oh yeah, I remember everything you said." She spun. Right into his chest. "I remember the two pulse point thing and the rogue pack thing, blabitty-blah, but I didn't think you were telling the truth."

He chuckled, and then cut his laugh short. "Why would I lie to you about something like that?"

"I thought you had a twisted sense of humor."

"Oh, my sense of humor is definitely twisted. But not about this. You look red." His hand touched her bare shoulder, radiating delicious warmth through her body. He took back his hand as if she'd shocked him. "Are you feeling okay?"

"Okay? No, Hayden Wolfie Dean, I am most definitely *not* okay!"

"Wolfie?" He grinned, shaking his head. "Is that the best you can come up with?"

She paced back and forth, to the windows and back to him again. Without warning, her skin flushed hot and her head pounded. Hayden had mentioned hot and cold flashes earlier. As if the clouds parted, she recalled every crazy part of their conversation.

"I'm a werewolf?" she screeched. "And you're a werewolf and you're really freaking old—"

"Whoa, no need to fight dirty." He threw up his hands. "I'm not old. For a werewolf, I'm in my prime."

"How old will I get?"

"About three hundred if you live alone, and a thousand if you bond with your fated mate. Theoretically speaking."

"A thousand?" Stars danced in front of her eyes. "As in, one thousand years. Wonderful. I'm going to be a horrible old woman. Bitter and really freaking hairy."

"You won't look much older than you do now," he said, his voice soothing to her ears. "You'll age gracefully. As for the bitter part, I think you're already there."

She gasped, and fought the urge to smack him.

"And *Gabriel* knows about the werewolves too," she rambled on. "He sent you the email, so he's in on this. How many more of you are there?"

"I'm not sure how many populate the world at this point, but we have hundreds of werewolves in the San Francisco Wolf Pack and there are hundreds of others in packs surrounding our area."

"Uh-huh, yeah," she said, nodding frantically, "and I'm going to *shift*—isn't that what you called it?—and grow a bunch of hair and howl at the moon, and oh God, that's not cute. I'll look like Chewbacca."

"I'm sure there are some people who think Chewbacca's cute." He laughed, hard and deep. This time, she did smack him, right in the shoulder. He cowered, probably for her benefit. "I'm kidding, slugger. You won't be anything like Chewy. You'll be dainty and sleek, most likely, and will have the same color coat as the hair on your head. It'll be dark and silky, and fall through my fingers just the same."

She softened. Damn him.

"This is so surreal. So freaking unbelievable. Do they make Nair for dogs?"

"Not that I know of, but you won't need—"

"It's hopeless." She slapped her forehead. It was ice cold. Clammy. "Does it hurt when it happens? When you shift?"

How could he be so calm about all this?

"Shifting is scary at first, so you naturally resist the change, which makes the process uncomfortable." He leaned against the bedpost and folded his arms over his chest. "But after that, it's the most freeing feeling in the world."

"Freeing?"

He nodded.

She rubbed the mark on her neck, and then eyed her wrist where his teeth had pierced her flesh. Vaguely, images took root in her mind. He'd held her hand. He'd apologized over the decision to bite her—she recalled the agony in his voice.

"You bit me," she whispered, remembering his tongue on her skin. "You freaking bit me. Right here. I can still feel where your teeth went in."

"I had to." His voice turned soft. "I didn't have any other option."

"You could've let me die."

He raised his chin in defiance. "That wasn't an option."

"Sure it was." She sucked in a short breath, and pushed out, "You said I would've died if you didn't bite me a second time. You didn't have to. You could've left me."

"I couldn't let you go." His dark eyes blazed with agony. "Not so soon after I'd found you. You can blame me if that makes this easier for you."

As her thoughts jumbled into an incomprehensible mess, Melina sucked her bottom lip into her mouth and bit softly. She became hyperaware that the only thing standing between their naked bodies was a fuzzy blanket and a terrycloth towel.

She suppressed the urge to toss the blanket on the bed and follow it down.

"You said you found me." Her heart thudded against her ribcage. "I don't know how you remember it, but you didn't. I was hired to interview you last year, and hired again this year."

He grabbed her by the wrist, and held it against his heart. His touch lit something in her hand, and buzzed into her chest. Her heart sped.

"I can hear your heart race when I touch you," he whispered, the subtle parting of his lips capturing her in a trance. "That only happens when a werewolf meets his match. In our race, we call that a Luminary bond. You're meant for me, Melina. No matter how we decide to live from this moment on, we're connected."

"Connected?"

"Fated mates."

"This is too much," she rasped out, struggling for air. Damn, her chest was tight. "Werewolves, fated mates, rogue wolves, Chewbacca hair. I don't know if I can wrap my head around it."

"I know," he breathed. "It's a lot to take in, but if you trust me, I can walk you through it."

She shook her head, but her heart beat 'yes'. "That's just it, Hayden. I don't know if I can trust you at all. You said you found me. That our touch proves we're meant to be. If our connection is so *intense*, where were you at that stupid awards show last year?"

"I had to touch you to know for sure. Our kiss in my office dispelled any doubt I had." He paused, brushing his thumb over the back of her hand. "On the night of the awards show, the rogues showed their dissent toward turned wolves. In order to squash any problems, my father asked that I take a born wolf from our pack to the event."

"But you took two women."

His lips quirked. "Go big or go home."

"So, if you had your way, you would've taken me?"

"If I had my way, Melina," he said, his voice rich and smooth as honey, "I'd take you every single day and twice on Sundays."

She went damp at the words.

"But you have to know, right from the start," he said, "that I don't have any intention of completing the Luminary bond with you."

Daggers to the heart.

She dismissed the gut-clench reaction. Was Hayden even what she wanted? And why was she thinking about him and their connection when she had much bigger issues to wrap her head around?

It was as if she couldn't resist him. Even if she was going to turn into a big ole hairy dog.

Maybe she'd be cute and dainty like Minnie…

God, she was stupid. This whole thing was too much.

"Our connection will draw us together like magnets," Hayden went on, "but only so far. We have to keep distance from one another."

He was totally breaking up with her, before they'd even started anything.

"Here comes the cold shoulder again. This time I'm ready for it." She ripped her hand from his and rubbed the spot on her hand where it'd warmed. "Let me guess. It's you, not me?"

She'd kissed a ton of frogs in her quest for the ultimate fairy tale, and each of them had used different, worn-out break-up lines.

"I'm the Alpha of the pack. Or, I will be," he corrected, digging into the closet. He yanked out a pair of dark-washed jeans and stepped into them. "As Alpha, I'll have a major target on my back to any wolf who wants to challenge my authority. Add the fact that I'm a turned wolf in the middle of a rogue uprising, and I might as well paint a target on your back, too. I won't let that happen."

The world *whooshed* in and out.

"You're talking too fast, and it's too much." She waved her hand in front of her face, wishing away the stars still shimmying around in her line of sight. "I'm barely keeping my hormones under control here, and now this Luminary talk? I don't get it. I don't know if I want to."

"I'm going to be Alpha, Melina. I'm going to rule. If someone has a bone to pick with me—"

"Clever wording." She couldn't help but joke through her cloud of confusion.

He sighed, kinking his neck to the side in that irritated way he'd perfected so well. "If someone wants to hurt me, they'll go for my mate first. I won't—I can't—do that to you."

Not only had she fallen for the most eligible bachelor of the year, she'd fallen for a werewolf. The *Alpha*.

She rubbed circles over her temples. Shouldn't she be worried about donning a coat of stinky wolf hair and growing fangs? Why were her thoughts preoccupied on Hayden turning her away?

"I don't know what's happening." Her heart gave a sickening thud. "I'm not thinking straight."

"I've been where you are, so I know the back and forth you're having with yourself. But inside, you know the truth about what's happening to you, and what needs to happen between us. You can feel it, right?"

Yeah, she could.

Despite her best efforts, she'd totally, hopelessly fallen in love with Hayden. She'd loved him from the start, she realized. The hard and true beat of her heart warned that she always would.

Surprisingly, after everything she'd learned the last twenty-four hours, *that* was what scared her the most.

Chapter Twenty

Sitting on the beach behind Hayden's house, Melina dug her toes into the sand and stared at the lineup of waves on the horizon. Slivers of moonlight illuminated the water as it churned and tumbled, rolling closer to shore. Cool sand and tiny pebbles smooshed between her toes, reminding her of summer days when her parents used to take her to Baker Beach on the very edge of the city. She'd always cherished those memories…

Taking a deep breath, Melina drew her knees against her chest and wrapped her arms around them.

She heard Hayden's footsteps striking over the sand before she spotted him. It seemed as if everything had changed in such a short amount of time. Her ears had become painfully sensitive, her sense of smell had heightened, and her lust for Hayden had become insatiable.

"You've been out here for an hour," he said, sitting beside her in the sand. He handed her a steaming mug of coffee— dark and bold, judging from the aroma. "I tried to give you some space, but the wind's picking up. Thought you might want something to warm you up."

She'd been cold earlier, but now, with her body running hot, the crisp air felt good. It was a reminder that she was alive, that she could feel something real and normal. The wind whirled, stirring loose pebbles over the beach. Hayden's enticing scent—spicy, crisp, and male—hit her nostrils, and made her go weak. She took a sip and breathed in deep when the sugar and vanilla cream hit her tongue.

"Stay out here much longer and you'll see the sun rise," he said, drinking from his own mug.

Without answering, Melina stared out over the waves, to where the dark blue ocean met the sky. It was probably three o'clock, a couple hours until daybreak. Although her body felt raw and worn, and her mind was drained beyond words, she couldn't sleep.

A new sun would bring a new world. A whole new reality and strange adjustments.

She wasn't ready to face any of it.

If only the dark could stay, even a little bit longer.

"Anything you want to talk about?" he asked, his voice a sexy rasp.

They'd gone 'round and 'round about the details of her transition. She was scared, but there wasn't anything she could do other than take it one day at a time. Hell, she was taking it one hour, *one minute*, at a time. Hayden had promised he'd be with her through it all, to help guide her through it. She believed him, easing some of the fears wracking through her.

But her heart still ached over one thing he'd glazed over.

"The Luminary bond," she said.

He nodded slowly, kicking his legs out in front of him. "It's the non-shifting equivalent of soul mates. It's the idea that there's one person out there for everyone."

"And you're it for me, huh?"

He chuckled. "Well you don't have to sound so miserable about it."

"No, it's not that…"

"Then what?"

She couldn't look at him, so she kept her gaze trained on the crashing waves in front of her. "You said our connection will grow, but only so far. You said you won't complete the bond with me, which means we'll never be together, right?"

"Right." He tipped back his mug and stared out over the horizon.

Prince Charming was sitting right beside her, but once again, he didn't want her. Not in the same way. When she thought of the future, she envisioned marriage and children, a home and career. She dreamed of having it all. Tied with a big ole red bow. But now she'd have to find someone else, and Hayden had ruined her. She'd constantly compare everyone to him, and they'd fall short. It was almost as if Hayden was asking her to choose—her heart over her dreams.

Cinderella managed to get her fairy tale. That *bitch*.

"If you're the one I'm supposed to be with," she said, stroking her mug, "how could I ever be happy with anyone else?"

"I don't want you to be with anyone else." Hayden spoke so harshly, it was nearly a growl. "I need you…" His words drifted.

He'd been about to say more. Melina could feel it. She could almost say the words herself. They were right on the tip of her tongue. And then they were gone.

"You think it's too dangerous for an Alpha to have a mate?" she probed. "Not us, specifically, but hypothetically speaking?"

Tipping back his mug, Hayden finished his coffee and then exhaled heavily. As if the weight of the world sat on his broad, muscular shoulders. "Under certain circumstances, yes. In the city right now, there's dissension from those who believe turned wolves are less worthy than born wolves."

"And they don't want you to rule?"

"Judging from what happened to you this weekend, they'll do anything to keep me from taking over the pack."

"Has it always been this way?" Her throat tightened. "I mean, when the rogues were in your pack, did you know they didn't want you to step up after your father died?"

"If any of my packmates had a problem with it, they must've kept it on lockdown. My father was always protective of me, so that might've been why. There were a few who voiced their prejudice from time to time, but I brushed them off. We all did. I never thought they'd separate from the pack and kill their own." He stared at the mug in his grasp. "They were never going to let me rule. I see that now, but I should've known it from the start."

Melina bit her lip as Hayden's partying and reckless behavior came to mind. She'd never studied psychology or anything, but if Hayden felt unworthy of the legacy his father left behind, he might be inclined to sabotage the whole thing. Probably easier to swallow the fact that he didn't become the leader from his own making, rather than not being good enough from within.

"Angus and Cara were amazing partners, in everything." Hayden looked to the sky, as if reading his next words in the stars. "They were perfect for one another, a power couple who garnered respect from everyone they met. But when Cara died, Angus lost it. He wandered the streets every night. He didn't eat well, and lost a ton of weight. Sometimes I'd talk to him, and I might as well have been talking to a blank slate. He wasn't the same man."

"I can imagine losing his wife was a harsh blow. Especially if they'd been together hundreds of years."

"No, you don't understand," he said, turning his entire body toward her. Moonlight danced over the hard lines of his face. "It wasn't losing Cara that made my father a living, breathing ghost. It was *loving* her. He cared for her so deeply that he lost himself. He was too involved, his heart too intertwined with hers. He loved her so much that he couldn't live without her."

The truth rumbled through her.

Hayden wasn't a womanizing playboy; he was simply afraid to love.

"So the natural alternative is to not love at all," she thought aloud.

"Better than having my heart ripped in half." He nodded. "I don't ever want to end up the way my father did at the end. No one should have to suffer that way."

Loneliness trickled into her heart, cold and agonizing, though something inside her warned the feeling wasn't coming from her at all. She'd somehow picked it up from him. His guard had been up from the moment she met him, she realized. It was the same wall he showed to the world instead of letting people in to see him for who he really was. The generous, caring Oz behind the curtain.

The *werewolf* behind the curtain.

No wonder he'd been content for the media to print stories of his partying. If they focused on the trivial parts of his life, they wouldn't dig deeper and look into the most secret part of him.

She'd misread him. Terribly.

Her heart snapped in two. "Do you think Angus would give up any of the moments he shared with his wife?"

"Hell no."

She paused, choosing her words carefully. "If he could go back, do you think he'd choose not to complete the Luminary bond thingy with her?"

"No, he wouldn't," he whispered. "And I know where you're going with this. Angus and Cara were born werewolves. They didn't have to overcome half of the obstacles that are in my way. The reason you're writing an article to improve my image isn't for a promotion. It's to show the pack that I've changed, that I can take the role of Alpha seriously. Not only do I have to prove my worth to the media, I have to prove to the voting council, the pack, and—"

"Yourself?"

He stared, and clamped his mouth shut. "I was going to say friends, but I guess you're right. There are things I need to prove to myself, too."

They sat in silence for what seemed like an eternity as waves slammed against the beach in the distance.

"How does a couple complete the Luminary bond?" Melina asked, determined to break through a few more of Hayden's walls. "Is it like a marriage ceremony?"

"Luminaries declare their undying love for one another during sex. There are words each recite—vows, I guess you could say—and that's it. It's rumored to be magical and soul-shattering, but I haven't done it so I can't say. After the bond, the couple is stronger and faster in wolf form, and they live longer."

"I remember you mentioning that." She shivered as she imagined going through the bond with the powerful man sitting next to her.

"Are you cold?" he asked, rubbing his hand up her arm. "Here."

As she protested, he shrugged out of his coat and draped it over her shoulders. It was warm and soft inside, and smelled like *him*. Tantalizingly masculine. She breathed in deep and let the spicy scent permeate every corner of her body.

"Even if I wanted to," he said softly, "I wouldn't want to put you in that position. An Alpha's mate is always on point, and always in the spotlight. And until the rogues are taken down, you'll be my Achilles heel, so to speak."

"Why live in fear that way?" She faced him, boldness streaking through her. "Why not take them down quickly and prove that you can rule better than any born wolf in the pack?"

He looked at her as though she'd sprouted three heads.

"What?" She smoothed her fly-aways. "Why are you looking at me like that?"

"You could take on the world, couldn't you?" He tightened the coat around her shoulders and cinched it closed below her neck. "I wish it was as easy as you seem to think it is. Problem is, we've been on the rogues' trail for a year, and can't seem to get anywhere. We hone in on a location, and they move before we can get there. If information leaks that someone is turning rogue, they disappear before we can question them. They're agile, have a seemingly endless supply of funds, and no moral compass. Not a good combination in an enemy force."

Didn't appear to be all that difficult from the outside looking in.

"Sounds like it's someone on the inside," she said simply. "Someone who knows your plan so it seems like they're one step ahead, but really they just know what you're going to do so they can prepare."

His dark eyes shadowed over as the wheels began to turn. "You're brilliant." Without warning, his hands cupped her cheeks. "You're also the most beautiful woman I've ever seen in my life." His worshipful gaze studied the features of her face. "I don't know where to kiss you first."

Her stomach flipped, but before she could respond, he planted the sweetest of kisses on the tip of her nose. Tilting her head down, he kissed her forehead, and then angled her face so that he could kiss her cheek.

Her eyes fluttered closed and her heart clenched, waiting, waiting, not-so-patiently waiting for his mouth to close over hers.

"If things were different," he whispered against her mouth. "I'd make you mine, right here on the sand."

She was still catching her breath when his lips found hers in the dark.

Chapter Twenty-One

A little after eight o'clock Monday morning, Hayden led the way into Melina's apartment, using his senses to detect any unwanted visitors. No unusual scents. Nothing out of the ordinary. Her front door was still locked, and everything seemed to be intact. Nothing stolen or missing, not a single piece of furniture overturned. Above all, there wasn't a single lingering werewolf scent for Hayden to pick up on.

He'd secretly hoped the werewolf who'd attacked Melina would've come back to her apartment to wait for her. He would've liked to rip his head off. It wouldn't solve a damn thing with the rogues, but he'd feel a hell of a lot better. He didn't even have a scent to fuel his search. All he had was the general area of the attack, which he'd promptly relayed to Gabriel, who'd taken the information to the council.

He'd also told Gabriel about Melina's suspicion that the person behind the attacks might be someone within the pack. Someone who would know about what they were going to do before they acted.

He didn't have a single lead.

As Hayden strode into Melina's living room, he fished his cell out of his pocket and checked his messages. Nothing since Gabriel's last text saying the council was going to vote on whether or not to send the pack's guards into Bernal Heights.

In this case, no news wasn't good news.

The rogues were still out there…

"Pack a few bags," Hayden said, following Melina down the hall to her bedroom. "You'll stay with me for a few weeks until the rogue business settles down."

"I still can't get over this." Shaking her head disbelievingly, Melina stripped the shirt from her body and flung it to the floor. "The idea of werewolves living on the streets of the city is crazy."

With a pained hiss, Hayden averted his eyes and headed to the closet. Using his peripheral vision, he watched her step out of her shorts and panties. He trembled down to the bone and forced his will power to remain intact.

"It may be crazy, but that doesn't make it any less true."

"And I'm going to stay with you?" She opened a drawer near her bed, removed a white lacy bra and matching panties, and put them on. "As in…at your beach house?"

She moved as if she were in slow motion, teasing him with every sensual movement, every flex and turn of her lean body. She wasn't moving any slower than normal, and she wasn't teasing him.

Except she was.

Had she said something? Was he supposed to answer? He swallowed cotton, and forced the lust to stop pounding through his veins.

"That was the plan," he said, remembering her question through the fog. "It's not safe for you to be alone right now. And I'm not sure how much the rogues know about you. It wouldn't be far-fetched to assume they've figured out where you live."

Wow. He'd somehow managed to sound coherent. As if every single thought wasn't revolving around Melina's gorgeous figure in dainty white lingerie. It was an image he wouldn't soon forget.

He brushed past her and headed for the closet. He could spend all day watching her change into new clothes and then stripping them from her body, but they didn't have time.

"We can reserve you a hotel under a fake name to make sure you're safe, and I'll stay with you, of course. I doubt I can find a room with a round, zebra-patterned bed, like I know you prefer, but you could make due for a while."

Pressing her lips together into a grin, Melina moved into the closet and came out wearing a blue dress with criss-cross patterns. Super short. Tight fit. Long sleeves. Paired with brown cowboy boots and a gold rose ring on her pinky finger.

"Magic," he breathed. "If I go in there, will I come out looking like Channing Tatum?"

Barking out a laugh, Melina dug beneath the bed and pulled out two giant cases of luggage. He let his curiosity get the best of him and strode into the closet. He had to see for himself.

"What the hell?" The breath ripped from his lungs.

"What?" Melina rushed into the closet behind him, horror in her eyes. "What is it?"

"How do you find anything in here?" He pushed aside hanger after hanger of fur, feathers, leather, and sequins. "Do you work at a circus?"

"You scared me," she said, hand over her heart. "I thought something was wrong."

"Something *is* wrong." He pinched the corner of something pink and furry and raised it high. "What's this?"

"High fashion." She bumped into his shoulder. "I guess I won't be needing fur anymore. Soon, I'll have a giant coat of my own." Her tone was bitter and dark, and even though she joked about it, Hayden could sense her anxiety.

"You shouldn't be wearing fur anyway," he said.

"It's faux." Smirking, she kinked her hips to the side. And just like that, all traces of anxiety disappeared from the space between them. "No werewolves were harmed in the making of my wardrobe."

"I'm telling you, it's not as bad as you're making it out to be," he said. "It's surprisingly natural."

"Oh yeah, I'm sure." Her tone was laced with snark. "By natural, you mean hairy, right? I'm going to have to shave with a weed-whacker."

"You're not." He laughed at the image. "You're only going to be covered with fur during the full moon, and only when you will it to happen. Every other time of month, your legs will be as silky-smooth as they are now."

Memories of Melina's legs wrapping around his waist hit him hard. Tampering down the desire firing through him, Hayden flicked a shimmery green something and a pink feathery headpiece.

"What is all this stuff?" he asked.

"The right side is off-the-runway clothes from this year, and the left is last year's specials. We're talking Gucci, Prada, Dior. All the gods."

"Gods?"

She nodded excitedly. "They rule my world."

"I'd rather rock it." Unable to hold back any longer, he gripped her hip and spun her into him. He nipped at her ear, even as the logical part of him warned against getting close to her again. "You definitely rock mine."

Her breath hitched as he pushed her against the wall of hanging clothes. He claimed her mouth and plunged his tongue past her lips, her little whimpers of delight feeding his desire. Surrounded by leopard prints, ponchos, fur, and glitter, Hayden skimmed his hands up and down her figure, gripped her tightly, and feasted on the sweetness of her mouth.

If they had more time…if one part of his brain wasn't worried about a rogue bursting in on them, catching him unaware, Hayden would've made love to Melina on her closet floor.

She could distract him so easily.

Too easily.

He palmed the flat span of her stomach and gently urged her back. "What's this?" he asked, holding up her hand and kissing the back. The gold ring on her pinky shone brightly in the closet light.

"My last name is Rosenthal, though I write under Melina Rae." She brushed her hand over the delicate gold petals. "The rose is a reminder not to lose myself."

He could understand why she'd chosen to wear the ring today. Especially under the circumstances.

It was a reality check, even for him.

"Your shelves are overflowing." He pointed to rack upon rack of heels, purses, and wallet-things. "How many bags does one woman need?"

"One for every outfit would be nice."

"I know you had particular tastes when it came to clothes, but I didn't know you were in this deep." He shook his head, taking in the sight, though his hand returned to her stomach. Gently, his fingers raked against her, gripping the loose material of her dress. "You'd be a perfect fit at *Eclipse*. No pun intended."

"That's what I've always thought, but if I don't get your article in tip-top shape, my editor won't pass it along to Lydia Hyde, and my chances will be shot."

There was another way to get Melina's foot in the door.

"I can pass your info along to Lydia." He shrugged, meeting her hungry gaze. "If I vouch for your work, she might read it in a different light."

"No way in hell," Melina snapped. "If I'm going to get the job, it's going to be because *I* earned it, not because *you* introduced me to someone you work with. Thank you, but no thank you." Removing his hand from her stomach, Melina escaped from the cage of his body and backed deeper into the closet. "Now would you go? I'll pack the bags."

"Don't have to tell me twice." He backed away, hands in the air, his fingers buzzing with the memory of her body. "What can I do to speed this process so we can get out of here?"

"I lost my phone somewhere after the rogues took me." She threw a pile of clothes onto the bed. And then another.

There was no way all those outfits were going to fit in the trunk. He should've traded the Bugatti for a minivan.

"My computer should be near the window in the living room," she hollered. "Can you check for an email from Sylvia Reinhart?"

The idea of invading her personal space rubbed him all kinds of wrong. "You want me to look through your private messages?"

"I've got nothing to hide." Her voice trailed off as she disappeared into the closet from hell. "Sylvia's my editor. I've usually emailed her by now, updating her on the progress of my article, but I've been preoccupied with everything else. She's probably going ape-shit."

"If you know she's going ape-shit, why do you need me to check?"

She peeked her head around the wall. "She's been known to fast forward deadlines, and if she has, I don't want to miss it. If you see something from her, would you open it and read it to me?"

She disappeared before he could answer. He found her computer where she'd said—on her desk near the large window overlooking Ashbury Street. Flipping open the lid of her MacBook Air, Hayden punched the space bar, bringing the computer to life.

"It needs a password," he called out, checking the street for anything out of the ordinary. Hippies. Clothing store. Cigar shop. Everything appeared fine. "Want to come out here and—"

"DickwadDean," she blurted. "Caps on Dick and Dean. All one word."

He flicked his tongue over his teeth. "Nice."

She laughed. "You stood me up. I was pissed."

"I'm beginning to get the picture."

As her email cued up, Hayden remarked how easily she'd asked him to log on to her computer and read her email. He'd known Gabriel for two-hundred years, and he still didn't trust the guy with his computer passcode. Melina was a different creature. Beyond her bizarre clothing choices, she wasn't afraid to let people get close to her.

He admired that about her. He sure as hell couldn't do it.

"There's an email." He read the subject line. "You'll have your work cut out for you. That's the heading."

"What?" she called out. "From Syliva?"

He opened the email, the breath freezing in his lungs when the image loaded in the body. He'd made the front page of *Celeb Entertainment Source*, and the front page of *Hollywood Hound*. Both magazines featured him in the buff, stealing the pants from a homeless man sprawled on a bench.

Hayden Dean Steals from the Homeless. Details Inside.

Dean's Drunken Binge. Arrested Records Documented.

"What's the—" Melina appeared beside him. He hadn't even heard her approach. "Is that…*you*?"

He nodded, the blood draining from his face.

"You were arrested?" she screeched. "When?"

"The night you were taken." His voice sounded rough, even to his ears. "I wasn't arrested. I was detained for questioning. That's why it took me so long to get to you."

Smacking her forehead, she bent beside him to get a better look at the covers. "They look bad and not too far-fetched, damn it. What where you doing?"

He paced around the couch centered in her living room. "When I left you at the pier, it was because I picked up the scent of a rogue in the parking garage. I shifted once I was inside, we fought, and he got away." Vengeance scorched through him, even now, days later. "I tried to get back to you, but I'd ripped through my clothes. One of the casualties of shifting, I'm afraid."

"Whoa, whoa, hold the phone. I'll ruin my clothes?" Her eyes went wide. "You didn't say *anything* about tearing through my clothes. No way. Nuh-uh. I want off this ride."

"You can wear clothes from Salvation Army, if you don't want to shred anything you have hanging up in there."

"Salvation…*Army*?"

"Believe me, Melina, your clothes situation is the least of our worries."

"You're right." But her tone didn't show it. "We've got a bigger problem here."

He could feel the honor of becoming Alpha slipping right through his fingers. His palms sweat. "I ripped through my clothes, and needed something to cover me. I tried to take the blanket off the homeless guy, which as it turns out, wasn't a blanket at all."

"Disaster." She closed down that email and opened another. "Wonder how much the people made from selling those pictures to the tabloids."

"Believe me, you don't want to know. It'll make you sick."

"I'm already there."

As she spun to face him, dark shadows shifted in her honey-brown eyes. "The magazines really are slanted, aren't they?"

"Every single one." He picked up the bags she'd dropped by the door. "Well, I do like to go out and have a couple drinks every now and again, but I'm usually arriving late to the bars, so I've only had a drink before closing."

"What about the fights?"

"I'm usually breaking it up, or defending a fool who couldn't stand up for himself."

"The women?"

"They were placeholders for you."

She sauntered closer. And then she threw her arms around his neck and crushed her mouth to his.

"Somehow I knew it. I really did," she said, as their lips parted. "I guess I just needed to hear you say it for it to be true. I'm going to write such a damned good article, everyone's going to forget about the tainted Hayden Dean they thought they knew before. And then you're going to get the promotion you're after."

He breathed hard, the taste of her lingering on his lips. "It's not a promotion, Melina. The governing council of the pack believes my image could taint the whole pack. They don't think I can be trusted because I don't take pack business seriously." His heart pounded out of his chest and his head spun. "Everything that's happened over the last year proves how selfish I am at the core — at least in their eyes. My fall from grace can easily be documented in the trail of magazine garbage."

She shot him an alarmed glare, her eyebrows drawing together. "You're worthy of this, Hayden. Turned wolf or born. Adopted or birthed." She brushed her hand over the stubble of his cheek. "You're Angus Dean's son. He chose you because he loved you, because he believed you were worthy to replace him. Now you only have to believe it yourself."

Gazing into her eyes, it was easy to believe her. He wanted to, but the damn ache in his chest had burned into a gaping hole of insignificance.

His phone buzzed from his pocket. Digging it out, Hayden swiped his finger over the screen and read the text from Gabriel:

Council voted against sending guards to Bernal Heights. WTF happened with picture in mag this a.m.? Council is pissed.

White hot pulses of fury surged through him. An innocent woman was kidnapped in the middle of the Embarcadero, attacked, and turned into a werewolf, and the city's most trusted council voted not to lift a damn finger?

What the hell was going on?

The world had flipped on its head, and his father was probably rolling in his grave. They'd made it their life's mission to *protect* the innocent and follow a set of rules that spoke of honor and courage.

This was horseshit.

"Time to go," he said, striding to the door.

"What is it?"

"I need to meet with the council." Good thing the Bugatti could tear through the miles. "Grab what you can. You're coming with me."

She dashed to her computer and tucked it under her arm. "This is all I really need. I have an idea on that trail of articles you mentioned. All I need is Wi-Fi and a couple hours with my computer."

On their way out the door, Melina said, "But first, do you mind dropping me off at *Celeb Crush's* office? Sylvia emailed back, just as I thought. She wants to meet this morning."

"Not happening," he bit out.

He wasn't letting her out of his sight.

"I think I can clean up your image so that this whole mess is behind you." She locked the door behind her. "But I need to meet with her first."

Something was brewing in that gorgeous head of hers.

"Okay," he conceded. "But tell her to meet you in my office."

"Done." She kissed him on the cheek before stomping down the stairs to the foyer. "Everything's going to be fine, Hayden. You'll see."

He wanted to believe her. He really did.

But he was about to storm into Dean, Hyde, & Hammer and demand the council revote to go after the rogues. His anger wasn't going to be received well.

And he wasn't backing down until they listened.

Chapter Twenty-Two

While Hayden went to talk with the council, Melina waited for Sylvia on the fifteenth floor of Dean, Hyde, & Hammer. Hayden had left Gabriel in the office to watch over her, to make sure no one from the pack came up unexpectedly. He'd sprawled on the leather couch near the big screen—Cardinals were playing and down by three—leaving Melina all alone in Hayden's office.

With thirty minutes to go until Sylvia arrived to talk about the new direction for the article, Melina pulled up the rolling chair behind Hayden's desk and started typing the thoughts on her mind.

She'd never written anything so fast in all her life. The words were at her fingertips as they streamed through her head. She breathed deep, tweaking words to make them fit, streamlining paragraphs that slowed the pace.

As she typed, she realized she'd been wrong to insist on those stupid image-improving phases. She'd told him to ditch his car (the one that'd saved her life as it sped away from the rogues), suggested that he change his attire (the clothes that accented the muscles her fingers loved to shadow so much), and compromise at work (with an unreasonable council that didn't support him).

He never had to change a thing about himself.

It was the perceptions of the outside world that had to change.

She had to change.

As she finished typing, tears welled in her eyes and her throat constricted.

Hayden wasn't perfect, but he was a good man. Decent and kind. People needed to see him for what he was.

Logging on to Dean, Hyde, & Hammer's Wi-Fi, Melina cued up Google and did a generic search for Hayden Dean. She scanned images and web hits, celebrity magazines and articles in the *San Francisco Chronicle*.

Just as she suspected, there was a definite flip in the paradigm when it came to Hayden Dean, right around a year ago. *About the time Angus died,* Melina thought. Before that, Hayden was a playboy, but besides the broken hearts, no one was seriously hurt. No fighting. No trashing hotel rooms. No stealing pants from bums and winding up in the clink.

"Knock, knock," Sylvia said from the doorway.

"I didn't hear the elevator come up," Melina said, suddenly uncomfortable to be sitting behind Hayden's desk. "Please, come in."

Over Sylvia's shoulder, Gabriel postured, and then hitched his chin at her back. Melina couldn't hear what he'd said, but something inside her hummed.

Everything okay?

It felt like a radio frequency in her head that was fuzzy and incomprehensible, that suddenly dialed in and became clear. When she'd watched Hayden and Gabriel interact at the aquarium benefit, they'd stared and nodded, and she remembered thinking they were somehow communicating without saying a word.

Maybe that's how werewolves in the pack spoke to one another…

"Yeah," she said aloud. "We're good."

"I know we are." Sylvia stared. "I don't need you to tell me that."

Nerves rattled in Melina's stomach. "I'm sorry." If she wasn't careful, she'd start to sound like a crazy person, hearing questions in her head and answering them aloud. As if things weren't already confusing. "I've been working on this month's column. It's nearly finished, and I think you're going to be pleasantly surprised at the direction."

Taking the seat in front of Hayden's desk, Sylvia pushed her thick-framed glasses up the tip of her nose and stared down at her. "What direction do you mean?"

Excitement flaring through her, Melina leaned over the desk and pressed her fingers together. "If I simply write the article as you asked, going over all of Hayden's good points and how he's changed this month, or how I've seen him change, why would anyone believe it? What reason would they have to believe this article over the hundreds of others that have painted him in such poor light?"

Sylvia stared. Stoic. Unreadable.

"I have to prove that the others were off-base," she went on. "By proving that there were stories behind the pictures and horrific headlines. Take this morning's headlines, for example."

"That's precisely the reason I wanted to talk to you." Sylvia swiped her tongue over her caked-red lips. "I've received direct word from a managing editor at *Eclipse* that they'd like you to take your article down a different avenue. And if you can keep the new order quiet, you're in at *Eclipse*. The job is yours."

Her spirit soared. "Really?"

"Really." Sylvia nodded. "They're ready to give you the opportunity of a lifetime. Double your annual *Celeb Crush* salary. Office with a view. Assistant already on staff. Unlimited off-the-runway picks as they come into the office and—"

"Did you say…" Her heart stuttered. "…unlimited off-the-runway picks?"

Sylvia smiled tightly. "Told you it was the opportunity of a lifetime. Don't exactly know why they're handing this offer to you, but there you have it." She smacked her lips together and folded her hands in her lap. Her Jackie-O suit was pink and perfectly tailored, her feet crossed in front of her. She'd always been a vision of grace, someone Melina had always looked up to. But there was something *off.* A heady scent that burned her nose. "There's another condition."

"Anything," Melina said.

"The article has to be written by tomorrow evening."

"Done." Anxiety ratcheted through her arms as her fingers twitched with the urge to type. "What does the editor need?"

"Do we have your word that you will keep this quiet?" Sylvia pierced her lips and sat ram-rod straight. "I was told to get a verbal guarantee."

Melina nodded. "I will."

"You're going to take the juiciest dirt you have on Hayden Dean, and expose it. You're to make sure he's taken out of the limelight all together. I've been instructed he's harboring an unnatural secret dark enough to do it." Sylvia glared over the rim of her glasses. "The managing editor who emailed me says you know what that is."

Melina could think of one big "unnatural" secret in particular. It'd make an unbelievable, jaw-dropping headline: *A Werewolf Among Us.*

Two weeks ago, Melina would've jumped at the chance to expose Hayden. She would've done damn near anything to get the job.

But now, something didn't sit right.

"I don't know," Melina said, scratching her head, trying to make sense of it all. "Who's the managing editor?"

Sylvia stared, her expression unreadable.

"Okay," Melina said. "Let me think about it for the day."

Think of a way out of it was more likely.

"I don't think you understand." Sylvia stood abruptly, jerking her bag over her shoulder. "The managing editors at *Eclipse* don't request, they command. When they give me an order that trickles to you, you make it happen or you become a ghost who used to work for my company."

Melina's mouth fell as confusion set in. From promotion to the threat of unemployment in two seconds flat. The back and forth gave her whiplash.

"I'm going to give you one piece of advice, Ms. Rae," Sylvia said, turning to leave. "Write the article the way they want it, or kiss your dreams goodbye. If you don't do this, you'll never work for another fashion magazine in the industry, *Celeb Crush* included."

The situation was black and white: expose Hayden the way she'd planned to anyway, or say farewell to her dream job.

"Okay," Melina said, her voice shaking. "I'll do it."

She had to find a way out. *Had to.*

There was no way she could turn on Hayden now.

"Good girl. You'll go far in this business." Sylvia smiled, slow and wicked. "You stick to following orders this way, and you'll get to the top the way I did."

As Sylvia left the office, still a vision of poise and grace, Melina realized the top wasn't sunshine and rainbows. It may've included endless supplies of money and all the Prada she could get her hands on, but the top wasn't easier with less stress.

The top sucked major ass.

Chapter Twenty-Three

Hayden burst through the doors to the conference room, garnering quizzical looks from Reagan, White, Mad Dog, and Lydia. They sat around an oblong table, piles of papers, maps, and magazines in front of them.

"Hayden," White said, rolling back from the table. "What's going on?"

"Why don't you tell me?" Hayden stared right into Lydia's beady black eyes. "I want to know how the council will explain its non-action in the crimes against an innocent non-shifter."

Lydia spread her arms to the chairs nearest him. "Why don't you sit, Hayden?"

Reagan and Mad Dog exchanged quiet words, though Hayden's heartbeat was thumping too loud through his ears for him to make them out. As far as Hayden was concerned, Reagan was loyal to Lydia, and White was loyal to him. Mad Dog was the wild card, the balance in the system who stood for what was right rather than holding loyalty to any one person. From the closeness between him and Reagan, it looked as if the tables had turned…out of Hayden's favor.

"We'd like answers as well," Lydia said, tossing a magazine across the table. It slid and spun, coming to a stop facing him. The headlines weren't good. He didn't have to see any more than the covers to know he'd sailed up Shit Creek. "We have reason to believe you shifted in public, and that's the reason you were left nude on the street."

"Is that true?" Mad Dog asked flatly.

Now was time for honesty. What good would it do to sugar coat things at this point? They were running the show behind his back, without his involvement. He would never lead the pack, he'd never rule.

"I was eating dinner at Pier 39 when I picked up the scent of a wolf in the parking garage across the street. I took off after him, shifted, and demanded answers. I was careful. No one saw me in wolf form." Hayden lifted his chin in defiance, ready to take whatever punishment they handed him. "He asked me to call him Rogue. He was part of the group that kidnapped Melina and—"

"You mean the non-shifter," Reagan corrected.

Way to rob her of her importance.

"No, I mean *Melina*." His heart beat true. "She's one of us now."

As the men mumbled their dissension to one another. Hayden postured, staring straight through Lydia. She was the only member of the council sitting silent. The only one who didn't seem surprised by the news.

"We hadn't heard about her transition," Mad Dog said, spinning toward Hayden. "We believed she escaped, you found her, and took her somewhere safe to recover."

Wonder who tipped them off to that much…

Gabriel, most likely.

"I helped her understand our society, the way it works, and its essential secrecy. I haven't talked to her about being inducted into the pack. I thought I'd do that during the next full moon." Hayden went palms down on the table. "But while I was away this weekend cleaning up the mess, this council voted to sit on their hands and do *nothing*. The rogues are only getting stronger, and if we sit idle much longer, we'll have to contend with another pack in our city. No one at this table wants that kind of conflict."

"That's not what we want," Mad Dog said, his baritone resonating through the room. "But we still don't know where to find Asher. If we go after the rogues, it'll be like killing ants. We need the queen, or the king, as it were, to end the attacks."

"If you have some sort of intelligence revealing where to find Asher," Reagan finished, "by all means, share what you know. Otherwise, more bloodshed is not the answer."

So that's why they'd voted not to move the guards. They didn't want to enter the ring until Asher stepped in, ready to fight.

"We can start by questioning the wolf at Howlands." Hayden glared at each one of them in turn. "See if he can identify his attacker. Asher took responsibility for the attack soon after it happened. He could've been there."

"You're grasping," White said.

"No, I'm determined."

"The wolf succumbed to his injuries Saturday night," Lydia blurted, cutting them short, "before we could get any leads from him."

Hayden wasn't surprised, and the flat-lined emotion irked him. "Was he guarded?"

Lydia shrugged. "That's not relevant anymore."

"Was he guarded?" He gritted his teeth together.

"No," Reagan said, putting a hand over Lydia's. "He was in critical condition from the moment he was brought in and wasn't expected to recover. There was no need to put guards at his door."

"No need?" Hayden bellowed. "You have someone in a hospital who could possibly ID a lead wolf in the rogue pack and you don't think it's relevant to protect him and the information he holds?"

White, Hayden's only freaking ally in all this, folded his hands over the table and stared at them, while everyone else looked on, indifferent. Unmoved.

"Fine." Hayden stood. "I'll go into Bernal Heights. I'll track down those rogues, starting with the church where Melina was being held. We won't call out all the guards, only a select few. It's not a full moon, so the ones who come with me should be born wolves."

"One of the reasons you're not fit to rule," Lydia said. "You can't even go into a hostile situation against our own kind unless it's during a full moon. We can't time our wars by the lunar cycle, Hayden. Somewhere deep down, don't you think the pack would do better with a different Alpha? One who is a born wolf?"

A growl reverberated from Hayden's chest and rumbled through the room. Adrenaline surged through him, mixing and churning with the vengeance in his gut. He charged around the table, aimed to take out Lydia's throat. She stood from the chair, arms at her sides while Reagan crouched defensively in front of her.

Fine.

He'd take them both out.

White caught Hayden around the waist and held him back. Barely. The guy was abnormally strong for being so old—undeniably due to the Luminary bond the councilman had completed with his mate of five-hundred years.

"Is that what this has come to?" Hayden spat over White's shoulder. "Has the council voted another Alpha?"

"No," White said, holding on to Hayden tight. "The promotion ceremony still takes place tomorrow night. But we have to be honest. Under the circumstances"—he nodded at the stack of magazines and their lies—"it doesn't look like you're taking your position in the pack seriously."

"The hell, you say." Hayden jerked out of his friend's grasp. "I feel like I'm the *only* one taking things seriously."

Mad Dog remained seated, watching the drama in the room unfold. Hayden eyed him carefully, waiting for him to spring into action. But he didn't.

"We've already voted to keep the guards at bay until Asher rears his head," White said. "We'll not vote until then."

"That's fine," Hayden said, jerking the leather coat over his shoulders. "Since you still haven't voted an Alpha, I'm still the heir apparent, which means I don't vote on council business. I can go into Bernal Heights by myself."

"You can't shift." White followed him to the door. "You won't be able to defend yourself against them."

"They attacked my Luminary, White. They'll come back for her." There. He said it. Laid it all out on the table.

White stared, his lips straining, the color matching his name.

"Justice has to be served," Hayden went on, hardening himself for war. "If I have to take matters into my own hands to make sure another innocent isn't harmed, so be it."

He stormed out the door.

"If you do this, you won't be voted Alpha," Lydia shouted, stopping him cold. "Whatever chance you had will be gone."

He turned back, hands clenching and unclenching. Mad Dog stared, his curious gaze flipping between Hayden and Lydia.

"You're disobeying a direct order from the council," White interjected, placing a hand on Lydia's shoulder. "Your interference could cause the pack dearly."

"Guess you have to decide, my man." Mad Dog raised his thick, bushy eyebrows. "Wouldn't be so hard to remain cool for a few days, and see if we can get a bead on Asher."

"No, it wouldn't be hard," Hayden said, the breath punching out of him. "But it also wouldn't be right. If this is the way the pack is going—ruled by cowards who'd rather sit back while innocent non-shifters and turned wolves are harmed—I don't want to be any part of it."

"Watch it," White said, grabbing Hayden's elbow. "Don't say something you'll regret later."

He looked his father's dear friend in the face. "I can protect the pack from the outside. But I can't be a part of the pack that refuses to take action when it's needed." He motioned to Lydia and Reagan, who stood as a solid wall on the opposite end of the room. "I won't."

As he spun on his heel and left the office, a dull ache spread through his chest, carving a hole.

Facing a rogue pack of wolves in human form had never been done before. Or if it had, the person hadn't lived to tell.

But for the first time in his life, there was a cause greater than him.

Chapter Twenty-Four

Charging into his bedroom on the opposite end of the fifteenth floor, Hayden went right for the nightstand and pulled out his special-made Glock. He attached the silencer, loaded it with heavy silver bullets, and popped the top on a spare ammunition box.

"What happened?" Gabriel asked from behind him.

"I'm going after them on my own."

"Excuse me?"

"You heard right." Hayden dumped the entire box into his pocket, and then shoved a Taser into the other. If bullets couldn't bring down the rogues, volts of electricity would stun them until he could get the upper hand. Spinning around, he faced his only friend. "The council is afraid to stand against the rogues."

Melina's familiar feminine scent struck him as she brushed past Gabriel and entered the room. Her scent warmed him from the inside out. He steeled himself against the feelings stirring inside his chest. He had to stay focused, had to remember why he was doing this.

The only way to keep Melina safe was to bring down every last rogue wolf in the city.

"Where are you going?" Worry tainted her tone. "Hayden? Talk to me."

He hadn't realized he'd been standing silent, the Glock resting against his side.

This was where it all began, Hayden thought. Where Gabriel had first told him the pack had hired Melina to write the article on him. At the time, he would've given his right arm not to have her follow him around. Now, he'd give his life to keep her safe.

"I've got an appointment," he said simply.

Her brows rose. "Oh yeah? Where?"

"Bernal Heights."

As realization set in, she covered her mouth with her hand.

"How many guards are going with you?" Gabriel asked, leaning against the doorframe.

"None." Hayden left the room before it closed in any more. "Just me."

They followed him out. He could feel their gazes trained on his back.

Melina brushed her hand along his. "But you said turned wolves can't shift unless there's a full moon."

"You've got one hell of a memory." He punched the elevator button as doubt pricked the hairs on the back of his neck. "Anyone ever tell you that?"

"It's suicide." Gabriel met Hayden as the steel doors opened. "I'm coming with you. You should have at least one wolf at your side."

"No." He spun, putting a hand up to stop Gabriel from joining him in the elevator. "I need you to stay with Melina. You're the only person I trust to protect her." He gripped his friend's hand tight and shook. "I'll be back in two hours. If you don't hear from me, use the secret elevator key, take her down to the basement and out the Alpha's escape tunnels. I don't know what's going on with the pack, but someone on the inside has to be giving information to the rogues. They're getting too strong, too fast, and the council is too hesitant to act. Something doesn't sniff right."

Gabriel nodded as if he understood, his blue eyes blazing bright. "Make those bastards howl for mercy."

Hayden smirked, anticipation singing through him. "It'll be my pleasure."

"You expect me to wait here like a good little girl?" Melina planted her hand on her hip. "Don't you know me better than that by now?"

"I do know you better than that." He roped his arms around her waist and dragged her against him. And then he bent her back and kissed her, infusing her with the light and hope and radiance she'd given him the last couple weeks. "And I'm so incredibly sorry."

"For what?"

"This." He pushed her off him and backed into the elevator, punching the button for the door to shut behind him.

"No!" She jolted forward, but it was too late.

Milliseconds before the doors hissed shut, he blew her a kiss through the opening. The elevator had never run so slowly. Each floor he descended felt more and more like he was farther away from heaven and closer to hell. When he reached the basement, Hayden jammed the elevator key into the lock near the buttons and turned. No matter how many times Melina punched the call button now, the elevator wouldn't return until Gabriel used his matching key to call it up.

Hayden sprinted through the basement to the doors leading to the parking garage, and then slid into his Bugatti. He tore through the city at breakneck speed, using the stop signs and red lights as general suggestions. Once he made it to Bernal Heights, he slowed to a crawl.

As he neared the corner of Valley and Church Street where he'd rescued Melina, he rolled down his windows and used his heightened senses to search out the stench of a rogue. The morning marine layer plumed over the street, and entered the car, shrouding Hayden in fresh fog. He breathed deep, praying it'd bring something—

There.

He swerved to the curb, killed the engine, and got out of the car, patting his pockets to double-check his weapons. Although he couldn't shift on command the way the rogues could, the bullets would slow them down and the Taser would stun them. Maybe, if he was lucky, he'd get a chance at Asher and find out who he worked for.

There were people out at this hour, strolling down the street, coming in and out of the myriad of mom-and-pop shops. He stalked past a pharmacy and liquor store, keeping his pace quick and sure. Darting across the street toward the English Gothic church, he glanced up at its massive granite spires, and ran around the back.

The door was unlocked.

Turning the handle, quietly, carefully, he let himself in.

The scent of werewolves was everywhere, nearly overpowering the aroma of Old English oil and aged wood. If Hayden didn't know better, he'd say they were surrounding him. Everywhere. In the stained-glass windows and walls. In the intricately arched ceiling.

They were still here.

Excitement hummed through him as he snaked through the pews, around towering beams that split the church in thirds.

Movement caught his eye from the back of the church.

Wolves. Three of them. Burly and dark haired. They

stalked through the aisles, the ridges of their backs raised in agitation. Sliding the Glock from his pocket, Hayden took aim. He could get one shot off. Maybe two. With his other hand, he gripped the Taser and pointed both weapons toward the wolves.

Growling reverberated from all around him. Damn acoustics in the church were blaring. Taking a step back down the middle aisle, Hayden watched as the wolves prowled, one up the middle, two on the sides.

Where's Asher? He projected through mind-speak.

The wolf coming at him curled his lip in defiance, revealing a set of hideous teeth.

Someone needs a teeth cleaning. Hayden pushed out the thought with a laugh.

Snarling into a howl, the wolf charged. Hayden crouched, fingers on both triggers. Without warning, the wolf skidded to a stop moments before he leaped. His eyes glazed over and his ears bent back.

The wolf was listening to something, and it wasn't him.

The wolf had pledged loyalty to another.

Hayden spun, searching out the leader of the new pack, the one who commanded the rogue.

"Hayden Dean," a gruff voice said from behind him. "Pleased to finally meet you."

He turned, ready to pop off a few shots. The werewolf was tall—over six-foot-six from what he could tell—with jet-black hair cut close to his scalp and a nasty scar slicing across his cheek. Hayden had never seen him before, but from his stature and menacing presence alone, he'd guess the werewolf was a former member of the guard.

"Asher, I presume," Hayden said, moving so that his back faced the wall.

"She said you would come, but I didn't believe her." Asher strode closer, his hands hidden behind his back. "What kind of an idiot do you have to be to come here knowing you can't defend yourself against us?"

"I came to talk some sense into you before it was too late."

Asher barked out a laugh. "You came to talk? Oh, now I'm intrigued." He perched on the edge of a pew, the leather pants stretching taut over his legs. "Go ahead, son of Angus, the Alpha who'll never be. Enlighten me. Tell me what I'm doing wrong and what you're doing right."

Hayden watched the wolves carefully as they inched closer.

"You can't possibly think the council is going to sit by and let you get away with starting a new pack in the city," Hayden said. "The guards will come for you eventually."

"You think I'm scared to stand against them?"

No, Asher didn't look scared. He looked ready for war.

"I'm not worried about the council." Asher patted his pocket. "I've got them right here."

Hayden sensed more wolves surround them. Whether they were outside or mobilizing in another part of the church, he couldn't be sure.

Things were about to go from bad to worse.

"Who do you work for?" Hayden spat, pulse spiking.

The silhouette of a woman appeared near the altar. "Me."

Chapter Twenty-Five

"Damn it, Lydia!" *He should've known.* "What the hell are you doing?"

Lydia traipsed down the stairs at the front, her hands clasped in front of her. The wolves bowed, their muzzles brushing the floor. Asher craned his neck over his shoulder to glare at her before returning his attention to Hayden.

"I'm taking control of the pack," Lydia said simply. "Both packs, actually. Puts me in a fine position, doesn't it? Don't look so surprised. You didn't seriously expect to rule after Angus died, did you?"

He stiffened, fury striking through his veins.

"You did?" She laughed. "Then it's true what they say: beauty or brains, but never both."

Asher chuckled as the wolves closed in. Two more, smaller and sleeker than the first group, emerged from behind the altar and fell behind their leader.

How fast could he fire off every round and reload? He could use the Taser on Asher, and drop a wolf or two before bolting to a better position…

"You were never going to rule." She paced in front of him like a lion in a cage, anxious to pounce. "Dean blood doesn't stream through your veins. You're not the leader Angus was. And you're inherently weaker than every born wolf in this room."

Her words stung, piercing through the wall Hayden had built up around his pride. But she didn't have to say any of it aloud. Those remarks had been on a permanent auto-loop through his mind from the day Angus took him in as his son.

But Lydia was wrong. That simple. Born wolves were no different from turned wolves with the exception of the timing of their shift. And he could take a few of these wolves down if the fight was one-on-one.

"You're a born wolf," he said, nudging his chin at her in defiance. "If you're stronger than I am, let's go a round."

"Oh, there was a time when I would've jumped at the chance to go a round with you." Licking her lips, she closed the distance between them and eyed him with heated intensity. "We could've been amazing together." She stepped back as he shivered in disgust. "But that was before Asher made me realize turned wolves are beneath us. They're not natural."

His finger tapped against the trigger as he took aim at one wolf before another…and then another.

"I'm just as natural as you are."

"No," Asher interrupted. "You're not. God made us this way. He linked us to the moon and blessed us with the ability to shift into these glorious creatures." He motioned to the rogue pack. "But you were born of an attack, a random act of violence. We were blessed by the Creator, and you were created from evil. Don't you see?"

"I see you're sick as fuck," Hayden snapped, fury shrinking the skin over his bones. "Holding on to this prejudice is going to break our society."

"No," Asher growled, "getting rid of the waste is going to

make our society purer, and stronger."

"The only thing born from hate will be more hate."

"He's not getting the picture," Lydia said, kinking her neck toward Asher. When her gaze returned to Hayden, it was filled with fiery determination. "Listen up, wannabe. Here's how this is going to work. You're going to be tortured in front of the pack during the next full moon, as an example of what will happen to turned wolves if they don't leave the city."

"The hell I am."

They wanted war, they were about to get it.

Letting the anger whipping through him take over, Hayden pointed the Taser at Asher and took a shot. He dodged, but the prongs caught him in the shoulder, dropping him onto his side. Hayden fired two quick rounds with his Glock—one at Lydia, the other at the wolf stalking in front of him.

Lydia dodged the bullet aimed for her, but the other hit square in the wolf's chest.

With a howl, the wolf leaped, canines bared. Anticipating the move, Hayden knelt and fired a second bullet into the wolf's belly. He dropped like a stone while Lydia disappeared behind a group of charging rogues.

He lost sight of her.

Jumping to his feet, Hayden reloaded a Taser cartridge and dropped the next wolf to charge his way. The dark-haired wolf fell to the carpet, twitching in agony. Hayden hurdled the nearest pew, and fired off the final rounds in his Glock. He couldn't tell which wolves he hit, and which he missed, but when the front doors to the church flew open, time stood still.

The wolf pack's guards had arrived, with White and Mad Dog leading the charge. Hayden counted twenty guards behind the councilmen, the ridges of their backs towering over five feet.

Victory sang through him.

His pack had come to join the fight.

Hayden's backup circled the room, corralling the rogues in the center. They snapped and charged, only to be driven back by the line of experienced guards.

Surrender, Mad Dog spoke through his thoughts, as he stalked the group of rogues. *Or we'll rip off your legs, skin them in the gutter, and feed you the bones.*

Damn. He was crazy intense, but they didn't call him Mad Dog for nothing.

Asher shook into full wolf form in a blink. Coarse dark fur flattened over his skin and muscles erupted where they weren't there before. He charged Hayden, his wide paws striking the floor like anvils. Thinking fast, Hayden charged right back and ate up the space between them. As Asher leaped, Hayden slid, just like he was sliding over home plate. He fired two quick rounds in Asher's chest, making sure the silver hit true.

The wolves in his command howled in distress as if they could feel the wound.

The split-second distraction was all the guards needed to surround the wolves completely and pin them to the ground.

As the guards took complete control over the rogues, Hayden scanned the church for Lydia. There. Sprinting down the main aisle toward the altar.

He took off after her, reloading.

"It's over," he shouted, keeping her trained in his sights. "If you give up now, you'll be tried for treason and rogue behavior, but you'll live to see another day."

"You think you're the only one who can give an ultimatum? I've got one better for you." Reaching the altar circled with stained glass, Lydia laughed in a string of wicked giggles that didn't suit her. Rays of sunlight slanted over her face, making her skin glow a devilish shade of orange. "If you disappear, your precious Luminary will live a happy, fulfilled life. If you remain on the path you're on, I'll kill her myself."

"You're hardly in a position to make a threat." He froze, finger twitching and ready to fire. "You're not in control over the council anymore, now that they know what you were plotting behind their backs, and you're not in control over the rogues."

Her attention shifted over his shoulder, where the rogues were shifting back to human form and being placed under wolf-pack arrest.

"I may have lost my grip on a few things, but I've got my hand in others," she whispered. "I've offered Melina the job of her dreams at *Eclipse*, as the sole editorial director of the fashion column. She was quite thrilled when I gave her the first assignment."

He rushed up the stairs. She backed against the altar, hands extended.

"I don't want you to mention her name, not ever again," he said, gripping her by the wrist. "You're under arrest for treason…"

She grinned from the side of her mouth before he could finish reading her rights. "Don't you want to know what she's going to write about?"

"I don't want to hear another word."

"Werewolves in the city," Lydia said. "Well, one werewolf in particular…You."

Panic latched onto his windpipe. "She wouldn't work for you and agree to that."

"Oh, she would and she will. It's already done." Lydia flicked her tongue over her teeth. "She's already accepted the position. I've got the contract she signed in my coat pocket. You can see for yourself, if you don't believe me."

"I'd have to be crazy to believe a word that came out of your mouth." Wrenching Lydia's arms behind her back, he dug into her coat pocket and pulled out a small envelope. "Is this it? The alleged contract?"

She nodded slowly. "I've made all of her dreams come true. You'll see."

Keeping her hands clasped together so she couldn't escape, Hayden shook the papers out of the envelope, and then nudged them open.

Eclipse's contract.

Melina's signature beside Lydia's. And today's date.

"Told you." Lydia twisted in his grasp. "She works for us now. I've given her everything. And for that, she's going to expose you to the world."

If he wasn't staring at the contract with his own eyes, he might not have believed it.

Working for *Eclipse* might've been her dream job, but she wouldn't expose him as a werewolf, would she? He forced his heartbeat to slow, and for confidence to remain in his heart, but doubt managed to wedge its way in. If she wrote an article exposing him, would people laugh it off as satire? Bizarre, unbelievable news? Or would she dig deep enough to be able to really prove it?

"I can see the doubt in your eyes," she whispered. "You know how much this means to her."

Yeah, he did.

He dragged her to the floor. She fought against his hold, but didn't shift. Putting a knee in her back, he swung her other wrist around and pinned her in place.

"With her position at *Eclipse*, Melina will be happy. That thought alone should be enough for you to leave the city and never look back," Lydia said, her face smothered against the carpet. "If you don't leave, every rogue in the city will be out for blood."

I could protect her.

"The hell you could."

He hadn't meant to project the thought.

"In case you hadn't noticed," he seethed into her ear, "your rogues are on lock-down."

She pushed out a maniacal laugh. "You think these rogues are the only ones out there? We're everywhere; working undercover as guards, interning at the law office. I've gotten to more people than you know, and we're *very* patient. We'll simply wait for the right time to strike. When your back is turned or when you least expect it. As your mate, Melina will always be a target. And you won't always be there to protect her." The words resonated deep, hitting him like a low blow. "You won't know who to trust."

She was right. Of course she was. The rogues in the church tonight weren't the only ones in the city. Not by a long shot. These were the only ones who happened to be in the vicinity when he showed up.

You won't always be there to protect her…

With a growl escaping from his throat, Hayden jerked Lydia to her feet and led her down the steps to join her rogues. He handed her off to Mad Dog, who dragged her out back as if he was taking out the trash.

White approached Hayden's side, his hands on his hips as he took in the scene. "Quite the party."

"Yeah." Hayden's chest squeezed. "Thanks for coming to back me up."

"We didn't only come to back you up," he said, leading Hayden out front. "We came to show loyalty to our Alpha."

As they pushed their way out the front doors, at least fifty packmates stood silent, in human form, bowing their heads.

Hayden felt his face scrunch. "But I'm not—"

"You *are* Alpha. Or at least you will be."

"I thought I wasn't worthy."

"Do these men look as if they think you're unworthy?"

He scanned the bowed heads, and the humbled gazes. "What changed? Lydia?"

"No, it was *you* who changed." White patted Hayden on the back, his touch warming through Hayden's coat. "Your father waited his entire life to see you put the pack's interest above your own." He paused, and covered his heart with his hand. "There is no greater sacrifice than putting your life above your brothers."

Hayden's throat burned with the threat of tears.

"Your father would've been proud of you, Hayden." White nodded and smiled, and Hayden imagined his father doing the same. "As far as the San Francisco Wolf Pack is concerned, it doesn't matter if you were born or turned. It's what's in your heart that's important. And in *your* heart, I find selfless love. *That,* my son, is the true heart of an Alpha. Now, kneel before the members of your pack to accept the position you were destined for."

His insides knotted. "The Alpha induction ceremony isn't scheduled until the next full moon."

"Now that you've proved your worth to the pack," White spread his arms wide, to the crowd of wolves surrounding them, "there's no need for a council vote. We've been waiting for this moment."

"But…" Inadequacy niggled in Hayden's gut. "…I'm not in wolf form. The induction ceremonies usually happen when the entire pack can be present as wolves."

"We can wait until the next full moon, if that's what you insist." White leaned in close. "But the men present today feel it's a sign of respect. You came here, defending the pack in human form. They want to bow to you in the same."

Heart in his throat, Hayden knelt before his father's friend and stared at the concrete.

"Hayden Dean, son of Angus, and rightful heir to the San Francisco Wolf Pack throne, do you solemnly swear to always have the pack's best interest at heart?"

"I do," he breathed.

He'd never meant any words more.

"Do you vow to protect the pack, honor its laws, and obey its customs?"

"I do."

"With the power vested in me," White said, "by the former Alpha, Angus Dean, I pronounce you the reigning Alpha of the San Francisco Wolf Pack."

Applause and hollers rang out from all around them as Hayden's packmates welcomed him as their leader. Something warmed in his chest, and sent chills scattering up and down his spine.

This was the moment he'd been dreaming of for the last year. He should've been thrilled, over the moon, ready to conquer the world.

But there was one thing missing...

"Melina." Lydia's words rang through his ears. *You won't always be there to protect her.* "I have to go," he said.

As he took off down Church Street with the contract in his back pocket, Hayden had the sickening feeling Lydia had one more trick up her sleeve.

Everywhere.

I've gotten to more people than you know.

He'd left Melina in Gabriel's care.

He'd never doubted him as a trusted friend...until now.

Chapter Twenty-Six

There's someone else I can't trust.

Lydia haunted Hayden long after she left his sight. All the way back to the law office, actually. Rogues were everywhere—he couldn't trust anyone anymore—but it was more than that.

Melina had taken the job at *Eclipse*.

He couldn't believe it.

Writing an article on him, exposing him as a wolf was underhanded and deceitful. The thought made him sick to his stomach. How could she even think about accepting a proposition from someone like Lydia?

No, that's not what bothered him most.

She chose the job over me.

Sickness bubbled into seething anger. He didn't blame her for taking the job—it was her dream. In no time, she'd be an asset to the magazine. They'd be lucky to have her. But that didn't mean the thought didn't piss him off.

She was going to write an article on him—the column of her career, probably—to use him to get ahead.

What kind of a person did that? He must not have known her as well as he thought he did…

Swerving into his usual spot, Hayden hopped out of his car and charged into the elevator. He jabbed the button and waited impatiently for the doors to open on his floor.

"Gabriel!" He stepped out, hands clenched into fists. "You still here?"

Silence. No wait, there was something in the distance. A printer spitting out pages. The sound came from his office.

She was here, finishing her article, most likely.

"Melina?" Following the sound, he stopped when he spotted her standing in front of his desk. Despite his anger, relief washed over him. Bitterness remained though, leaving a nasty taste in his mouth. "You're here."

Safe and sound.

"Oh my God, I'm so glad you're okay." She started to move toward him, but stopped suddenly as if something held her back. Her features were strained, her face pale. "I've been worried sick."

Although it killed him, he gave her the space she clearly needed and remained in the doorway.

"I thought you'd be checking out your new office by now," he said, leaning against the doorjamb.

She frowned. "Why would I be doing that?"

"Because I know all about the job. I have the proof right here." As he removed the contract from his back pocket and threw it to the ground at her feet, his heart drummed in his ears. "I can't believe you'd side with the traitor over me—over us."

"I did take the job, but I'm writing—"

"I don't care. Not anymore. You can save the excuses. I've asked the guards to come up and escort you out."

She swallowed hard, but didn't move a muscle.

Something was off.

"Where's Gabriel?" A musky smell invaded his senses. Someone was in the room. "He still here?"

The corners of her lips twitched. And then her eyes shifted to the left side of his office, to the space between his desk and the wall-to-wall window. "He stepped out for a few minutes."

Lie.

"Is he coming back?"

She nodded, shaking.

Another lie.

"Why don't you step out here with me so we can talk." *What the hell was going on?* "Melina? What do you say?"

Beads of sweat trickled down her temple. She was in trouble. Putting a finger to his lips, Hayden crouched low and scanned the shadows slanting over the floor. A thick, unmoving form lay near the window.

Gabriel...

Something moved behind his desk, shifting the dim rays of light. And then the unmistakable sound of a bullet sliding into the chamber filled the air. Jerking upright, Hayden cut his shocked breath short.

The intruder held a gun to the back of Melina's head.

Hayden froze, blood to bone.

"Reagan," he pleaded, tone flat. "You don't want to do this. Put the gun down."

He should've known Lydia would have Reagan in her back pocket...

"I'm the one giving orders around here now." Lydia's most trusted confidant snarled, and moved around the desk, closer to Melina. "Guns have that effect. Everyone listens when they're staring down the barrel. Don't they, sweetheart?" Snatching Melina around the waist, he dragged her against him and shoved the barrel of the gun to her temple.

Pulses of white-hot fury shot through Hayden's muscles as she winced.

"Tell your boyfriend to back off," Reagan seethed into her ear.

Leaning her weight against him, Melina blinked quickly. "He's not my boyfriend."

Oh, God. This wasn't the time to argue about petty shit.

Do what he says.

Reagan smirked and stared Hayden down over Melina's shoulder. "You can deny it all you want, but it's not going to save him now. I can sense the connection between you."

As Hayden's shoulder began to round forward, he suppressed a growl.

"I'm not trying to save anyone." She swallowed hard. "I'm just letting you know that killing me isn't going to affect him the way you think it will. Didn't you hear him when he walked in? He's called the guards on me. They're on their way up."

Holding the gun square to her temple, Reagan's finger moved to the trigger. "Then I guess you're expendable."

"No, wait." Hayden put up his hands in surrender. "I'm the one you want. Take me instead. She's meaningless." *Heart clench.* "The guards will deal with her if you let her go. I've already arranged it."

He hadn't set up a thing, but Reagan didn't need to know that.

"You already *arranged* it?" Melina stared him down as if she didn't have a gun held to her head. "To hell with both of you."

And then, with lightning-quick speed, she threw her head back, striking Reagan in the nose.

Groaning, Reagan's finger squeezed the trigger in reflex. "You bitch!"

She whacked his wrist, twisted away from him, and then jabbed him in the throat with the side of her hand. Bowling over in pain, Reagan coughed out a blood-curdling curse.

As Hayden kicked the gun out of reach and wrenched

Reagan's arms behind his back, the guards burst through the emergency stairwell door.

Reinforcements.

Melina was going to be all right.

"You really did call them?" Mouth dropped open, Melina stepped aside as they carted Reagan out. "I thought you were blowing smoke. You know, for effect."

He had been. The guards must've seen the situation unravel over the security cameras.

"There's a packmate down over here," Hayden said, focusing on Gabriel. He knelt at his side and felt for a pulse. Strong beats thumped against his fingers. "He'll be all right, but he needs to be treated. She does, too."

"I'm fine." Folding her arms over her chest, Melina sat on the edge of his desk and crossed one leg over the other. "I can take care of myself."

The only reason she was able to do so much damage to Reagan was because he wasn't expecting her to fight back. And he wasn't in wolf form. If he'd had time to shift before the guards arrived, it would've been an entirely different story. Not that he'd tell her any of that.

"You should still be checked out," Hayden said, as three guards escorted Gabriel to the elevators. "Just to be sure."

"If you insist." She hopped off his desk, and faced him, fire burning in her eyes. "Seeing as how you called them to deal with me in the first place."

God, everything was such a mess.

He was happy she was safe, but if she'd drop him so easily for a damned job, how could he trust her intentions or her feelings? How could he believe a word out of her mouth? Whether what they shared was between two people in love or material for the next juicy article?

He couldn't live, or love, that way.

"You'll be safe with them," he said, anxiety knotting in

the pit of his stomach. "But don't forget to grab your article off the printer."

"You bastard." She fumed, eyes narrowing to slits. "After everything we've been through, you really think I would throw it away for a stupid job?"

"Of course I do. That's exactly what happened. The proof is still crumpled over there on the floor." He steeled himself against her. "I don't blame you, Melina. You've always deserved better than what I could give you. You'll be amazing at *Eclipse*."

Shaking her head, Melina planted her hands on her hips and huffed. "For the record, I wasn't going to expose you—the article is about Lydia and the corruption in the company. But you can read it for yourself since I know you don't trust me." She turned on her heel and stormed out of his office. Two stomps and she spun around. "And you're right about that last part. I *do* deserve better than you."

He was still standing in the same spot, staring toward the elevators, long after she'd gone. He couldn't calm down. Air rushed out of his lungs. His heartbeat wouldn't slow. Stabbing pain had begun to pierce his temples. He might as well have been breaking in two—cracking straight down the middle.

When strength trickled back to his legs, Hayden stumbled to the printer and picked up the few pages she'd printed. The more he skimmed, the more he felt like an asshole.

Corruption at Eclipse.
Lydia Hyde behind it all...

Not a single mention of werewolves. His name didn't appear once.

"Damn it!" He crumpled the papers into a wad and chucked them toward the trash bin. She'd been telling the truth. She hadn't planned to expose him at all. "I should've known. I'm a raging idiot...and I don't deserve her."

Truer words were never spoken.

Hayden charged toward the elevators, and stopped at the wolf painting.

"She's better off without me," he mumbled, standing in the exact place where she'd admired the painting. "She does deserve better. And she'll be safer without me at her side, screwing everything up."

Saying the words aloud didn't make him believe them anymore.

Hayden roared, scrubbing his hands through his hair. And then he snapped.

Chapter Twenty-Seven

"I have to get the hell out of here."

He punched the elevator button and counted the seconds until the cage arrived. The metal box shook and trembled as he pounded against the mirrors, letting the fury spiraling in his gut take him over.

He longed to shift and burst through this body, taking his most primal form. He couldn't shift right now, of course, but it didn't lessen the overwhelming urge.

There were a million and a half reasons why he and Melina couldn't be together. The danger she'd be in as his mate, especially now that he was officially going to be the Alpha, and Lydia's threat alone were reasons enough.

Even if he could get past those, even if he believed he could protect her, it didn't change the fact that eventually, he'd be alone again. If he felt this torn up leaving her now, how would it be later in life, after they'd bonded and grown old together?

The pain would tear his chest in half, he was sure of it.

The elevator doors opened. Gabriel stood in the

basement, hands on his hips. A bandage wound around his head, but other than that, he appeared normal.

"Gabriel." Hayden forced his temper to cool. "How do you feel?"

"Fine," he said, nodding. "Better than fine. The guards fixed me up with this stupid head wrap and a bunch of feel-good meds. I'm flying high for the next hour. They wanted me to walk laps through the building. Stimulate the blood or some shit."

"Glad to hear it. I didn't like seeing you laid out that way."

"Reagan took a cheap shot. Caught me off guard." Gabriel smirked. "But from what I hear, your lady returned the favor for me. Speaking of, how are you doin', Hulk?"

"Hulk?"

Gabriel motioned to the metal rail in Hayden's grasp.

Shit. He must've torn the sucker off in his blind rage. He chucked it into the back of the elevator and marched out into the lobby. Gabriel followed on his heels.

"Hey man, you're in no form to go out. You look like you're about to burst out of your skin." Gabriel grabbed Hayden by the elbow. He jerked it out of his friend's grasp. "Where are you headed?"

"Fuck if I know." He wanted to run to Melina and haul her against him. Tell her how much he ached to have her in his life. "I'm going somewhere I can breathe."

"What happened up there?" Gabriel stood in front of him, his arms folded over his chest. "Between you and Melina?"

"I broke it off. Ended it. Killed it." Hayden slapped his arms against his sides. "I accused her of using me to get a leg up in her career. I drove her so far away, she won't be coming back. It's probably for the better, anyway. In order for her to live a long and happy life, she can't be anywhere near me."

"That's what you think?"

Lydia's threat still echoed through his head.

Melina would never be safe. Not while there were rogues roaming the city. He couldn't protect her every second of every day. Melina wasn't the type to be caged, and he couldn't do that to her.

"It's what I know." Something cracked in Hayden's chest. "I have to get out of here."

Gabriel followed him into the parking garage. "Do you love her?"

That was the question of the hour, of the week, of his life, wasn't it? Melina was everything he never knew he'd always wanted. She was his fated mate, but their connection went deeper than that. She was intelligent with a razor sharp wit that had him rolling on multiple occasions. She was drop-dead gorgeous, and somehow managed to see him for who he really was.

She'd looked deeper than anyone else ever had. She'd broken down his walls and made him *feel* when he'd been cold and achingly lonely for so long.

"I love her more than I've ever loved another." Picking up his pace, Hayden dug through his pocket and unlocked the Bugatti's doors. "I love her enough to leave her. Does that answer your question?"

As Hayden slid into the driver's seat, Gabriel grabbed the doorframe. "You're crazy to let her walk away from you," Gabriel said, "but if you're sure this is what you want, I won't stop you."

"Good." Hayden brought the engine to life. "Now get the hell out of my way."

"Wait. One more thing," Gabriel said. "If you're not going to be with her, do you mind if I give her a go?"

Possessiveness rumbled through Hayden's veins. "You'll stay away from her or we are no longer packmates." Biting out the words, he saw nothing but a haze of red. "Do you hear me, traitor?"

"So you don't want her, but you don't want anyone else to have her, either?" Gabriel nodded as if he hadn't heard Hayden's threat. "Oh, she'll live a long and happy life, all right. A long and lonely one, if you have anything to say about it."

His connection to Melina would never, ever fade. He couldn't handle losing her. Not now, not ever.

Never to another.

He was dying inside, his chest aching with loneliness.

But the mere notion of her being with someone else—

His stomach recoiled before he could finish the thought.

Melina would eventually find someone like Gabriel or another werewolf in their pack. That fact was inevitable. They wouldn't be fated mates, and wouldn't share the same connection and chemistry he'd experienced with her, but the new someone would fill a void. He'd fill the empty spot in her bed, and in her heart.

Hayden trusted his packmates to a certain degree, but not with her life, or her heart. If something happened, if they hurt a single hair on her head, he'd rip theirs clean off.

No one could protect her the way he could...

If he spent time with her now—even a few minutes kissing her heart-shaped lips, ghosting his hands over her mane of silky-black hair—he'd cherish those memories forever.

He'd never regret a single moment.

Hayden extended his hand to his friend. "I know this sounds odd, but thank you."

"Glad I could clarify a few things for you." Grinning like the cat that ate the canary, Gabriel took Hayden's hand. "I thought it might take a desperate measure to get you to see the writing on the wall. You two are perfect together. She's the only one who can put up with your shit."

As Hayden realized he'd been joking about asking Melina out, relief washed over him.

"Son of a bitch." Choking out a laugh, Hayden smacked

Gabriel's hand away. "You're a piece of work."

"A masterpiece, some might say." Gabriel turned, starting his walk toward the lobby. "You know there's a benefit at the de Young Museum tonight…it's a black-tie poker tournament. Nationally televised. Ten-thousand dollar buy-in. If you play your cards right, you might be able to land a date."

"I like the way you think." Hayden's wheels turned, though doubt settled in. After behaving so badly and turning Melina away, would she go? Would she forgive him? "Do you have a date?"

"Ah, you know me," he said, grinning. "I'm too indecisive to pick just one."

Someday, a woman was going to come along and show Gabriel the true meaning of soul mate. Only then would he know how truly satisfying it was to love one woman, and know, unequivocally, that she was his for all eternity.

And that's exactly what Melina had given him.

Chapter Twenty-Eight

After passing by the guards stationed outside the gate to her complex, Hayden charged into the foyer. Harsh rays of afternoon sunlight streamed through the windows facing the street, illuminating the tears and stains on the red-carpeted stairs. He marched down the narrow hall to her apartment and rapped on the door. He waited, tapping his foot, and biting his lip. He thrust his hands in his pockets. Pulled them out and rubbed his hands on his pants. Scanned the hall one way, and then the other.

"Just a second," Melina's voice rang out from inside.

His heart leapt.

And then the unmistakable sound of sniffling hit his ears. Something rustled behind the door. She'd been crying...

"Damn it." Remorse flooded him, drying out his throat and tightening his middle. He rested his hand on the door and let his head fall. "Melina? It's me."

How could he ever make it up to her?

"I'm coming." Her voice sounded strained. Had she been crying all day?

The lock twisted, and then the door opened. Her eyes were red, her cheeks pale, yet her chin was raised in a notion of strength.

"What are you doing here?" she asked, folding her arms over her chest.

"Melina." He reached out to cup her cheek in his hand.

She dodged before he touched her face. "What do you want?"

To touch you, hold you, and kiss away your tears.

He swallowed hard, and gazed into those soft brown eyes. She was so beautiful. Angelic and innocent…only there was fire to her. A fierceness that exuded from her spirit, a spark that had him burning to claim her.

"Hayden?" She leaned down to catch his gaze. "Are you going to say something or did you just want to stand in my hall?"

He couldn't straighten out the words tangling in his mind.

"Because if this is how the conversation is going to go," she said, "I can get you a chair."

She was strong-willed, even now. Offering him a seat in the hallway rather than inviting him inside was the ultimate snub to the Alpha of her new pack. But she didn't care. She stood her ground anyway.

He would've expected nothing less from an Alpha's mate.

He smiled through the fog in his mind and shook his head. "I don't need a chair." *I need you. More than the useless air filling my lungs.* "I came back to ask you something."

Why couldn't he spit it out?

He'd been so ready to tell her everything that was spinning in his head and heart, but now that he was face to face with her, staring at the red rings around her eyes, he couldn't think of anything but how much he'd hurt her. And how he'd never be able to make it right, no matter how he tried.

One word at a time, moron.

"Okay." Melina sniffled, and his heart cracked a little more. "Go ahead and ask what you need to ask."

Oh, he'd hurt her bad. She'd put up a wall; he could feel the cold chill of a massive ice sheet forming between them.

• • •

Melina gazed into Hayden's tumultuous chocolate-brown eyes and forced herself to take a deep breath. She couldn't get her hopes up. He wasn't here to apologize or declare his undying love for her. He was probably going to talk about the guards following her every move. How it was going to be a horrible violation of her privacy for a while.

But he looked so damned torn up about it. A thin sheen of sweat covered his forehead. His hands were trembling, though he tried to hide it by clenching and unclenching them into fists.

"Would you go to the de Young Museum with me tonight?" He blurted the words quickly, in one rambled string. "I have two tickets. I'd be honored if you'd accompany me."

"You really should get your mood swings checked out." She narrowed her eyes at him. "Because if you think I've forgotten the last things you said to me a few short hours ago, you're insane."

Keeping his gaze trained on hers, he nodded slowly. "You're angry, as you should be."

"I don't need your permission."

"No, you certainly don't." His gaze lowered to her mouth. "But your lips are damn sexy when they pout that way."

As the anger rose in her belly, something softened inside her chest. A warm blush bloomed over her skin, and the urge to melt into his arms almost overtook her. Almost. Would she always be drawn to him this way? Even if he thought he was a puppet-master who could toy with her emotions?

"You don't get to tell me my lips are sexy." She fought to keep the wall of indifference in place. "Not anymore."

How could he have thought she'd write an article exposing him as a werewolf? He must not have felt the same things she did.

"I was under a ton of pressure before." His shoulders dropped forward. "I was the asshole of all assholes."

She nodded. "The King Asshole."

"The Alpha Asshole."

She fought a smirk. "You should tattoo that to your forehead so every woman you date from here on out knows what they're getting into. It'd be good advertising."

And it'd save a ton of broken hearts.

His expression turned grave. "You're the only woman who'll be in my life from this moment until the day I die. I'm sorry I haven't proven that to you thus far, but if you'd let me, I'd like to make this a new start."

She leaned against the doorjamb to steady herself.

"You said I sided against you…" She swallowed down the tears straining her throat. "…how could you think I'd do that? After everything?"

"God, Melina, I'm so sorry." He looked the part, but he was good at playing the role people needed him to play. "I'm an idiot for not trusting you."

"You could say it until you're blue in the face." As she twisted his words, remorse flickered through her. "It doesn't matter. It's over."

She loved and trusted him. He didn't share the sentiments. *Fine.* She'd have to move on.

He exhaled heavily. "I thought the only way you could live a full and happy life was if I wasn't at your side."

"You honestly think I'd fall at your feet with a simple apology?"

He didn't need to respond. The truth was written all over

his face.

"I was trying to do the right thing, struggling to find a way to keep you safe. I didn't realize I'd be committing myself to a lifetime of misery." He paled. "I shouldn't have let Lydia poison what I knew to be true for myself. I should've trusted you—trusted us. But I can't go back. All I know is that I belong with you. And there's nothing I'd love more than to build a life with you and prove how perfect we are together."

Deep down in her core, she felt the same, but she'd heard him say those lovingly sweet things before, and words had only gotten them so far.

"No one can protect you the way I can," he said.

He was right on that part. She never felt safer than she did when he was at her side.

He reached out for her hand. "No one can love you the way I can, either."

Her middle hollowed out as his fingers brushed over hers. His touch sparked something inside her—a deep-rooted desire, a need to snuggle up next to him and breathe in his comforting scent.

How could she live without him?

Wait—would she be pledging her life to someone who would flip a switch and cast her aside? It wasn't only earlier in his office, but at the awards show last year, too.

She wasn't sure.

"Hayden—"

"You don't have to decide right now," he said, squeezing her hand. "If you think you could forgive me, come with me to a black-tie event at the de Young tonight. I'll come by and wait outside your door at six. If you don't come out, I'll take that as a sign that you don't ever want to see me again. It'll be a hard reality for me to accept, but I'll have to learn to deal with it. As an Alpha's mate, you'll always have the protection of the guards. And you'll never have to see me again, if that's what you truly wish." He lifted her hand, and brushed his lips over her knuckles. "Please forgive me."

And then, after another, softer kiss in the heart of her hand, he closed his eyes and turned away.

Six o'clock.

She only had a few hours to make the biggest decision of her life. Her heart was already leaping in early-expectation, but her mind—her mind teetered between courage and doubt.

Chapter Twenty-Nine

"Aww, sweetie. You look gorgeous," Colleen said as Melina opened the front door to her apartment. "Spanx doesn't really scream black tie to me, but whatever." She shrugged. "To each her own."

Melina pushed Colleen through the door and kicked it shut behind her before anyone spotted her in her flesh-toned sausage-stuffer. "I'm putting on the dress last," Melina said, double-checking the time. "What's in the bag?"

"I came bearing gifts!" Colleen dropped the bag and removed its contents. "Vodka to watch with your favorite movie: *The Devil Wears Prada*."

"That sounds like a killer date night." Grinning, Melina planted her hands on her hips. "But I might not be here for it."

"You still haven't made up your mind whether or not you're going with him?"

Melina shook her head as nerves rattled through her.

"Well, I'm getting started." Colleen started streaming the movie, and flopped onto Melina's bed. "If you decide to answer the door, I'll wish you well and watch the movie by myself. If you don't, we'll get plastered, watch it together, and vote on the best outfits. Win-win for me."

This whole situation had given Melina a serious case of déjà vu.

"I'm just glad the shoe's on the other foot this time," Colleen went on.

"There's still a chance he'll stand me up." Pulling her gold Prada gown off the hanger, Melina stepped into it and twirled in front of the mirror. It had a bustier top and silk skirt. Brighter on the top, more muted on the bottom. Draping train, with a glimpse of her feet in front. And it was absolutely show-stopping. She spun, eyeing the large bow tied at the back of her neck. "But I don't think he will."

"And you *really* haven't made up your mind?" Colleen kicked off her heels and dropped back on the bed. "The Prada dress you're wearing says something different."

"Part of me is all fluttery and anxious, and can't wait for him to knock on that door." Melina slipped into the bathroom and touched up her makeup. "But another part of me feels like I might be asking for disappointment."

The opening song for *The Devil Wears Prada* cued up. Melina peeked around the bathroom wall. All those city girls, glamming up for their big day. She felt like one of them, minus one teeny-tiny thing…most of them were leaving an apartment where a man was tangled in their bed sheets. She didn't have anyone but Colleen, a bottle of Grey Goose, and a movie. Trying not to think about the grim reality facing her, Melina shoved a few bobby pins into the hair she'd pulled back from her face, dashed on sweet vanilla perfume, and hopped into her strappy Prada heels.

"So what are you waiting for?" Colleen unscrewed the top on the vodka and poured two glasses, filled to the rim. "What's going to make your decision?"

With a huff, Melina perched on the edge of the bed. "I

don't know. I guess I'm waiting for the moment to strike me. Something that'll make me wake up and know absolutely, positively that he didn't mean those things he said. You didn't hear him, Colleen. It seemed so easy for him to push me out of his life."

"I still don't understand," Colleen said. "It feels like you're leaving out a part of the story. What reason would he have to break up with you? You said everything was going great, he was exceeding your expectations, and then—*wham!*—you're out on your ass."

She hadn't told Colleen all the details—she'd left out every mention of werewolves. Maybe, when the time was right, she'd share the truth with her best friend. On second thought, if Colleen knew about their secret society, would she say something? Would she freak out and expose them? If she did, it wouldn't do anything but thrust her into the limelight, for all the wrong reasons. She'd become a target of the wolf pack. How far would they go to silence the truth? Would they hurt her?

No, Melina decided. The only way to keep Colleen safe was to keep her separate from the lives of the wolves in the city. She'd have to live in secret, keeping Colleen completely out of it.

Shit…

"You just went pale," Colleen said. "Drink up, sister."

Melina took her drink and tipped it back. She'd just committed the same sin as Hayden. She'd just decided, whole-heartedly, that it was safer for someone to be kept on the outside of the wolf pack society.

Was that all Hayden had been trying to do?

Could he really, truly love her, even though he hadn't said those three little words yet?

She wrung her hands in front of her and checked the time. He'd be here any—

A knock on the door had Melina and Colleen jumping to their feet.

"Holy shit," Colleen said. "He's here. What are you going to do?"

Blinking quickly to stop the tears from falling, Melina threw her arms around Colleen's neck and squeezed. "I know you can't understand this, but you just helped me make up my mind."

"I did?" She beamed. "I don't know what I did, but I'm glad I could be of service."

Adjusting her dress, Melina swept to the door and paused, hand to handle.

And then slowly, heart in her throat, she opened the door.

Hayden stood in front of her, a single, gold-tipped rose in his hand. His dark eyes were fraught with worry, and his full lips had pressed into a hard line.

"Thank God." He spoke softly, as if he couldn't catch his breath. "I'm so glad you're here."

She smirked, feeling weightless. Bold. "I live here."

"Yeah." He seemed to tremble. "You do."

His hair was slicked back, and his face clean-shaven, accentuating the ruggedness of his jaw. He stood tall, wearing a Prada suit and black bow tie.

"Melina," he said, handing her the preserved flower, "you wear a gold ring on your finger to remind you of where you come from and who you are. I want this to remind you that I know who you are, too…" He wrapped his free hand around her back and tugged her into his arms. "Just like this rose, you are dainty and perfect, sweet, beautiful, elegant, with the softest petals." He lifted her hand and brushed his lips over the back of her knuckles.

"Thank you." She melted as he buried his head against her neck and breathed in deep. "That was sweet."

She belonged with him, wrapped tight in his arms. For

always.

This—*right here*—was her fairy tale.

"No fur coat tonight?" He pulled back, a sly grin curling his lips.

"No," she said, cheeks heating. "I'll have another opportunity to wear fur this month. I'll save it for then."

His lips twitched as if he was holding back a laugh. "You look amazing."

"Thanks." She tugged on his lapel. "You do, too."

"Ah-hem." Colleen made a noise from behind her.

Melina turned and introduced the two of them. Colleen curtsied as if she were the princess getting picked up for the ball, and then made a rude gesture with her hands when he glanced back down the hall. After handing Colleen the rose and asking if she'd put it in water, Melina snatched her bag, and shut the door behind her. Judging from the gesture, Colleen had more than given Melina her blessing. Apparently, she wasn't going to be waiting up for her to come home.

"Are you ready?" Hayden asked, planting a soft kiss on her shoulder.

Melina took his hand. "Absolutely."

Hayden led her down the stairs, his hand gently resting on the small of her back. And when they exited the doors to the apartment complex, a limo waited at the curb.

"Where's the Bugatti?" she asked, sliding into the limo.

After catching the train of her gown and holding it up for her to adjust, Hayden got in behind her and scooted close. "There's this really intelligent woman I know, who said if you want to make a good impression, you should drive something classy, something that shows you're ready to take on certain responsibilities."

"You *were* listening."

"I listen to everything you say."

She lit up, from the inside out. But she liked the way

the Bugatti clung to curves, and the way he handled the car. Powerful and assured. The way he handled her between the sheets, actually.

Turned out she liked a lot of things about Hayden... exactly the way he was. No image alterations necessary.

But he still hadn't said he loved her...

"So where are we going?" she asked as the limo drove toward Golden Gate Park.

"There's a poker tournament benefiting inner-city youth at the de Young Museum tonight." He put his hand on her knee, and brushed his thumb up and down along her inner thigh. She shivered as lightning rods of delicious sensation shot between her legs. "Do you play?"

She'd play with him all night long if he said the word...

"I know the basics, but nothing fancy."

"Don't worry, I'll be at your side to help you." He patted her leg, and then leaned in to kiss her cheek. "Thanks for coming tonight. I'm so relieved you opened the door."

"I wasn't sure what I was going to do until the last minute, to be honest."

He rubbed his hands up and down his thighs as they rounded the park and approached the museum. "I expected that, and I don't deserve a second chance from you, but you have to know...sending you away from me like that was one of the hardest things I've ever done in my life. It felt like I was ripping my heart out of my chest."

She knew the feeling well. She'd felt the same way.

"You don't have to protect me by keeping me shielded from the dangers of the rogues." She took his hand and weaved her fingers through his. "We can face them together."

He cupped her chin in his hands. "You're unbelievably brave, the way you take on the world. You aren't afraid to take risks in life, or love. I stand to learn a lot from you."

Was he kidding?

She wasn't the one who took off to challenge a pack of wolves.

She shook her head. "I'm not brave."

"Don't do that." He ghosted his thumb over her cheek and held her still. "Never underestimate yourself that way. When the rogues kidnapped you, you escaped on your own. You busted Reagan's nose when he held you at gunpoint, and just offered to face the wolves again. I know you have a fairy tale in your head and think you're the damsel in distress in all this. But I know better. You're the heroine. No," he corrected, planting a feather-soft kiss on her lips. "You're *my* heroine."

As the limo pulled up to the curb, she lost herself in this moment, and in this man. She coiled her arms around his neck and kissed him with all the passion in her heart and soul. Her lips tingled, and her heart clenched, as his mouth slanted over hers. He kissed her, open-mouthed, both hands softly cupping her face.

This was her fairy tale.

He was it.

She didn't need a castle, a white horse, a crown, or even—gasp!—Prada. She needed him. With every fiber of her being. She needed him like the very air in her lungs.

"When I said I loved you," she breathed against his lips. "I meant it. You don't have to say it back until you're ready, but—"

"I love you, Melina Rae Rosenthal. And I don't want to be apart from you again. Not for one day, one hour, one minute."

Her heart stuttered, and she fought to breathe. Outside the limo, cameras flashed and crowds of people waited for Hayden to emerge.

"I can't make a promise that we'll never fight," he went on, "or that I'll never piss you off and make you want to leave, because I will. I'll probably screw something up because that's what I've done best for the last two-hundred years. I can't promise you a life without pain or loss, but I'll be at your side the whole time. And it'll be worth it in the end."

Something erupted inside her. Her mouth dried. Her stomach ached. Tears rolled down her cheeks. She was a blubbering mess. Removing the handkerchief from his pocket, he wiped away her tears.

"Don't cry, doll."

She smiled into a laugh, as tears caught on her lashes.

Doll.

She used to hate that word. But coming from the right person, the pet name was kind of freaking adorable. He could call her Doll until the day she died, and she'd be the happiest woman on earth, as long as he said it exactly the way he did now. Filled with love and total adoration.

"Ready to go out there and fuel the circus?" He nudged his chin at the parade of reporters lining the red carpet.

"I'm ready." She kissed him, slow and tender, and then leaned over his lap to pull on the handle. "But I should be asking you that question. From the moment we step on that carpet, they're going to know we're together. You won't be able to avoid the truth about our relationship the way you're attached to my side this way."

He eyed the hand that still gripped her knee. "Yet I'm not moving."

Her thighs dimpled with gooseflesh. "Are you sure you're ready for this?" For a relationship. To go public with us. To declare to the world, essentially, that she was his only. "For what tonight brings?"

"Hell yes."

She trembled as his lips caught hers in a smoldering kiss. Her heart filled with joy and gratitude, but most of all…love.

"Totally, completely, I'm yours," she whispered against his mouth.

"And I'm the luckiest werewolf in the world for it," he said, taking her hand. "Come on. Let's go show them what love looks like."

And then Hayden Dean, playboy, mogul, businessman, and *Alpha wolf,* led her down the red carpet as if she were his queen.

Chapter Thirty

Melina never thought the day would come.

Shifting for the first time was nerve-wracking, even though Hayden had spent the last few weeks prepping her for what was to come. He'd said it wasn't too painful, but it could be really uncomfortable if she wasn't completely relaxed. If she didn't accept the change whole-heartedly, it'd be harder. He said not to think about how she'd look in wolf form, or the pain she might feel.

The concept was like someone telling her not to think about elephants.

Yeah, okay.

Elephant. Elephant. Elephant.

She took one last, long look at herself in his bathroom mirror. She fluffed her dark strands as they fell over her shoulder, and then laughed at how absolutely ridiculous the thought was.

She'd just primped...to become a wolf.

Sighing, she adjusted her shirt—the one Hayden would love—and stepped into the bedroom of his Moss Beach home. The night was dark, but the full moon shone brightly through the windows, illuminating the room with a cool white glow.

"Hayden?" she called, tiptoeing into the hall.

"Downstairs."

Wringing her hands, Melina traipsed downstairs and into the kitchen. Hayden stood in front of the French doors leading onto the deck, bare-chested, with a pair of black running shorts slung low on his hips. A sense of calm eased its way through her at the sight. Stealing behind him, she wrapped her arms around him and nuzzled her face against his bare back. She could hear his heart beat, steady and true. She could feel his lungs expand and deflate. Both things warmed her and quieted her nerves completely.

"Your article came out today." He gazed at her over his shoulder.

She hadn't realized today was the day. Nerves flared through her. "How is it?"

Papers rumpled over his shoulder. She leaned around him, and noticed he held *Eclipse* in his hands.

"You have a knack for exposing the truth about people." He flipped the page that showed a picture of Lydia's desk, how full it was before, and how empty it was now that she'd been fired. "We never had reason to suspect she was stealing millions from the company and hiding it in accounts overseas. Are you sure you don't want to take the job at *Eclipse*? It's what you've worked your whole life for."

"Yeah, I'm sure." She nodded against his back, and then let him spin around in her arms. "I think I want to start up a local off-the-runway rental store. Packmates get a discount, of course."

She'd already started up the website, and looked at the upfront costs. They were doable, and she was surprisingly stoked about the idea. She'd actually get to work with the clothes hands-on this way, rather than sitting behind a desk and writing articles about fashion. And as a bonus, she'd get to go to all the fashion shows.

Hayden had already promised to take her to Fashion Week, if she wanted to kick-start her new business. He supported her dreams; reason number two million why she loved him.

"If that's what you want, you could have it." He kissed the tip of her nose. "You have the know-how, the work ethic, and the crazy sense of fashion."

"Crazy?" She stepped back so he could get a good, hard look of tonight's outfit. "What do you think of this?"

His mouth dropped as he eyed her hungrily, making her quiver. "I thought you hated the 49ers!"

He held her finger and made her do a little spin. She wore a small 49ers jersey that hugged her breasts and a pair of red booty shorts that hid little.

"Oh, I still hate 'em," she said, planting her hands on her hips. "But you said I'd rip through my clothes during the shift. This was the only outfit I could think of where I wouldn't mind if it got torn to shreds."

"If only I had a Raider jersey to do the same." He laughed, nodding. "But I don't own anything that hideous. Now that you have your outfit picked out, are you ready?"

She nodded, unable to speak.

"It's going to be okay," he said, and grabbed a rolled up blanket off the table. "You'll see."

Taking her hand, Hayden led her out the French doors onto the deck, and then down a set of stairs to the beach. Once they reached the sand, the crashing sound of the waves was deafening. The moon's glow illuminated everything, shining on the long stretch of white sand, the trees sheltering them from view, and the angry waves crashing against the shore.

There wasn't a hint of breeze, or threat that anyone would see them.

No wonder Hayden had bought this house.

It was perfect.

He fluffed out the blanket on the sand, and then met her at the edge of the water. She dipped her feet in, and lost her balance when the water sucked back to sea.

After tonight, would this feel different? Would *she* be different?

"Everything will be exactly the same as it is now," he said, as if reading her mind. "The water will feel the same lapping against your feet. Your heart will pump the same blood, and beat for me as it does now."

She leaned back against him as he wrapped his arms around her.

"Okay," she said. "What now?"

He spun her in his arms. "Can you feel the moon tugging on something inside you?"

She shrugged. "I'm not sure."

"Close your eyes. Concentrate."

As she did, the sound of the waves hummed through her ears and slowed her heart rate. Her skin chilled. And then, right there, a low hum fluttered in her belly.

"That's it," he murmured beside her. "Now focus on that. Feel it gather into a ball in your gut. Clench your abs, and wait for the hum to wave through your arms and legs."

She did as she was told, focusing, clenching, willing that hum to spread through her. To her surprise, it did. She smiled as her entire body tingled, head to toe.

"Now," he said, as his hand found her back, "push outward as if you were trying to communicate with me through your thoughts. But instead of your thoughts, project the transition."

Clenching her back teeth together, she fixated all her energy on that humming feeling, hunched over, hardened her abs, and then let the sensations rip through her.

Pinching her eyes tight, Melina dropped to her knees, dizzy and tired. When she opened her eyes again, Hayden stood in front of her in wolf form.

God, he was magnificent.

He stood tall, the ridge on his back arched high. His coat was fluffy, his fur dark brown with traces of black. And his eyes—they gripped her with their tenderness.

Wait, was he…

Yes, I'm the wolf from the painting in my office. He spoke through her thoughts. *My father painted it of me before he died.*

You are *cute and cuddly!*

He stiffened, raising his chin in defiance. *I am not.*

Okay, you're menacing and scary, she lied. *Definitely the most lethal wolf I've ever seen.*

He probably would be all of those things if he were facing an enemy, she realized. But now, in front of her this way, he was…*safe.*

His eyes softened. *I don't mind being cute and cuddly… for you. But that's where it ends.*

How can you hear what I'm thinking?

It's called mind-speak, he said. *As long as I'm your Alpha, you'll be able to hear me, and anyone else in our pack. While you were going through transition, you gained the ability to communicate this way in both of your forms. It should be clearer now that you've shifted into a wolf, but—*

What do you mean, now that I've shifted into a wolf?

The lips on his muzzle curled back into a funny looking smile. *Look at your hands, Melina.*

She glanced down at her hands. Only she didn't have hands. Dark, furry paws had replaced them. She jumped, as electric currents of surprise zipped through her.

Holy shit, I'm a wolf!

A striking one, if I say so myself. He nuzzled his face against hers. *But I may be biased.*

That didn't hurt at all. Sweet relief washed over her as she stared at the shreds of the 49er jersey at her feet. *That was fast. And I still feel like myself.*

Didn't I tell you?

Yeah, but contrary to what you think, you don't know everything.

She nipped at him, and then took off down the beach. She ran in the surf, relishing the power and strength surging through her. It felt oddly natural, her paws hitting the sand and kicking it up behind her. The wind soaring over her body and ruffling her fur.

She was in tune with everything: the salt on the breeze, the crisp feel of the water, and the sound of every rustling branch in the trees behind them.

Whimpering in delight, she glanced behind her and watched as Hayden chased her down. She took off, propelling her legs to churn over faster. He caught her not far down the beach, and bumped into her side.

You're glorious, he said, his voice echoing through her head. *The most beautiful wolf I've ever seen.*

Her heart melted, right then and there. It was beyond strange, but being with Hayden this way felt right. The attack by the rogue had been horrible and the whole process frightening, but look what'd come out of it.

She'd be with Hayden for hundreds of years.

Just like this, he said.

Are you going to be able to hear everything I think? she asked, slowing in the surf. *Because that could be bad. It might surprise you how much I think about fashion.*

I won't hear everything, but it'll take a while for you to learn which thoughts to project and which to keep to yourself. It's a learning process, like everything else.

Something told her that Hayden would be there always, showing her the ropes. As much as she enjoyed being in this form, she wanted to talk to him, rub her hands over his glorious body, and explain to him how she was feeling in this moment...with him.

So how do I shift back?

He kept pace with her as they strolled back toward the blanket he'd laid in the sand. *You do the same thing you did to shift into a wolf. You focus on the tugging in your stomach, harden it into a ball, and let it explode through you. It should feel close to the same.*

As they reached the blanket, Melina did as he explained, channeling the energy into her shift. She closed her eyes, imagined how she looked before, and had the sudden urge to shake. As she trembled, head to tail, her fur flattened to smooth skin, and her legs were beneath her once more. Beside her, Hayden sat back on his haunches and howled to the moon. And then, with a solid shake, he was sitting beside her, golden tan skin, bulging muscles and hard lines.

"Do you do this all the time?" she asked, excitement roaring through her. "Like, all night, every full moon?"

"I don't, but we could." He laid flat on his back, and then pointed to the trees surrounding them. "I own the beach, so we'd have all the privacy we could ask for."

She nestled herself beside him, her head in the crook of his arm. "There's one more thing I want to ask for."

"Anything." He kissed the top of her head.

"Will you make me your Luminary?"

He turned on his side, facing her. "Are you sure you're ready for that?"

"For forever? With you?"

He nodded, his eyes lighting fire in the dark.

"Absolutely."

He kissed her, gently, with achingly soft lips, and then

slipped his tongue into her mouth. She whimpered into him as he caught her, wrapping her in his arms. His tongue searched her mouth with languid strokes, sparking both love and lust in her veins.

She was on fire. Burning for him.

Rubbing her hands up and down his back, she pulled him on top of her. He settled between her legs, his thick length positioned at her center. He braced himself on his elbows, and then ghosted his hands over her hair.

"I love you, Melina," he whispered.

It wasn't only the words that had her heart pinching. It was the look of love in his eyes, the adoration in his touch as he ran his fingers through her hair, the promise in his kiss.

He kissed her forehead, her nose, her lips, untying her. And then, when she was quivering with need, he eased himself inside her. She gasped, stretching to the fullest as he worked his way deeper. He caught her mouth, ripping the air from her lungs as she whimpered and cried out for him to plunge deeper.

As their hips met and the rhythm sped, he rose up to look into her eyes.

"You're so hot." He thrust harder, his heavy-lidded eyes glazed with lust. "You're going to burn me."

She stilled beneath him. "That doesn't sound pleasant. Want me to stop?"

"Never."

Hayden thrust his tongue past her lips and worked her mouth as his cock worked inside her. She was consumed by him to the point of delirium. Mind, body, and soul. He thrust harder, slanting his mouth over hers as their bodies moved over the blanket as one. And then, when every sensation in her body was heightened, on edge and begging for release, he braced himself on one arm and slid the other one between their bodies. He teased her clit, nipped at her bottom lip, and with one final, feather-soft touch, she broke apart beneath him. As the orgasm rocked her hips against his, her most sensitive flesh milked his shaft relentlessly.

He reared up, every muscle in his body flexed with tension.

"The…vows." The words were staccato and raspy, as if he couldn't spare one extra ounce of energy to say them properly. "Take…my hands."

She put her hands over her head, palms up. He filled them with his own and then groaned as he lowered his head to her mouth to claim her again.

"Palm to palm," he mumbled against her lips. "Heart to heart, from this moment on…" He trailed off as she coiled her thighs around his hips and tugged against him, driving him deeper into her heat. "…we never shall part."

She tingled with awareness, beneath her skin and bone. It was unexplainable, magical, but for reasons she couldn't explain, Melina knew he'd touched her soul.

"You have to…" He groaned, plunging into her. "…say them back."

As she rolled her hips against him, the familiar sensations pulsed in her core. "Palm to palm, heart to heart, from this moment on…" She paused, unable to catch her breath. And then, when he tightened, gasping for release, his eyes hazy with desire, she pitched into a second, stronger, orgasm. "…we never shall part."

He cried out her name, his hips flush against hers as he erupted into her still-clenching depths. Fireworks of ecstasy ripped through her, exploding into brilliant starbursts of passion that left her weak and powerless.

They were one.

She'd thought they were close before, but nothing could compare to this. There was nothing on earth that could separate them now.

"You're mine." He collapsed on top of her, his face buried

in her hair. "And I'm yours."

Relishing the pressure of his body over hers, Melina brushed her hands up and down the muscles on his back. "For all eternity."

He rose up on shaky hands and kissed her, setting fire to the love in her heart. "I can't wait to get started."

With the sound of the waves crashing in the distance, Hayden laid back and tugged Melina against him. And then, staring at the stars, they made plans for the future. There would be adorable children and homes filled with light and laughter: one in the city and one near the ocean. And there would *always* be Prada, glorious and perfect, just like their love.

Acknowledgments

Firstly, I have to thank my agent, Nalini Akolekar, and my editor, Candace Havens, for their confidence in my writing ability, their devotion to the craft, and patience. Above all, patience—especially after two-hundred-sixty pages of this manuscript went kaput. Thanks to Katie Clapsadl and Curtis Svehlak for working so hard behind the scenes so that I can focus on writing the book.

Love and hugs to my support group of family and friends. Thanks to Elisa Dane, Virna DePaul, Susan Hatler, Vanessa Kier, Laurie Shaw, Aggie Smith, Lora Walker, and Monica Wunderlich, for unwavering faith and friendship.

To Justin, Kelli, and Gavin…my heart.

About the Author

New York Times and *USA TODAY* bestselling author Kristin Miller writes sweet and sassy contemporary romance and paranormal romance of all varieties. Kristin has degrees in psychology, English, and education, and taught high school and middle school English before crossing over to a career in writing. She lives in Northern California with her alpha male husband and their two children. She loves chocolate way more than she should and the gym less. You can usually find her in the corner of a coffee shop, laptop in front of her and mocha in hand, using the guests around her as fuel for her next book.

Don't miss the rest of the **San Francisco Wolf Pack**
series

BEAUTY AND THE WEREWOLF

WHAT A WEREWOLF WANTS

Also by Kristin Miller

THE SEATTLE WOLF PACK SERIES

GONE WITH THE WOLF

FOUR WEDDINGS AND A WEREWOLF

SO I MARRIED A WEREWOLF

A DARK AND DIRTY TALE SERIES

DESIRING RED

DOMINATING RED

DANGEROUSLY RED

***Discover more paranormal romance titles from
Entangled...***

DRAKON'S PROMISE
a *Blood of the Drakon* novel by N.J. Walters

Darius Varkas is a drakon. He's neither human nor dragon. He's both. He and his brothers are also the targets of an ancient order who want to capture all drakons for their blood, which can prolong a human's life. When Sarah Anderson finds a rare book belonging to the Knights of the Dragon, she's quickly thrust into a dangerous world of secrets and shifters. And when the Knights realize Sarah has a secret of her own, she becomes just as much a target as Darius. Her scary dragon shifter just might be her best chance at survival.

FLYING THROUGH FIRE
a *Dark Desires* novel by Nina Croft

Thorne's willpower has been honed over ten thousand years. He might want Candy, but the last thing he needs is an infatuation with a young, impetuous werewolf. Candy makes him lose control, and that could have disastrous consequences. As the threat escalates and they become separated by time and space, Candy must find a way back to him, because while Thorne alone has the power to defeat the dragons, only together can they finally bring peace to the universe.

THE HUNT
a *Shifter Origins* novel by Harper A. Brooks

Prince Kael has just lost his father to an assassin, and he's the next target. A murderer is on the loose, the kingdom is in disarray, and Kael is determined to make the person responsible for killing his father pay. But falling for the beautiful Cara, panther-shifter assassin and main suspect his father's murder, wasn't part of the plan. He's not at all sure she did it, and he finds himself going against everything he's ever known just to claim her.